ON DANGEROUS GROUND

ON DANGEROUS GROUND

Jack Higgins

LONDON NEW YORK SYDNEY TORONTO

Printed and bound in Germany
by Graphischer Großbetrieb Pößneck GmbH
A member of the Mohndruck printing group

For Sally Palmer
with love

PROLOGUE

CHUNGKING

AUGUST 1944

The pilot, Flight Lieutenant Joe Caine of RAF Transport
Command, was tired, frozen to the bone, his hands clamped
to the control column. He eased it forward and took the
plane down, emerging from low cloud at three thousand
feet into driving rain.

The aircraft ploughing its way through heavy cloud and
thunderstorm was a Douglas DC3, the famous Dakota, as
much a workhorse for the American Air Force as for the
RAF who together operated them out of the Assam

airfields of North India, flying supplies to Chiang Kai-shek's Chinese Army. On their way they had to negotiate the infamous Hump, as it was known to Allied aircrews, the Himalayan mountains, trying to survive in some of the worst flying conditions in the world.

'There she is, Skipper,' the second pilot said. 'Dead ahead. Three miles.'

'And the usual lousy black-out,' Caine said, which was true enough. The inhabitants of Chungking were notoriously lazy in that respect and there were lights all over the place.

'Well, here we go,' he said.

'Message from control tower,' the wireless operator called from behind.

Caine switched on to VHF and called the tower. 'Sugar Nan here. Is there a problem?'

'Priority traffic coming in. Please go round,' a neutral voice said.

'For God's sake,' Caine replied angrily, 'I've just clocked one thousand miles over the Hump. We're tired, cold and almost out of fuel.'

'VIP traffic to starboard and below you. Go round. Please acknowledge.' The voice was firm.

The second pilot looked out of the side, then turned. 'About five hundred feet below, Skipper. Another Dakota. A Yank from the look of it.'

'All right,' Caine said wearily and banked to port.

The man who stood on the porch of the Station Commander's office staring up into the rain, listening to the sound of the first Dakota coming in, wore the uniform of a Vice-Admiral of the Royal Navy, a trenchcoat over his shoulders. His name was Lord Louis Mountbatten and he was cousin to the King of England. A highly decorated war hero, he was also Supreme Allied Commander Southeast Asia.

The American General in steel-rimmed spectacles who emerged behind him, pausing to light a cigarette, was General 'Vinegar Joe' Stilwell, Mountbatten's deputy and also Chief of Staff to Chiang Kai-shek. The greatest expert on China of anyone in the Allied forces, Stilwell was also fluent in Cantonese.

He perched on the rail. 'Well, here he comes, the great Chairman Mao.'

'What happened to Chiang Kai-shek?' Mountbatten asked.

'Found an excuse to go up-country. It's no use, Louis, Mao and Chiang will never get together. They both want the same thing.'

'China?' Mountbatten said.

'Exactly.'

'Yes, well, I'd like to remind you this isn't the Pacific, Joe. Twenty-five Jap divisions in China and, since the start of their April offensive, they've been winning. No one knows that better than you. We need Mao and his Communist Army. It's as simple as that.'

They watched the Dakota land. Stilwell said, 'The Washington viewpoint is simple. We've given enough lend-lease to Chiang.'

'And what have we got for it?' Mountbatten asked. 'He sits on his backside doing nothing, saving his ammunition and equipment for the civil war with the Communists when the Japs are beaten.'

'A civil war he'll probably win,' Stilwell said.

'Do you really think so?' Mountbatten shook his head. 'You know, in the West Mao and his people are looked upon as agrarian revolutionaries, that all they want is land for the peasants.'

'And you don't agree?'

'Frankly, I think they're more Communist than the Russians. I think they could well drive Chiang Kai-shek out of mainland China and take over after the war.'

3

'An interesting thought,' Stilwell told him, 'but if you're talking about making friends and influencing people, that's up to you. Washington won't play. Fresh supplies of arms and ammunition must come from your people, not American sources. We'll have a big enough problem handling Japan after the war. China is your baby.'

The Dakota came towards them and stopped. A couple of waiting ground crew wheeled steps forward and waited for the door to open.

'So you don't think I'm asking dear old Mao too much?'

'Hell, no!' Stilwell laughed. 'To be honest, Louis, if he agrees, I don't see how you'll be getting very much in return for all that aid you intend to give him.'

'Better than nothing, old sport, especially if he agrees.'

The door swung open; a young Chinese officer emerged. A moment later Mao Tse-tung appeared. He paused for a moment, looking towards them, wearing only a simple uniform and cap with the red star, then he started down the steps.

Mao Tse-tung, Chairman of the Chinese Communist Party, was at that time fifty-one, a brilliant politician, a master of guerrilla warfare and a soldier of genius. He was also the implacable foe of Chiang Kai-shek and the two sides had been engaged in open warfare instead of taking on the Japanese together.

In the office he sat behind the Station Commander's desk, the young officer behind him. To one side of Mountbatten and Stilwell stood a British Army Major. His left eye was covered by a black eye-patch and the badge in his cap was that of the Highland Light Infantry. A Corporal wearing the bonnet of the same regiment stood against the wall behind him, a cardboard office file under his left arm.

Stilwell said in fluent Cantonese, 'I'll be happy to translate for these proceedings, Chairman Mao.'

Mao sat facing him, face enigmatic, then said in excellent

4

English, an ability he seldom advertised, 'General, my time is limited.' Stilwell stared at him in astonishment and Mao said to Mountbatten, 'Who is this officer and the man with him?'

Mountbatten said, 'Major Ian Campbell, Chairman, one of my aides. The Corporal is his batman. Their regiment is the Highland Light Infantry.'

'Batman?' Mao enquired.

'A soldier servant,' Mountbatten explained.

'Ah, I see.' Mao nodded enigmatically and turned to Campbell. 'The Highlands of Scotland, am I right? A strange people. The English put you to the sword, turned your people off their land and yet you go to war for them.'

Ian Campbell said, 'I am a Highlander, flesh and bone, a thousand years behind me, Laird of Loch Dhu Castle and all around, like my father and his before me, and if the English need a helping hand now and then, why not?'

Mao actually smiled and turned to Mountbatten. 'I like this man. You should lend him to me.'

'Not possible, Chairman.'

Mao shrugged. 'Then to business. I have little time. I must make the return journey in no more than thirty minutes. What do you offer me?'

Mountbatten glanced at Stilwell who shrugged and the Admiral said to Mao, 'Our American friends are not able to offer arms and ammunition to you and your forces.'

'But everything the Generalissimo needs they will supply?' Mao asked.

He stayed surprisingly calm and Mountbatten said, 'I believe I have a solution. What if the RAF flew in ten thousand tons a month over the Hump to Kunming, assorted weapons, ammunition and so forth.'

Mao selected a cigarette from an old silver case and the young officer lit it for him. The Chairman blew out a long plume of smoke. 'And what would I have to do for such munificence?'

'Something,' Mountbatten said. 'I mean, we have to have something. That's only fair.'

'And what would you have in mind?'

Mountbatten lit a cigarette himself, walked to the open door and looked out at the rain. He turned. 'The Hong Kong Treaty, the lease to Britain. It expires 1 July 1997.'

'So?'

'I'd like you to extend it by one hundred years.'

There was a long silence. Mao leaned back and blew smoke to the ceiling. 'My friend, I think the rains have driven you a little crazy. Generalissimo Chiang Kai-shek rules China, the Japanese permitting, of course.'

'But the Japanese will go,' Mountbatten said.

'And then?'

The room was very quiet. Mountbatten turned and nodded. The Corporal clicked his heels and passed the file to Major Campbell who opened it and took out a document which he passed across the desk to the Chairman.

'This is not a treaty but a covenant,' Mountbatten said. 'The Chungking Covenant, I call it. If you will read it and approve it with your signature above mine, you will agree to extend, if you ever control China, the Hong Kong Treaty by a hundred years. In exchange, His Majesty's Government will supply you with all your military needs.'

Mao Tse-tung examined the document, then glanced up. 'Have you a pen, Lord Mountbatten?'

It was the Corporal who supplied one, moving in quickly. Mao signed the document. Major Campbell produced three more copies and laid them on the table. Mao signed each one, Mountbatten countersigned.

He handed the pen back to the Corporal and stood up. 'A good night's work,' he said to Mountbatten, 'but now I must go.'

He started for the door and Mountbatten said, 'A moment, Mr Chairman, you're forgetting your copy of the covenant.'

Mao turned. 'Later,' he said. 'When it has been counter-signed by Churchill.'

Mountbatten stared at him. 'Churchill?'

'But of course. Naturally this should not delay the flow of arms, but I do look forward to receiving my copy signed by the man himself. Is there a problem?'

'No.' Mountbatten pulled himself together. 'No, of course not.'

'Good. And now, I must go. There is work to do, gentlemen.'

He went out and down the steps followed by the young officer, crossed to the Dakota and climbed in. The door was closed, the steps wheeled away, the plane started to taxi and Stilwell burst into laughter.

'God help me, that's the weirdest thing I've seen in years. He certainly is a character. What are you going to do?'

'Send the damn thing to London for Churchill's signature, of course.' Mountbatten turned back in the entrance and said to Major Campbell, 'Ian, I'm going to give you a chance to have dinner at the Savoy. I want you on your way to London as soon as possible with a dispatch from me for the Prime Minister. Did I hear another plane land?'

'Yes, sir, a Dakota from Assam.'

'Good. Give orders for it to be refuelled and turned around.' Mountbatten glanced at the Corporal. 'You can take Tanner with you.'

'Fine, sir.'

Campbell shuffled the papers to put them in the file and Mountbatten said, 'Three copies. One for Mao, another for the Prime Minister and the third for President Roosevelt. Didn't I sign four?'

'I took the liberty of making an extra copy, sir, just in case of accidents,' Campbell said.

'Good man, Ian,' Mountbatten nodded. 'On your way then. Only one night out at the Savoy then straight back.'

'Of course, sir.'

Campbell saluted and went out followed by Tanner. Stilwell lit a cigarette. 'He's a strange one, Campbell.'

'Lost his eye at Dunkirk,' Mountbatten said. 'Got a well earned Military Cross. Best aide I ever had.'

'What's all this Laird of Loch Dhu crap?' Stilwell said. 'You English are really crazy.'

'Ah, but Campbell isn't English, he's Scots and, more than that, he's a Highlander. As Laird of Loch Dhu he heads a sect of Clan Campbell and that, Joe, is a tradition that existed before the Vikings sailed to America.'

He walked to the door and stared out at the driving rain. Stilwell joined him. 'Are we going to win, Louis?'

'Oh, yes,' Mountbatten nodded. 'It's what will come after that bothers me.'

In Campbell's quarters, Tanner packed the Major's hold-all with military thoroughness while Campbell shaved. They had been together since boyhood, for Tanner's father had been a gamekeeper on the Loch Dhu estate, and together they endured the shattering experience of Dunkirk. When Campbell had first worked for Mountbatten at Combined Operations Headquarters in London he had taken the Corporal with him as his batman. The move to Southeast Asia Command had followed that. But to Jack Tanner, good soldier with a Military Medal for bravery in the field to prove it, Campbell would never be anything else but the Laird.

The Major came out of the bathroom drying his hands. He adjusted the black eye-patch and smoothed his hair then pulled on his tunic. 'Got the briefcase, Jack?'

Tanner held it up. 'The papers are inside, Laird.'

He always gave Campbell the title when they were alone. Campbell said, 'Open it. Take out the fourth copy, the extra copy.'

Tanner did as he was told and passed it to him. The single sheet of paper was headed Supreme Allied Commander Southeast Asia Command. Mao had signed it, not only in English, but in Chinese, with Mountbatten countersigning.

'There you are, Jack,' Campbell said as he folded it. 'Piece of history here. If Mao wins, Hong Kong will stay British until 1 July 2097.'

'You think it will happen, Laird?'

'Who knows. We've got to win the war first. Pass me my Bible, will you?'

Tanner went to the dresser where the Major's toilet articles were laid out. The Bible was about six inches by four with a cover of embossed silver, a Celtic cross standing out clearly. It was very old. Campbells had carried it to war for many centuries. It had been found in the pocket of the Major's ancestor who had died fighting for Bonnie Prince Charlie at Culloden. It had been recovered from the body of his uncle, killed on the Somme in 1916. Ian Campbell took it everywhere.

Tanner opened it. The inside of the Bible's cover was also silver. He felt carefully with his nail, it sprang open, revealing a small hidden compartment. Campbell folded the sheet of paper to the appropriate size and fitted it in, closing the lid.

'Top secret, Jack, only you and I know it's there. Your Highland oath on it.'

'You have it, Laird. Shall I put it in the hold-all, Laird?'

'No, I'll carry it in my map pocket.' There was a knock at the door, Tanner went to open it and Flight Lieutenant Caine stepped in. He was carrying heavy flying jackets and boots.

'You'll need these, sir. We'll probably have to go as high as twenty thousand over part of the Hump. Bloody freezing up there.'

The young man looked tired, dark circles under his eyes. Campbell said, 'I'm sorry about this. I know you've only just got in.'

'That's all right, sir. I carry a co-pilot, Pilot Officer Giffard. We can spell each other. We also have a navigator and wireless operator. We'll make out.' He smiled. 'One can hardly say no to Lord Mountbatten. All the way to Delhi on this one I see.'

'That's right. Then onwards to London.'

'Wish I was doing that leg of the trip.' Caine opened the door and looked out at the rain. 'Never stops, does it? What a bloody country. I'll see you at the plane, sir.' He went out.

Campbell said, 'Right, Jack, let's get moving.'

They pulled on the flying boots, the heavy sheepskin jackets. Finally ready, Tanner picked up his hold-all and the Major's.

'On your way, Jack.'

Tanner moved out. Campbell glanced around the room, reached for his cap and put it on, then he picked up the Bible, put it in the map pocket of his flying jacket and fastened the flap. Strange, but he felt more than tired. It was as if he had reached the end of something. His Highland blood speaking again. He shrugged the feeling off, turned and went out into the rain, following Tanner to the Dakota.

To Kunming from Chungking was four hundred and fifty miles. They took the opportunity of refuelling and then pressed on to the most hazardous section of the trip, the five hundred and fifty miles over the Hump to the Assam airfields.

Conditions were appalling – heavy rain and thunderstorms and the kind of turbulence that threatened to break the plane up. Several hundred aircrew had died making this run over the past couple of years; Campbell knew that. It was probably the most hazardous flying duty in the RAF or the USAF. He wondered what persuaded men to volunteer for such work and, while thinking about it, actually managed some sleep, only surfacing as they came into their Assam destination to refuel.

The onward trip to Delhi was another eleven hundred miles and a completely different proposition. Blue skies, considerable heat and no wind to speak of. The Dakota coasted along at ten thousand feet and Caine left the flying to Giffard, came back and tried to get a couple of hours' sleep.

Campbell dozed again and came awake to find the wireless operator shaking Caine by the shoulder. 'Delhi in fifteen minutes, Skipper.'

Caine got up, yawning. He grinned at Campbell. 'Piece of cake this leg, isn't it?'

As he turned away there was an explosion. Pieces of metal flew off the port engine, there was thick black smoke and, as the propeller stopped turning, the Dakota banked and dived steeply, throwing Caine off his feet.

Campbell was hurled against the bulkhead behind with such force that he was almost knocked senseless. The result was that he couldn't really take in what was happening. There was a kind of nightmare as if the world was breaking up around him, the impact of the crash, the smell of burning and someone screaming.

He was aware of being in water, managed to focus his eyes and found himself being dragged through a paddy field by a wild-eyed Tanner, blood on his face. The Corporal heaved him on to a dyke then turned and hurried back, knee-deep in water, to the Dakota which was burning fiercely now. When he was halfway there it blew up with a tremendous explosion.

Debris cascaded everywhere and Tanner turned and came back wearily. He eased the Major higher on the dyke and found a tin of cigarettes. His hand shook as he lit one.

'Are we it?' Campbell managed to croak.

'So it would appear, Laird.'

'Dear God.' Campbell's hands moved over his chest. 'The Bible,' he whispered.

'Dinna fash yourself, Laird, I'll hold it safe for you.'

Tanner took it from the map pocket and then all sounds faded for Campbell, all colour, nothing now but quiet darkness.

In Chungking Mountbatten and Stilwell were examining on the map the relentless progress of the advancing Japanese who had already overrun most of the Allied airfields in eastern China.

'I thought we were supposed to be winning the war,' Stilwell said.

Mountbatten smiled ruefully. 'So did I.'

Behind him, the door opened and an aide entered with a signal flimsy. 'Sorry to bother you, sir, but this is from Delhi marked urgent.'

Mountbatten read it then swore softly. 'All right, you can go.'

The aide went out. Stilwell said, 'Bad news.'

'The Dakota Campbell was travelling in lost an engine and crashed just outside Delhi. It fireballed after landing. By all accounts the documents and my dispatches went with it.'

'Is Campbell dead?'

'No, that Corporal of his managed to get him out. All the crew were killed. It seems Campbell received a serious head injury. He's in a coma.'

'Let's hope he hangs in there,' Stilwell said. 'Anyway, something of a set-back for you, your Chungking Covenant going up in flames. What will you do? Try to get Mao to sign another one?'

'I doubt if I'll ever get close enough to him again. It was always an "anything is better than nothing" situation. I didn't really expect much to come out of it. Anyway, in my experience Chinese seldom give you a second bite at the cherry.'

'I agree,' Stilwell said. 'In any case, the wily old bastard is probably already regretting putting his signature to that thing. But what about his supplies?'

'Oh, we'll see he gets those because I want him actively on our side taking on the Japanese. The Hong Kong business was never serious, Joe. I thought we ought to get something out of the deal if we could and the Hong Kong thing was all that the Prime Minister and I could come up with. Not that it matters now, we've got far more serious things to consider.' He walked back to the wall map. 'Now, show me exactly where those Japanese forward units are.'

1993

London

ONE

Norah Bell got out of the taxi close to St James's Stairs on Wapping High Street. She paid off the cab driver and walked away, a small, hippy, dark-haired girl in leather jacket, tight black mini-skirt and high-heeled ankle boots. She walked well with a sort of total movement of the whole body. The cab driver watched her put up her umbrella against the heavy rain, sighed deeply and drove away.

She paused on the first corner and bought an *Evening Standard*. The front page was concerned with only one thing, the arrival of the American President in London that day to meet with both the Israeli and British Prime

Ministers to discuss developments in the Palestinian situation. She folded the newspaper, put it under her left arm and turned the corner of the next street, walking down towards the Thames.

The youth standing in a doorway opposite was perhaps eighteen and wore lace-up boots, jeans and shabby bomber jacket. With the ring in his left nostril and the swastika tattooed on his forehead, he was typical of a certain type of gang animal that roamed the city streets in search of prey. She looked easy meat and he went after her quickly, only running in at the last minute to grab her from behind, one hand over her mouth. She didn't struggle, went completely still, which should have told him something, but by then he was beyond reason, charged with the wrong kind of sexual excitement.

'Just do as you're told,' he said, 'and I won't hurt you.'

He urged her into the porch of a long-disused warehouse, pushing against her. She said, 'No need to be rough.'

To his amazement she kissed him, her tongue flickering in his mouth. He couldn't believe his luck as, still clutching her umbrella, she moved her other hand down between them, brushing against his hardness.

'Jesus,' he moaned and kissed her again, aware that her hand seemed to be easing up her skirt.

She found what she was looking for, the flick knife tucked into the top of her right stocking. It came up, the blade jumped and she sliced open the left side of his face from the corner of the eye to the chin.

He screamed, falling back. She said calmly, putting the point under his chin, 'Do you want some more?'

He was more afraid than he had ever been in his life. 'No, for God's sake, no!'

She wiped the blade on his jacket. 'Then go away.'

He moved out into the rain, then turned, holding a handkerchief to his face. 'Bitch! I'll get you for this.'

'No you won't.' Her accent was unmistakably Ulster Irish. 'You'll find the nearest casualty department as fast as you can, get yourself stitched up and put the whole thing down to experience.'

She watched him go, closed the knife, slipping it back in the top of the stocking, then she turned and continued down towards the Thames, moving along the waterfront, finally pausing at an old warehouse. There was a small Judas gate in the main entrance. She opened it and went in.

It was a place of shadows, but at the far end there was a glass office with a light in it. It was reached by a flight of wooden stairs. As she moved towards it, a young, dark-skinned man moved out of the darkness, a Browning Hi-Power in one hand.

'And who might you be?' she asked.

The door of the office was opened and a small man with dark tousled hair wearing a reefer jacket appeared. 'Is that you, Norah?'

'And who else?' she replied. 'Who's your friend?'

'Ali Halabi, meet Norah Bell. Come away up.'

'I'm sorry,' the Arab said.

She ignored him and went up the stairs; he followed, noting with approval the way her skirt tightened over her hips.

When she went into the office the man in the reefer coat put his hands on her shoulders. 'God help me, but you look good enough to eat,' and he kissed her lightly on the lips.

'Save the blarney.' She put her umbrella on the desk, opened her handbag and took out a packet of cigarettes. 'Anything in a skirt, Michael Ahern. I've known you too long.'

She put a cigarette in her mouth and the Arab hurriedly took out a lighter and lit it for her. He turned to Ahern. 'The lady is part of your organisation?'

'Well, I'm not with the bloody IRA,' she said. 'We're Prods, mister, if you know what that means.'

'Norah and I were in the Ulster Volunteer Force together and then the Red Hand of Ulster,' Ahern said. 'Until we had to move on.'

Norah laughed harshly. 'Until they threw us out. A bunch of old women, that lot. We were killing too many Catholics for their liking.'

'I see,' Ali Halabi said. 'Is it Catholics who are your target or the IRA?'

'The same difference,' she said. 'I'm from Belfast, Mr Halabi. My father was an Army Sergeant, killed in the Falklands War. My mother, my kid sister, my old grandad, all the family I had in the world, were killed in a street bomb planted by the IRA back in eighty-six. You might say I've been taking my revenge ever since.'

'But we are open to offers,' Ahern said amiably. 'Any revolutionary organisation needs money.'

The Judas gate banged below. Ali took the gun from his pocket and Ahern moved to the door. 'Is that you, Billy?'

'As ever was.'

'Would that be Billy Quigley?' Norah asked.

'Who else?' Ahern turned to Ali. 'Another one the Red Hand threw out. Billy and I did some time together in the Maze prison.'

Quigley was a small, wiry man in an old raincoat. He had faded blond hair and a careworn face that was old beyond his years.

'Jesus, is that you, Norah?'

'Hello, Billy.'

'You got my message?' Ahern said.

'Yes, I drop in to the William of Orange in Kilburn most nights.'

Ahern said to Ali, 'Kilburn is what you might call the Irish quarter of London. Plenty of good Irish pubs there,

Catholic and Protestant. This, by the way, is Ali Halabi from Iran.'

'So what's it all about?' Quigley demanded.

'This.' Ahern held up the *Evening Standard* with the headline about the American President. 'Ali here represents a group of fundamentalists in Iran called the Army of God. They, shall we say, deeply deplore Arafat's deal with Israel over the new status of Palestine. They are even more unhappy with the American President presiding over that meeting at the White House and giving it his blessing.'

'So?' Quigley said.

'They'd like me to blow him up for them while he's in London, me having a certain reputation in that field.'

'For five million pounds,' Ali Halabi said. 'Don't let us forget that.'

'Half of which is already on deposit in Geneva.' Ahern smiled. 'By God, Billy, couldn't we give the IRA a run for their money with a million pounds to spend on arms?'

Quigley's face was pale. 'The American President? You wouldn't dare, not even you.'

Norah laughed that distinctive harsh laugh. 'Oh, yes he would.'

Ahern turned to her. 'Are you with me, girl?'

'I wouldn't miss it for the world.'

'And you, Billy?' Quigley licked dry lips and hesitated. Ahern put a hand on his shoulder. 'In or out, Billy?'

Quigley smiled suddenly. 'Why not. A man can only die once. How do we do it?'

'Come down below and I'll show you.'

Ahern led the way down the steps and switched on a light at the bottom. There was a vehicle parked in a corner covered by a dust sheet which he pulled away, revealing a grey British Telecom van.

'Where in the hell did you get that?' Quigley demanded.

'Someone knocked it off for me months ago. I was going to leave it outside one of those Catholic pubs in Kilburn with five hundred pounds of Semtex inside and blow the hell out of some Sinn Fein bastards, but I decided to hang on to it until something really important turned up.' Ahern smiled cheerfully. 'And now it has.'

'But how do you intend to pull it off?' Ali demanded.

'Hundreds of these things all over London. They can park anywhere without being interfered with because they usually have a manhole cover up while the engineers do what they have to do.'

'So?' Quigley said.

'Don't ask me how, but I have access through sources to the President's schedule. Tomorrow he leaves the American Embassy in Grosvenor Square at ten o'clock in the morning to go to Number Ten Downing Street. They take the Park Lane route, turning into Constitution Hill beside Green Park.'

'Can you be sure of that?' Norah asked.

'They always do, love, believe me.' He turned to Quigley and Ali. 'You two, dressed in Telecom overalls which are inside the van, will park halfway along Constitution Hill. There's a huge beech tree. You can't miss it. As I say, you park, lift the manhole cover, put up your signs and so on. You'll be there at nine-thirty. At nine-forty-five you walk away through Green Park to Piccadilly. There are some men's toilets. You can get rid of your overalls there.'

'And then what?' Ali demanded.

'I'll be in a car, waiting with Norah for the golden moment. As the President's cavalcade reaches the Telecom van I'll detonate by remote control.' He smiled. 'It'll work, I promise you. We'll probably kill everyone in the cavalcade.'

There was silence; a kind of awe on Quigley's face and Norah was excited, face pale. 'You bastard,' she said.

'You think it will work?'

'Oh, yes.'

He turned to Ali. 'And you? You're willing to take part?'

'An honour, Mr Ahern.'

'And you, Billy?' Ahern turned to him.

'They'll be singing about us for years,' Quigley said.

'Good man yourself, Billy.' Ahern looked at his watch. 'Seven o'clock. I could do with a bite to eat. How about you, Norah?'

'Fine,' she said.

'Good. I'm taking the Telecom van away now. I shan't be returning to this place. I'll pick you two up in the Mall at nine o'clock in the morning. You'll arrive separately and wait at the park gates across from Marlborough Road. Norah will be behind me in a car. You two will take over and we'll follow. Any questions?'

Ali Halabi was incredibly excited. 'I can't wait.'

'Good, off you go now. We'll leave separately.' The Arab went out and Ahern turned to Quigley and held out his hand. 'A big one this, eh, Billy?'

'The biggest, Michael.'

'Right, Norah and I will go now. Come and open the main gate for us. I'll leave you to put out the lights and follow on.'

Norah climbed into the passenger seat, but Ahern shook his head. 'Move into the rear out of sight and pass me one of those orange jackets. We've got to look right. If a copper sees you he might get curious.'

It said British Telecom across the back of the jacket. 'It'll never catch on,' she told him.

He laughed and drove out into the street, waving at Quigley who closed the gate behind them. He travelled only a few yards then swung into a yard and switched off the engine.

'What is it?' she demanded.

23

'You'll see. Follow me and keep your mouth shut.'

He opened the Judas gate gently and stepped in. Quigley was in the office; they could hear his voice and, when they reached the bottom of the stairs, they could even hear what he was saying.

'Yes, Brigadier Ferguson. Most urgent.' There was a pause. 'Then patch me through, you silly bugger, this is life or death.'

Ahern took a Walther from his pocket and screwed on a silencer as he went up, Norah behind him. The door was open and Quigley sat on the edge of the desk.

'Brigadier Ferguson?' he said suddenly. 'It's Billy Quigley. You said only to call you when it was big. Well this couldn't be bigger. Michael Ahern and that bitch Norah Bell and some Iranian named Ali Halabi are going to try to blow up the American President tomorrow.' There was a pause. 'Yes, I'm supposed to be in on it. Well, this is the way of it . . .'

'Billy boy,' Ahern said, 'that's really naughty of you.' As Quigley turned he shot him between the eyes.

Quigley fell back over the desk and Ahern picked up the phone. 'Are you there, Brigadier? Michael Ahern here. You'll need a new man.' He replaced the receiver, turned off the office light and turned to Norah. 'Let's go, my love.'

'You knew he was an informer?' she said.

'Oh, yes, I think that's why they let him out of the Maze prison early. He was serving life, remember. They must have offered him a deal.'

'The dirty bastard,' she said. 'And now he's screwed everything up.'

'Not at all,' Ahern said. 'You see, Norah, it's all worked out exactly as I planned.' He opened the van door and handed her in. 'We'll go and get a bite to eat and then I'll tell you how we're really going to hit the President.'

★

In 1972, aware of the growing problem of terrorism, the British Prime Minister of the day ordered the setting up of a small élite intelligence unit which became known rather bitterly in intelligence circles as the Prime Minister's private army, as it owed allegiance only to the office.

Brigadier Charles Ferguson had headed the unit since its inception, had served many Prime Ministers and had no political allegiance whatsoever. His office was on the third floor of the Ministry of Defence, overlooking Horseguards Avenue. He had been working late when Quigley's call was patched through. He was a rather untidy looking man in a Guards tie and tweed suit and was standing looking out of his window when there was a knock at the door.

The woman who entered was in her late twenties and wore a fawn trouser suit of excellent cut and black horn-rimmed glasses that contrasted with close-cropped red hair. She could have been a top secretary or PA. She was in fact a Detective Chief Inspector of Police from Special Branch at Scotland Yard, borrowed by Ferguson as his assistant after the untimely death in the line of duty of her predecessor. Her name was Hannah Bernstein.

'Was there something, Brigadier?'

'You could say so. When you worked with anti-terrorism at Scotland Yard did you ever come across a Michael Ahern?'

'Irish terrorist, Orange Protestant variety. Wasn't he Red Hand of Ulster?'

'And Norah Bell?'

'Oh, yes,' Hannah Bernstein said. 'A very bleak prospect, that one.'

'I had an informer, Billy Quigley, in deep cover. He just phoned me to say that Ahern was masterminding a plot to blow up the American President tomorrow. He'd recruited Quigley. Bell is involved and an Iranian named Ali Halabi.'

'Excuse me, sir, but I know who Halabi is. He belongs to Army of God. That's an extreme fundamentalist group very much opposed to the Israeli-Palestine accord.'

'Really?' Ferguson said. 'That is interesting. Even more interesting is that Quigley was shot dead while filling me in. Ahern actually had the cheek to pick up the phone and speak to me. Told me it was him. Said I'd need a new man.'

'A cool bastard, sir.'

'Oh, he's that all right. Anyway, notify everyone. Scotland Yard anti-terrorist unit, MI5 and security at the American Embassy. Obviously the Secret Service men guarding the President will have a keen interest.'

'Right, sir.'

She turned to the door and he said, 'One more thing. I need Dillon on this.'

She turned. 'Dillon, sir?'

'Sean Dillon. Don't pretend you don't know who I mean.'

'The only Sean Dillon I know, sir, was the most feared enforcer the IRA ever had and, if I'm right, he tried to blow up the Prime Minister and the War Cabinet in February nineteen-ninety-one during the Gulf War.'

'And nearly succeeded,' Ferguson said; 'but he works for this Department now, Chief Inspector, so get used to it. He only recently completed a most difficult assignment on the Prime Minister's orders that saved the Royal Family considerable grief. I need Dillon, so find him. Now, on your way.'

Ahern had a studio flat in what had been a warehouse beside the canal in Camden. He parked the Telecom van in the garage then took Norah up in what had been the old freight hoist. The studio was simply furnished, the wooden floor sanded and varnished, a rug here and there, two or three large sofas. The paintings on the wall were very modern.

'Nice,' she said, 'but it doesn't seem you.'

'It isn't. I'm on a six months' lease.'

He opened the drinks cabinet, found a bottle of Jameson Irish whiskey and poured some into two glasses. He offered her one, then opened a window and stepped out on to a small platform overlooking the canal.

'What's going on, Michael?' she said. 'I mean, we don't really stand much of a chance of blowing up the President on Constitution Hill. Not now.'

'I never thought for a moment that I could. You should remember, Norah, that I never let my left hand know what my right is doing.'

'Explain,' she said.

'Because of Quigley's phone call, wherever the President goes tomorrow they'll be on tenterhooks. Now, follow my reasoning. If there is an abortive explosion on his intended route to Number Ten Downing Street, everyone heaves a sigh of relief, especially if they find what's left of Halabi there.'

'Go on.'

'They won't expect another attempt the same day in an entirely different context.'

'My God,' she said. 'You planned this all along; you used Quigley.'

'Poor sod.' Ahern brushed past her and helped himself to more whiskey. 'Once they have their explosion they'll think that's it, but it won't be. You see, tomorrow night at seven-thirty, the American President, the Prime Minister and selected guests board the river boat *Jersey Lily* at Cadogan Pier on the Chelsea Embankment for an evening of frivolity and cocktails, cruising the Thames past the Houses of Parliament, ending up at Westminster Pier. The catering is in the hands of Orsini and Co., by whom you and I are employed as waiters.' He opened a drawer and took out two security cards. 'My name is Harry Smith – nice and innocuous. You'll note the false moustache and horn-rimmed glasses. I'll add those later.'

'Mary Hunt,' Norah said. 'That does sound prim. Where did you get my photo?'

'An old one I had. I got a photographer friend to touch it up and add the spectacles. They intend a cocktail party on the forward deck, weather permitting.'

'What about weapons? How would we get through security?'

'Taken care of. An associate of mine was working as a crew member until yesterday. He's left two silenced Walthers wrapped in cling film at the bottom of the sand in a fire bucket in one of the men's restrooms and that was after the security people did their checks.'

'Very clever.'

'I'm no kamikaze, Norah, I intend to survive this. We hit from the upper decks. With silenced weapons, he'll go down as if he's having a heart attack.'

'And what happens to us?'

'The ship has an inflatable tender on a line at the stern. My associate checked it out. It has an outboard motor. In the confusion, we'll drop in and head for the other side of the river.'

'As long as the confusion is confusion enough.'

'Nothing's perfect in this life. Are you with me?'

'Oh, yes,' she said. 'To the end, Michael, whatever comes.'

'Good girl.' He put an arm round her and squeezed. 'Now, could we go and get something to eat? I'm starving.'

TWO

'A strange man, Sean Dillon,' Ferguson said.

'I'd say that was an understatement, sir,' Hannah Bernstein told him.

They were sitting in the rear of Ferguson's Daimler, threading their way through the West End traffic.

'He was born in Belfast, but his mother died in childbirth. His father came to work in London, so the boy went to school here. Incredible talent for acting. He did a year at the Royal Academy of Dramatic Art and one or two roles at the National Theatre. He also has a flair for languages, everything from Irish to Russian.'

'All very impressive, sir, but he still ended up shooting people for the Provisional IRA.'

'Yes, well that was because his father, on a trip home to Belfast, got caught in some crossfire and was killed by a British Army patrol. Dillon took the oath, did a fast course on weaponry in Libya and never looked back.'

'Why the switch from the IRA to the international scene?'

'Disenchantment with the glorious cause. Dillon is a thoroughly ruthless man when he has to be. He's killed many times in his career; but the random bomb that kills women and children? Let's say that's not his style.'

'Are you trying to tell me he actually has some notion of morality?'

Ferguson laughed. 'Well, he certainly never played favourites. Worked for the PLO, but also as an underwater specialist for the Israelis.'

'For money, of course.'

'Naturally. Our Sean does like the good things in life. The attempt to blow up Downing Street, that was for money. Saddam Hussein was behind that. And yet eighteen months later he flies a light plane loaded with medical supplies for children into Bosnia and no payment involved.'

'What happened, did God speak down through the clouds to him or something?'

'Does it matter? The Serbs had him, and his prospects, to put it mildly, looked bleak. I did a deal with them which saved him from a firing squad. In return he came to work for me, slate wiped clean.'

'Excuse me, sir, but that's a slate that will never wipe clean.'

'My dear Chief Inspector, there are many occasions in this line of work when it's useful to be able to set a thief to catch one. If you are to continue to work for me, you'll have to get used to the idea.' He peered out as they turned into Grafton Street. 'Are you sure he's at this place?'

'So they tell me, sir. His favourite restaurant.'

'Excellent,' Ferguson said. 'I could do with a bite to eat myself.'

Sean Dillon sat in the upstairs bar of Mulligan's Irish Restaurant and worked his way through a dozen oysters and half a bottle of Krug champagne to help things along as he read the evening paper. He was a small man, no more than five feet five, with hair so fair that it was almost white. He wore dark cord jeans, an old black leather flying jacket, a white scarf at his throat. The eyes were his strangest feature, like water over a stone – clear, no colour – and there was a permanent slight ironic quirk to the corner of his mouth, the look of a man who no longer took life too seriously.

'So there you are,' Charles Ferguson said and Dillon glanced up and groaned. 'No place to hide, not tonight. I'll have a dozen of those and a pint of Guinness.'

A young waitress standing by had heard. Dillon said to her in Irish, 'A fine lordly Englishman, a *colleen*, but his mother, God rest her, was Irish, so give him what he wants.'

The girl gave him a smile of true devotion and went away. Ferguson sat down and Dillon looked up at Hannah Bernstein. 'And who might you be, girl?'

'This is Detective Chief Inspector Hannah Bernstein, Special Branch, my new assistant and I don't want you corrupting her. Now, where's my Guinness?'

It was then that Hannah Bernstein received her first shock for, as Dillon stood, he smiled and it was like no smile she had ever seen before, warm and immensely charming, changing his personality completely. She had come here wanting to dislike this man, but now . . .

He took her hand. 'And what would a nice Jewish girl

31

like you be doing in such bad company? Will you have a glass of champagne?'

'I don't think so, I'm on duty.' She was slightly uncertain now and took a seat.

Dillon went to the bar, returned with another glass and poured Krug into it. 'When you're tired of champagne, you're tired of life.'

'What a load of cobblers,' she said, but took the glass.

Ferguson roared with laughter. 'Beware this one, Dillon, she ran across a hoodlum emerging from a supermarket with a sawn-off shotgun last year. Unfortunately for him she was working the American Embassy detail that week and had a Smith and Wesson in her handbag.'

'So you convinced him of his wicked ways?' Dillon said.

She nodded. 'Something like that.'

Ferguson's Guinness and oysters appeared. 'We've got trouble, Dillon, bad trouble. Tell him, Chief Inspector.'

Which she did in a few brief sentences. When she was finished, Dillon took a cigarette from a silver case and lit it with an old-fashioned Zippo lighter.

'So, what do you think?' she asked.

'Well, all we know for certain is that Billy Quigley is dead.'

'But he did manage to speak to the Brigadier,' Hannah said. 'Which surely means Ahern will abort the mission.'

'Why should he?' Dillon said. 'You've got nothing except the word that he intends to try and blow up the President sometime tomorrow. Where? When? Have you even the slightest idea, and I'll bet his schedule is extensive!'

'It certainly is,' Ferguson said. 'Downing Street in the morning with the PM and the Israeli Prime Minister. Cocktail party on a river steamer tomorrow night and most things in between.'

'None of which he's willing to cancel?'

'I'm afraid not.' Ferguson shook his head. 'I've already had a call from Downing Street. The President refuses to change a thing.'

Hannah Bernstein said, 'Do you know Ahern personally?'

'Oh, yes,' Dillon told her. 'He tried to kill me a couple of times and then we met for face-to-face negotiations during a truce in Derry.'

'And his girl-friend?'

Dillon shook his head. 'Whatever else Norah Bell is, she isn't that. Sex isn't in her bag. She was just an ordinary working-class girl until her family was obliterated by an IRA bomb. These days she'd kill the Pope if she could.'

'And Ahern?'

'He's a strange one. It's always been like a game to him. He's a brilliant manipulator. I recall his favourite saying. That he didn't like his left hand to know what his right hand was doing.'

'And what's that supposed to mean?' Ferguson demanded.

'Just that nothing's ever what it seems with Ahern.'

There was a small silence then Ferguson said, 'Everyone is on this case. We've got them pumping out a not very good photo of the man himself.'

'And an even more inferior one of the girl,' Hannah Bernstein said.

Ferguson swallowed an oyster. 'Any ideas on finding him?'

'As a matter of fact I have,' Dillon said. 'There's a Protestant pub in Kilburn, the William of Orange. I could have words there.'

'Then what are we waiting for?' Ferguson swallowed his last oyster and stood up. 'Let's go.'

The William of Orange in Kilburn had a surprising look of Belfast about it, with the fresco of King William victorious at the Battle of the Boyne on the whitewashed wall at one side. It could have been any Orange pub in the Shankill.

'You wouldn't exactly fit in at the bar, you two,' Dillon said as they sat in the back of the Daimler. 'I need to speak to a man called Paddy Driscoll.'

'What is he, UVF?' Ferguson asked.

'Let's say he's a fund-raiser. Wait here. I'm going round the back.'

'Go with him, Chief Inspector,' Ferguson ordered.

Dillon sighed. 'All right, Brigadier, but I'm in charge.'

Ferguson nodded. 'Do as he says.'

Dillon got out and started along the pavement. 'Are you carrying?' he asked.

'Of course.'

'Good. You never know what will happen next in this wicked old world.'

He paused in the entrance to a yard, took a Walther from his waistband at the rear, produced a Carswell silencer and screwed it into place; then he slipped it inside his flying jacket. They crossed the cobbled yard through the rain, aware of music from the bar area where some loyalist band thumped out 'The Sash My Father Wore'. Through the rear window was a view of an extensive kitchen, and a small, grey-haired man seated at a table doing accounts.

'That's Driscoll,' Dillon whispered. 'In we go.' Driscoll, at the table, was aware of some of his papers fluttering in a sudden draft of wind, looked up and found Dillon entering the room, Hannah Bernstein behind him.

'God bless all here,' Dillon said, 'and the best of the night yet to come, Paddy, me old son.'

'Dear God, Sean Dillon.' There was naked fear on Driscoll's face.

'Plus your very own Detective Chief Inspector. We *are* treating you well tonight.'

'What do you want?'

34

Hannah leaned against the door and Dillon pulled a chair over and sat across the table from Driscoll. He took out a cigarette and lit it. 'Michael Ahern. Where might he be?'

'Jesus, Sean, I haven't seen that one in years.'

'Billy Quigley? Don't tell me you haven't seen Billy because I happen to know he drinks here regularly.'

Driscoll tried to tough it out. 'Sure, Billy comes in all the time, but as for Ahern . . .' He shrugged. 'He's bad news that one, Sean.'

'Yes, but I'm worse.' In one swift movement Dillon pulled the Walther from inside his flying jacket, levelled it and fired. There was a dull thud, the lower half of Driscoll's left ear disintegrated and he moaned, a hand to the ear, blood spurting.

'Dillon, for God's sake!' Hannah cried.

'I don't think He's got much to do with it.' Dillon raised the Walther. 'Now the other one.'

'No, I'll tell you,' Driscoll moaned. 'Ahern did phone here yesterday. He left a message for Billy. I gave it to him around five o'clock when he came in for a drink.'

'What was it?'

'He was to meet him at a place off Wapping High Street, a warehouse called Olivers. Brick Wharf.'

Driscoll fumbled for a handkerchief, sobbing with pain. Dillon slipped the gun inside his flying jacket and got up. 'There you are,' he said. 'That didn't take long.'

'You're a bastard, Dillon,' Hannah Bernstein said as she opened the door.

'It's been said before.' Dillon turned in the doorway. 'One more thing, Paddy, Michael Ahern killed Billy Quigley earlier tonight. We know that for a fact.'

'Dear God!' Driscoll said.

'That's right. I'd stay out of it if I were you,' and Dillon closed the door gently.

★

'Shall I call for back-up, sir?' Hannah Bernstein said as the Daimler eased into Brick Wharf beside the Thames.

Ferguson put his window down and looked out. 'I shouldn't think it matters, Chief Inspector. If he was here, he's long gone. Let's go and see.'

It was Dillon who led the way in, the Walther ready in his left hand, stepping through the Judas gate, feeling for the switch on the wall, flooding the place with light. At the bottom of the steps he found the office switch and led the way up. Billy Quigley lay on his back on the other side of the desk. Dillon stood to one side, shoving the Walther back inside his flying jacket and Ferguson and Hannah Bernstein moved forward.

'Is that him, sir?' she asked.

'I'm afraid so.' Ferguson sighed. 'Take care of it, Chief Inspector.'

She started to call-in on her mobile phone and Ferguson turned and went down the stairs followed by Dillon. He went out into the street and stood by a rail overlooking the Thames. As Dillon joined him, Hannah Bernstein appeared. Ferguson said, 'Well, what do you think?'

'I can't believe he didn't know that Billy was an informer,' Dillon said.

Ferguson turned to Hannah. 'Which means?'

'If Dillon's right, sir, Ahern is playing some sort of game with us.'

'But what?' Ferguson demanded.

'There are times for waiting, Brigadier, and this is one of them,' Dillon said. 'If you want my thoughts on the matter, it's simple. We're in Ahern's hands. There will be a move tomorrow, sooner rather than later. Based on that, I might have some thoughts, but not before.'

Dillon lit a cigarette with his old Zippo, turned and walked back to the Daimler.

★

It was just before nine the following morning when Ahern drove the Telecom van along the Mall, stopping at the park gates opposite Marlborough Road. Norah followed him in a Toyota saloon. Ali Halabi was standing by the gates dressed in a green anorak and jeans. He hurried forward.

'No sign of Quigley.'

'Get in.' The Arab did as he was told and Ahern passed him one of the orange Telecom jackets. 'He's ill. Suffers from chronic asthma and the stress has brought on an attack.' He shrugged. 'Not that it matters. All you have to do is drive the van. Norah and I will lead you to your position. Just get out, lift the manhole cover then walk away through the park. Are you still on?'

'Absolutely,' Halabi said.

'Good. Then follow us and everything will be all right.'

Ahern got out. Halabi slid behind the wheel. 'God is great,' he said.

'He certainly is, my old son.' Ahern turned and walked back to Norah parked at the kerb in the Toyota.

Norah went all the way round, passing Buckingham Palace, turning up Grosvenor Place and back along Constitution Hill by the park. On Ahern's instructions she pulled in at the kerb opposite the beech tree and paused. Ahern put his arm out of the window and raised a thumb. As they moved away, the Telecom van eased into the kerb. There was a steady flow of traffic. Ahern let her drive about fifty yards then told her to pull in. They could see Halabi get out. He went round to the back of the van and opened the doors. He returned with a clamp, leaned down and prised up the manhole cover.

'He's working well, is the boy,' Ahern said.

He took a small plastic remote control unit from his

pocket and pressed a button. Behind them the van fireballed and two cars passing it, caught in the blast, were blown across the road.

'That's what dedication gets for you.' Ahern tapped Norah on the shoulder. 'Right, girl dear. Billy told them they'd get an explosion and they've got one.'

'An expensive gesture. With Halabi gone we won't get the other half of the money.'

'Two and a half million pounds on deposit in Switzerland, Norah, not a bad pay day, so don't be greedy. Now let's get out of here.'

It was late in the afternoon, with Ferguson still at his desk at the Ministry of Defence, when Hannah Bernstein came in.

'Anything new?' he asked.

'Not a thing, sir. Improbable though it sounds, there was enough of Halabi left to identify, his fingerprints anyway. It seems he must have been on the pavement, not in the van.'

'And the others?'

'Two cars caught in the blast. Driver of the front one was a woman doctor, killed instantly. The man and woman in the other were going to a sales conference. They're both in intensive care.' She put the report on his desk. 'Quigley was right, but at least Ahern's shot his bolt.'

'You think so?'

'Sir, you've seen the President's schedule. He was due to pass along Constitution Hill at about ten o'clock on the way to Downing Street. Ahern must have known that.'

'And the explosion?'

'Premature. That kind of thing happens all the time, you know that, sir. Halabi was just an amateur. I've looked at his file in depth. He had an accountancy degree from the London School of Economics.'

'Yes, it all makes sense – at least to me.'

'But not to Dillon. Where is he?'

'Out and about. Nosing around.'

'He wouldn't trust his own grandmother, that one.'

'I suppose that's why he's still alive,' Ferguson told her. 'Help yourself to coffee, Chief Inspector.'

At the studio flat in Camden Ahern stood in front of the bathroom mirror and rubbed brilliantine into his hair. He combed it back, leaving a centre parting, then carefully glued a dark moustache and fixed it in place. He picked up a pair of horn-rimmed spectacles and put them on, then compared himself with the face on the security pass. As he turned, Norah came in the room. She wore a neat black skirt and white blouse. Her hair was drawn back in a tight bun. Like him she wore spectacles, rather large ones with black rims. She looked totally different.

'How do I look?' she said.

'Bloody marvellous,' he told her. 'What about me?'

'Great, Michael. First class.'

'Good.' He led the way out of the bathroom and crossed to a drinks cabinet. He produced a bottle of Bushmills and two glasses. 'It's not champagne, Norah Bell, but it's good Irish whiskey.' He poured and raised his glass. 'Our country too.'

'Our country too,' she replied, giving him that most ancient of loyalist toasts.

He emptied his glass. 'Good. All I need is our box of cutlery and we'll be on our way.'

It was around six-thirty when Ferguson left the Ministry of Defence with Hannah Bernstein and told his driver to take him to his flat in Cavendish Square. The door was opened by Kim, the ex-Gurkha Corporal who had been his man-servant for years.

'Mr Dillon has been waiting for you, Brigadier.'

'Thanks,' Ferguson said.

When they went into the living room Dillon was standing by the open french window, a glass in his hand. He turned. 'Helped myself. Hope you don't mind.'

'Where have you been?' Ferguson demanded.

'Checking my usual sources. You can discount the IRA on this one. It really is Ahern and that's what bothers me.'

'Can I ask why?' Hannah Bernstein said.

Dillon said, 'Michael Ahern is one of the most brilliant organisers I ever knew. Very clever, very subtle, and very, very devious. I told you, he doesn't let his left hand know what his right is doing.'

'So you don't think he's simply shot his bolt on this one?' Ferguson said.

'Too easy. It may sound complicated to you, but I think everything from Quigley's betrayal and death to the so-called accidental explosion of the Telecom van on the President's route was meant to happen.'

'Are you serious?' Hannah demanded.

'Oh, yes. The attempt failed so we can all take it easy. Let me look at the President's schedule.'

Hannah passed a copy across and Ferguson poured himself a drink. 'For once I really do hope you're wrong, Dillon.'

'Here it is,' Dillon said. 'Cocktail party on the Thames riverboat *Jersey Lily*. The Prime Minister, the President and the Prime Minister of Israel. That's where he'll strike, that's where he always intended, the rest was a smokescreen.'

'You're mad, Dillon,' Ferguson said. 'You must be,' and then he turned and saw Hannah Bernstein's face. 'Oh, my God,' he said.

She glanced at her watch. 'Six-thirty, sir.'

'Right,' he said, 'let's get moving. We don't have much time.'

★

At the same moment, Ahern and Norah were parking the Toyota in a side street off Cheyne Walk. They got out and walked down towards Cadogan Pier. There were police cars by the dozen, uniformed men all over the place and at the boarding point a portable electronic arch that everyone had to pass through. Beside it were two large young men in blue suits.

Ahern said, 'Secret Service, the President's bodyguard. I think they get their suits from the same shop.'

He and Norah wore their identity cards on their lapels and he grinned and passed a plastic box to one of the Secret Servicemen as they reached the arch. 'Sorry to be a nuisance, but there's two hundred knives, spoons and forks in there. It might blow a fuse on that thing.'

'Give it to me and you go through,' the Secret Serviceman said.

They negotiated the arch and he opened the plastic box and riffled the cutlery with his hand. At that moment several limousines drew up.

'For Christ's sake, man, it's the Israeli Prime Minister,' his colleague called.

The Secret Serviceman said to Ahern, 'You'll have to leave this box. On your way.'

'Suit yourself.' Ahern went up the gangplank followed by Norah. At the top he simply slipped through a door and, following a plan of the ship he had memorised, led the way to a toilet area.

'Wait here,' he told Norah and went into the men's restroom marked number four.

There was a man washing his hands. Ahern started to wash his hands also. The moment the man left, he went to the red fire bucket in the corner, scrabbled in the sand and found two Walthers wrapped in cling film, each with a silencer on the end. He slipped one into the waistband of his trousers at the rear and concealed the other inside his uniform blazer. When he went outside he checked that no one was around for the moment and passed the second Walther to Norah, who slipped it into the inside breast pocket of her blazer under the left armpit.

'Here we go,' he said.

At that moment a voice with a heavy Italian accent called, 'You two, what are you doing?' When they turned a grey-haired man in black coat and striped trousers was coming along the corridor. 'Who sent you?'

Ahern, already sure of his facts, said, 'Signor Orsini. We were supposed to be at the buffet at the French Embassy, but he told us to come here at the last minute. He thought you might be short-handed.'

'And he's right.' The Head Waiter turned to Norah. 'Canapés for you and wine for you,' he added to Ahern. 'Up the stairs on the left. Now get moving,' and he turned and hurried away.

The Prime Minister and the President had already boarded and the crew were about to slip the gangway when Ferguson, Dillon and Hannah drew up in the Daimler. Ferguson led the way, hurrying up the gangway and two Secret Servicemen moved to intercept him.

'Brigadier Ferguson. Is Colonel Candy here?'

A large, grey-haired man in a black suit and striped tie hurried along the deck. 'It's all right. Is there a problem, Brigadier?'

'These are aides of mine, Dillon and Chief Inspector Bernstein.' Behind him the gangway went down as the crew cast off and the *Jersey Lily* started to edge out into the Thames. 'I'm afraid there could be. The explosion this morning? We now believe it to be a subterfuge. You've had a photo of this man Ahern. Please alert all your men. He could well be on the boat.'

'Right.' Candy didn't argue and turned to the two

Secret Servicemen. 'Jack, you take the stern, George, go up front. I'll handle the President. Alert everybody.'

They all turned and hurried away. Ferguson said, 'Right, let's try to be useful in our own small way, shall we?'

There was music on the night air provided by a jazz quartet up in the prow, people crowding around, mainly politicians and staff from the London embassies, the President, the Prime Minister and the Israeli Prime Minister moving among them, waiters and waitresses offering wine and canapés to everyone.

'It's a nightmare,' Ferguson said.

Candy appeared, running down a companionway. 'The big three will all say a few words in about ten minutes. After that we continue down past the Houses of Parliament and disembark at Westminster Pier.'

'Fine.' Ferguson turned to Dillon as the American hurried away. 'This is hopeless.'

'Maybe he's not here,' Hannah said. 'Perhaps you're wrong, Dillon.'

It was as if he wasn't listening to her. 'He'd have to have a way out.' He turned to Ferguson. 'The stern, let's look at the stern.'

He led the way to the rear of the ship quickly, pushing people out of the way, and leaned over the stern rail. After a moment he turned. 'He's here.'

'How do you know?' Ferguson demanded.

Dillon reached over and hauled in a line and an inflatable with an outboard motor came into view. 'That's his way out,' he said. 'Or it was.' He reached over, opened the snap link that held the line and the inflatable vanished into the darkness.

'Now what?' Hannah demanded.

At that moment a voice over the tannoy system said, 'Ladies and Gentlemen, the Prime Minister.'

Dillon said, 'He isn't the kind to commit suicide so he

wouldn't walk up to him in the crowd.' He looked up at the wheelhouse perched on top of the ship, three levels of decks below it. 'That's it. It has to be.'

He ran for the steps leading up, Hannah at his heels, Ferguson struggling behind. He looked along the first deck which was deserted and started up the steps to the next. As he reached it, the Prime Minister said over the tannoy, 'I'm proud to present to you the President of the United States.'

At the same moment as Dillon reached the deck he saw Michael Ahern open the saloon door at the far end and enter, followed by Norah Bell carrying a tray covered by a white napkin.

The saloon was deserted. Ahern moved forward and looked down through the windows to the forward deck where the President stood at the microphone, the British and Israeli Prime Ministers beside him. Ahern eased one of the windows open and took out his gun.

The door opened gently behind him and Dillon moved in, his Walther ready. 'Jesus, Michael, but you never give up, do you.'

Ahern turned, the gun against his thigh. 'Sean Dillon, you old bastard,' and then his hand swung up.

Dillon shot him twice in the heart, a double thud of the silenced pistol that drove him back against the bulkhead. Norah Bell stood there, frozen, clutching the tray.

Dillon said, 'Now, if there was a pistol under that napkin and you thinking about reaching for it, I'd have to kill you, Norah, and neither of us would like that, you being a decent Irish girl. Just put the tray down.'

Very slowly, Norah Bell did as she was told and placed the tray on the nearest table. Dillon turned, the Walther swinging from his right hand and said to Ferguson and Hannah, 'There you go, all's well that ends well.'

Behind him Norah hitched up her skirt, pulled the flick

knife from her stocking and sprang the blade, plunging it into his back. Dillon reared up in agony and dropped his Walther.

'Bastard!' Norah cried, pulled out the knife and thrust it into him again.

Dillon lurched against the table and hung there for a moment. Norah raised the knife to strike a third blow and Hannah Bernstein dropped to one knee, picked up Dillon's Walther and shot her in the centre of the forehead. At the same moment Dillon slipped from the table and rolled on to his back.

It was around midnight at the London Clinic, one of the world's greatest hospitals, and Hannah Bernstein sat in the first floor reception area close to Dillon's room. She was tired, which in the circumstances was hardly surprising, but a diet of black coffee and cigarettes had kept her going. The door at the end of the corridor swung open and, to her astonishment, Ferguson entered followed by the President and Colonel Candy.

'The President was returning to the American Embassy,' Ferguson told her.

'But in the circumstances I felt I should look in. You're Chief Inspector Bernstein, I understand.' The President took her hand. 'I'm eternally grateful.'

'You owe more to Dillon, sir. He was the one who thought it through, he was the one who knew they were on board.'

The President moved to the window and peered in. Dillon, festooned with wires, lay on a hospital bed, a nurse beside him.

'How is he?'

'Intensive care, sir,' she said. 'A four-hour operation. She stabbed him twice.'

'I brought in Professor Henry Bellamy of Guy's Hospital,

Mr President,' Ferguson said. 'The best surgeon in London.'

'Good.' The President nodded. 'I owe you and your people for this, Brigadier, I'll never forget.'

He walked away and Colonel Candy said, 'Thank God it worked out the way it did; that way we can keep it under wraps.'

'I know,' Ferguson said. 'It never happened.'

Candy walked away and Hannah Bernstein said, 'I saw Professor Bellamy half an hour ago. He came to check on him.'

'And what did he say?' Ferguson frowned. 'He's going to be all right, isn't he?'

'Oh, he'll live, sir, if that's what you mean. The trouble is Bellamy doesn't think he'll ever be the same again. She almost gutted him.'

Ferguson put an arm round her shoulder. 'Are you all right, my dear?'

'You mean am I upset because I killed someone tonight? Not at all, Brigadier. I'm really not the nice Jewish girl Dillon imagines. I'm a rather Old Testament Jewish girl. She was a murderous bitch. She deserved to die.' She took out a cigarette and lit it. 'No, it's Dillon I'm sorry for. He did a good job. He deserved better.'

'I thought you didn't like him,' Ferguson said.

'Then you were wrong, Brigadier.' She looked in through the window at Dillon. 'The trouble is I liked him too much and that never pays in our line of work.'

She turned and walked away. Ferguson hesitated, glanced once more at Dillon, then went after her.

THREE

AND TWO MONTHS later in another hospital, Our Lady of Mercy in New York, on the other side of the Atlantic as darkness fell, young Tony Jackson clocked in for night duty. He was a tall, handsome man of twenty-three who had qualified as a doctor at Harvard Medical School the year before. Our Lady of Mercy, a charity hospital mainly staffed by nuns, was not many young doctors' idea of the ideal place to be an intern.

But Tony Jackson was an idealist. He wanted to practise real medicine and he could certainly do that at Our Lady of Mercy, who could not believe their luck at getting their hands on such a brilliant young man. He loved the nuns, found the vast range of patients fascinating. The money was poor, but in his case money was no object. His father, a successful Manhattan attorney, had died far too early from cancer, but he had left them well provided for. In any case, his mother, Rosa, was from the Little Italy district of New York with a doting father big in the construction business.

Tony liked the night shift, that atmosphere peculiar to hospitals all over the world, and it gave him the opportunity to be in charge. For the first part of the evening he worked on the casualty shift, dealing with a variety of patients, stitching slashed faces, handling as best he could junkies who were coming apart because they couldn't afford a fix. It was all pretty demanding, but slackened off after midnight.

He was alone in the small canteen having coffee and a sandwich when the door opened and a young priest looked in. 'I'm Father O'Brien from St Marks. I had a call to come and see a Mr Tanner, a Scottish gentleman. I understand he needs the last rites.'

'Sorry, Father, I only came on tonight, I wouldn't know. Let me look at the schedule.' He checked it briefly then nodded. 'Jack Tanner, that must be him. Admitted this afternoon. Age seventy-five, British citizen. Collapsed at his daughter's house in Queens. He's in a private room on level three, number eight.'

'Thank you,' the priest said and disappeared.

Jackson finished his coffee and idly glanced through *The New York Times*. There wasn't much news, an IRA bomb in London in the city's financial centre, an item about Hong Kong, the British Colony in China which was to revert to Chinese control on 1 July 1997. It seemed that the British governor of the colony was introducing a thoroughly democratic voting system while he had the chance and the Chinese government in Peking were

48

annoyed, which didn't look good for Hong Kong when the change took place.

He threw the paper down, bored and restless, got up and went outside. The elevator doors opened and Father O'Brien emerged. 'Ah, there you are, Doctor. I've done what I could for the poor man, but he's not long for this world. He's from the Highlands of Scotland, would you believe? His daughter is married to an American.'

'That's interesting,' said Jackson. 'I always imagined the Scots as Protestant.'

'My dear lad, not in the Highlands,' Father O'Brien told him. 'The Catholic tradition is very strong.' He smiled. 'Well, I'll be on my way. Good night to you.'

Jackson watched him go then got in the elevator and rose to the third level. As he emerged, he saw Sister Agnes, the night duty nurse, come out of room eight and go to her desk.

Jackson said, 'I've just seen Father O'Brien. He tells me this Mr Tanner doesn't look good.'

'There's his chart, Doctor. Chronic bronchitis and severe emphysema.'

Jackson examined the notes. 'Lung capacity only twelve per cent and the blood pressure is unbelievable.'

'I just checked his heart, Doctor. Very irregular.'

'Let's take a look at him.'

Jack Tanner's face was drawn and wasted, the sparse hair snow white. His eyes were closed as he breathed in short gasps, a rattling sound in his throat at intervals.

'Oxygen?' Jackson asked.

'Administered an hour ago. I gave it to him myself.'

'Aye, but she wouldn't give me a cigarette.' Jack Tanner opened his eyes. 'Is that no the terrible thing, Doctor?'

'Now, Mr Tanner,' Sister Agnes reproved him gently. 'You know that's not allowed.'

Jackson leaned over to check the tube connections and noticed the scar on the right side of the chest. 'Would that have been a bullet wound?' he asked.

'Aye, it was so. Shot in the lung while I was serving in the Highland Light Infantry. That was before Dunkirk in nineteen-forty. I'd have died if the Laird hadn't got me out and him wounded so bad he lost an eye.'

'The Laird, you say?' Jackson was suddenly interested, but Tanner started to cough so harshly that he almost had a convulsion. Jackson grabbed for the oxygen mask. 'Breathe nice and slowly. That's it.' He removed it after a while and Tanner smiled weakly. 'I'll be back,' Jackson told him and went out.

'You said the daughter lives in Queens?'

'That's right, Doctor.'

'Don't let's waste time. Send a cab for her now and put it on my account. I don't think he's got long. I'll go back and sit with him.'

Jackson pulled a chair forward. 'Now, what were you saying about the Laird?'

'That was Major Ian Campbell, Military Cross and Bar, the bravest man I ever knew. Laird of Loch Dhu Castle in the Western Highlands of Scotland, as his ancestors had been for centuries before him.'

'Loch Dhu?'

'That's Gaelic. The black loch. To us who grew up there it was always the Place of Dark Waters.'

'So you knew the Laird as a boy?'

'We were boys together. Learned to shoot grouse, deer and the fishing was the best in the world, and then the war came. We'd both served in the reserve before it all started so we went out to France straight away.'

'That must have been exciting stuff?'

'Nearly the end of us, but afterwards they gave the

Laird the staff job working for Mountbatten. You've heard of him?'

'Earl Mountbatten, the one the IRA blew up?'

'The bastards, and after all he did in the war. He was Supreme Commander in Southeast Asia with the Laird as one of his aides and he took me with him.'

'That must have been interesting.'

Tanner managed a smile. 'Isn't it customary to offer a condemned man a cigarette?'

'That's true.'

'And I am condemned, aren't I?'

Jackson hesitated then took out a pack of cigarettes. 'Just as we all are, Mr Tanner.'

'I'll tell you what,' Tanner said. 'Give me one of those and I'll tell you about the Chungking Covenant. All those years ago I gave the Laird my oath, but it doesn't seem to matter now.'

'The what?' Jackson asked.

'Just one, Doc, it's a good story.'

Jackson lit a cigarette and held it to Tanner's lips. The old man inhaled, coughed then inhaled again. 'Christ, that's wonderful.' He lay back. 'Now, let's see, when did it all start?'

Tanner lay with his eyes closed, very weak now. 'What happened after the crash?' Jackson asked.

The old man opened his eyes. 'The Laird was hurt bad. The brain, you see. He was in a coma in a Delhi hospital for three months and I stayed with him as his batman. They sent us back to London by sea and by then the end of the war was in sight. He spent months in the brain-damage unit for servicemen at Guy's Hospital, but he never really recovered and he had burns from the crash as well and almost total loss of memory. He came so close to death early in forty-six that I packed his things and sent them home to Castle Dhu.'

'And did he die?'

'Not for another twenty years. Back home we went to the estate. He wandered the place like a child. I tended his every want.'

'What about family?'

'Oh, he never married. He was engaged to a lassie who was killed in the London blitz in forty. There was his sister, Lady Rose, although everybody calls her Lady Katherine. Her husband was a baronet killed in the desert campaign. She ran the estate then and still does, though she's eighty now. She lives in the gate lodge. Sometimes, rents the big house for the shooting season to rich Yanks or Arabs.'

'And the Chungking Covenant?'

'Nothing came of that. Lord Louis and Mao never managed to get together again.'

'But the fourth copy in the Laird's Bible; you saved that. Wasn't it handed over to the authorities?'

'It stayed where it was in his Bible. The Laird's affair after all and he not up to telling anyone much of anything.' He shrugged. 'And then the years had rolled by and it didn't seem to matter.'

'Did Lady Katherine ever come to know of it?'

'I never told her. I never spoke of it to anyone and he was not capable and, as I said, it didn't seem to matter any longer.'

'But you've told me?'

Tanner smiled weakly. 'That's because you're a nice boy who talked to me and gave me a cigarette. A long time ago, Chungking in the rain and Mountbatten and your General Stilwell.'

'And the Bible?' Jackson asked.

'Like I told you, I sent all his belongings home when I thought he was going to die.'

'So the Bible went back to Loch Dhu?'

'You could say that.' For some reason Tanner started to laugh and that led to him choking again.

Jackson got the oxygen mask and the door opened and Sister Agnes ushered in a middle-aged couple. 'Mr and Mrs Grant.'

The woman hurried forward to take Tanner's hand. He managed a smile, breathing deeply, and she started to talk to him in a low voice and in a language totally unfamiliar to Jackson.

He turned to her husband, a large amiable looking man. 'It's Gaelic, Doctor; they always spoke Gaelic together. He was on a visit. His wife died of cancer last year back in Scotland.'

At that moment Tanner stopped breathing. His daughter cried out and Jackson passed her gently to her husband and bent over the patient. After a while he turned to face them. 'I'm sorry, but he's gone,' he said simply.

There it might have ended except for the fact that, having read the article in *The New York Times* on Hong Kong and its relations with China, Tony Jackson was struck by the coincidence of Tanner's story. This became doubly important because Tanner had died in the early hours of Sunday morning and Jackson always had Sunday lunch, his hospital shifts permitting, at his grandfather's home in Little Italy where his mother, since the death of his grandmother, kept house for her father in some style.

Jackson's grandfather, after whom he had been named, was called Antonio Mori and he had been born by only a whisker in America because his pregnant mother had arrived from Palermo in Sicily just in time to produce her baby at Ellis Island. Twenty-four hours only, but good enough and little Antonio was American born.

His father had friends of the right sort, friends in the Mafia. Antonio had worked briefly as a labourer until these friends had put him into first the olive oil and then the restaurant business. He had kept his mouth shut and always done as he was told, finally achieving wealth and prominence in the construction industry.

His daughter hadn't married a Sicilian, he accepted that, just as he accepted the death of his wife from leukaemia. His son-in-law, a rich Anglo-Saxon attorney, gave the family respectability. His death was a convenience. It brought Mori and his beloved daughter together again, plus his fine grandson, so brilliant that he had gone to Harvard. No matter that he was a saint and chose medicine. Mori could make enough money for all of them because he was Mafia, an important member of the Luca family whose leader, Don Giovanni Luca, in spite of having returned to Sicily, was *Capo di tutti Capi*: Boss of all the Bosses in the whole of the Mafia. The respect that earned for Mori couldn't be paid for.

When Jackson arrived at his grandfather's house, his mother, Rosa, was in the kitchen supervising the meal with the maid, Maria. She turned, still handsome in spite of grey in her dark hair, kissed him on both cheeks then held him off.

'You look terrible. Shadows under the eyes.'

'Mama, I did the night shift. I lay on my bed three hours then I showered and came here because I didn't want to disappoint you.'

'You're a good boy. Go and see your grandfather.'

Jackson went into the sitting room where he found Mori reading the Sunday paper. He leaned down to kiss his grandfather on the cheek and Mori said, 'I heard your mother and she's right. You do good and kill yourself at the same time. Here, have a glass of red wine.'

Jackson accepted it and drank some with pleasure. 'That's good.'

'You had an interesting night?' Mori was genuinely interested in his grandson's doings. In fact he bored his friends with his praises of the young man.

Jackson, aware that his grandfather indulged him, went to the french window, opened it and lit a cigarette. He turned. 'Remember the Solazzo wedding last month?'

'Yes.'

'You were talking with Carl Morgan; you'd just introduced me.'

'Mr Morgan was impressed by you, he said so.' There was pride in Mori's voice.

'Yes, well you and he were talking business.'

'Nonsense, what business could we have in common?'

'For God's sake, grandfather, I'm not a fool and I love you, but do you think I could have reached this stage in my life and not realised what business you were in?'

Mori nodded slowly and picked up the bottle. 'More wine? Now tell me where this is leading.'

'You and Mr Morgan were talking about Hong Kong. He mentioned huge investments in skyscrapers, hotels and so on and the worry about what would happen when the Chinese Communists take over.'

'That's simple. Billions of dollars down the toilet,' Mori said.

'There was an article in the *Times* yesterday about Peking being angry because the British are introducing a democratic political system before they go in ninety-seven.'

'So where is this leading?' Mori asked.

'I am right in assuming that you and your associates have business interests in Hong Kong?'

His grandfather stared at him thoughtfully. 'You could say that, but where is this leading?'

Jackson said, 'What if I told you that in nineteen-forty-four Mao Tse-tung signed a thing called the Chungking

Covenant with Lord Louis Mountbatten under the terms of which he agreed that, if he ever came to power in China, he would extend the Hong Kong Treaty by one hundred years in return for aid from the British to fight the Japanese?'

His grandfather sat there staring at him then got up, closed the door and returned to his seat.

'Explain,' he said.

Jackson did so and, when he was finished, his grandfather sat thinking about it. He got up and went to his desk and came back with a small tape recorder. 'Go through it again,' he said. 'Everything he told you. Omit nothing.'

At that moment Rosa opened the door. 'Lunch is almost ready.'

'Fifteen minutes, *cara*,' her father said. 'This is important, believe me.'

She frowned, but went out, closing the door. He turned to his grandson. 'As I said, everything,' and he switched on the recorder.

When Mori reached the Glendale Polo ground later that afternoon it was raining. There was still a reasonable crowd huddled beneath umbrellas or the trees because Carl Morgan was playing and Morgan was good, a handicap of ten goals indicating that he was a player of the first rank. He was fifty years of age, a magnificent looking man, six feet in height with broad shoulders and hair swept back over his ears.

His hair was jet black, a legacy of his mother, niece of Don Giovanni, who had married his father, a young army officer, during the Second World War. His father had served gallantly and well in both the Korean and Vietnam wars, retiring as a Brigadier General to Florida where they enjoyed a comfortable retirement thanks to their son.

All very respectable, all a very proper front for the son

who had walked out of Yale in 1965 and volunteered as a paratrooper during the Vietnam War, emerging with two Purple Hearts, a Silver Star and a Vietnamese Cross of Valour. A war hero whose credentials had taken him into Wall Street and then the hotel industry and the construction business, a billionaire at the end of things, accepted at every social level from London to New York.

There are six chukkas in a polo game lasting seven minutes each, four players on each side. Morgan played forward because it gave the greatest opportunity for total aggression, and that was what he liked.

The game was into the final chukka as Mori got out of the car and his chauffeur came round to hold an umbrella over him. Some yards away, a vividly pretty young woman stood beside an estate car, a Burberry trenchcoat hanging from her shoulders. She was about five foot seven with long blonde hair to her shoulders, high cheekbones, green eyes.

'She sure is a beautiful young lady, Mr Morgan's daughter,' the chauffeur said.

'Stepdaughter, Johnny,' Mori reminded him.

'Sure, I was forgetting, but with her taking his name and all. That was a real bad thing her mother dying like that. Asta, that's kind of a funny name.'

'It's Swedish,' Mori told him.

Asta Morgan jumped up and down excitedly. 'Come on, Carl, murder them!'

Carl Morgan glanced sideways as he went by, his teeth flashed and he went barrelling into the young forward for the opposing team, slamming his left foot under the boy's stirrup and lifting him, quite illegally, out of the saddle. A second later he had thundered through and scored.

The game won, he cantered across to Asta through the rain and stepped out of the saddle. A groom took his pony, Asta handed him a towel then lit a cigarette and passed it to him. She looked up, smiling, an intimacy between them that excluded everyone around.

'He sure likes that girl,' Johnny said.

Mori nodded. 'So it would appear.'

Morgan turned and saw him and waved and Mori went forward. 'Carl, nice to see you. And you, Asta.' He touched his hat.

'What can I do for you?' Morgan asked.

'Business, Carl; something came up last night that might interest you.'

Morgan said, 'Nothing you can't talk about in front of Asta, surely?'

Mori hesitated. 'No, of course not.' He took the small tape recorder from his pocket. 'My grandson, Tony, had a man die on him at Our Lady of Mercy Hospital last night. He told Tony a hell of a story, Carl. I think you could be interested.'

'OK, let's get in out of the rain.' Morgan handed Asta into the estate car and followed her.

Mori joined them. 'Here we go.' He switched on the tape recorder.

Morgan sat there after it had finished, a cigarette drooping from the corner of his mouth, his face set.

Asta said, 'What a truly astonishing story.' Her voice was low and pleasant, more English than American.

'You can say that again.' Morgan turned to Mori. 'I'll keep this. I'll have my secretary transcribe it and send it to Don Giovanni in Palermo by coded fax.'

'I did the right thing?'

'You did well, Antonio.' Morgan took his hand.

'No, it was Tony, Carl, not me. What am I going to do with him. Harvard Medical School, the Mayo Clinic, a brilliant student, yet he works with the nuns at Our Lady of Mercy for peanuts.'

58

'You leave him,' Morgan said. 'He'll find his way. I went to Vietnam, Antonio. No one can take that away from me. You can't argue with it, the rich boy going into hell when he didn't need to. It says something. He won't be there for ever, but the fact that he was will make people see him as someone to look up to for the rest of his life. He's a fine boy.' He put a hand on Mori's shoulder. 'Heh, I hope I don't sound too calculating.'

'No,' Mori protested. 'Not at all. He's someone to be proud of. Thank you, Carl, thank you. I'll leave you now. Asta.' He nodded to her and walked away.

'That was nice,' Asta told Morgan. 'What you said about Tony.'

'It's true. He's brilliant, that boy. He'll end up in Park Avenue, only, unlike the other brilliant doctors there, he'll always be the one who worked downtown for the nuns of Our Lady of Mercy, and that you can't pay for.'

'You're such a cynic,' she said.

'No, sweetheart, a realist.' He slid behind the wheel. 'Now, let's get going. I'm famished. I'll take you out to dinner.'

They had finished their meal at The Four Seasons, were at the coffee stage, when one of the waiters brought a phone over. 'An overseas call for you, sir. Sicily. The gentleman said it was urgent.'

The voice over the phone was harsh and unmistakable. 'Carlo. This is Giovanni.'

Morgan straightened in his seat. 'Uncle?' He dropped into Italian. 'What a marvellous surprise. How's business?'

'Everything looks good, particularly after reading your fax.'

'I was right to let you know about this business then?'

'So right that I want you out of there on the next plane. This is serious business, Carlo, very serious.'

'Fine, Uncle. I'll be there tomorrow. Asta's with me. Do you want to say hello?'

'I'd rather look at her, so you'd better bring her with you. I look forward to it, Carlo.'

The phone clicked off; the waiter came forward and took it from him. 'What was all that about?' Asta said.

'Business. Apparently Giovanni takes this Chungking Covenant thing very seriously indeed. He wants me in Palermo tomorrow. You too, my love. It's time you visited Sicily,' and he waved for the head waiter.

The following morning they took a direct flight to Rome, where Morgan had a Citation private jet standing by for the flight to Punta Raisa Airport, twenty miles outside Palermo. There was a Mercedes limousine waiting with a chauffeur and a hard looking individual in a blue nylon raincoat with heavy cheekbones and the flattened nose of the prize fighter. There was a feeling of real power there, although he looked more Slav than Italian.

'My uncle's top enforcer,' Morgan whispered to Asta, 'Marco Russo.' He smiled and held out his hand. 'Marco, it's been a long time. My daughter, Asta.'

Marco managed a fractional smile. 'A pleasure. Welcome to Sicily, *signorina*, and nice to see you again, *signore*. The Don isn't at the town house, he's at the Villa.'

'Good, let's get moving then.'

Luca's villa was outside a village at the foot of Monte Pellegrino, which towers into the sky three miles north of Palermo.

'During the Punic Wars the Carthaginians held out against the Romans on that mountain for three years,' Morgan told Asta.

'It looks a fascinating place,' she said.

'Soaked in blood for generations.' He held up the local

paper which Marco had given him. 'Three soldiers blown up by a car bomb last night, a priest shot in the back of the neck this morning because he was suspected of being an informer.'

'At least you're on the right side.'

He took her hand. 'Everything I do is strictly legitimate, Asta, that's the whole point. My business interests and those of my associates are pure as driven snow.'

'I know, darling,' she said. 'You must be the greatest front man ever. Grandad Morgan a General, you a war hero, billionaire, philanthropist and one of the best polo players in the world. Why, last time we were in London, Prince Charles asked you to play for him.'

'He wants me next month.' She laughed and he added, 'But never forget one thing, Asta. The true power doesn't come from New York. It lies in the hands of the old man we're going to see now.'

At that moment they turned in through electronic gates set in ancient fifteen-foot walls and drove through a semi-tropical garden towards the great Moorish villa.

The main reception room was enormous, black and white tiled floor scattered with rugs, seventeenth-century furniture from Italy in dark oak, a log fire blazing in the open hearth and french windows open to the garden. Luca sat in a high-backed sofa, a cigar in his mouth, hands clasped over the silver handle of a walking stick. He was large, at least sixteen stone, his grey beard trimmed, the air of a Roman Emperor about him.

'Come here, child,' he said to Asta and, when she went to him, kissed her on both cheeks. 'You're more beautiful than ever. Eighteen months since I saw you in New York. I was desolated by your mother's unfortunate death last year.'

'These things happen,' she said.

'I know. Jack Kennedy once said, anyone who believes there is fairness in this life is seriously misinformed. Here, sit beside me.' She did as she was told and he looked up at Morgan. 'You seem well, Carlo.' He'd always insisted on calling him that.

'And you, Uncle, look wonderful.'

Luca held out his hand and Morgan kissed it. 'I like it when your Sicilian half floats to the surface. You were wise to contact me on this Chungking business and Mori showed good judgement in speaking to you.'

'We owe it to his grandson,' Morgan said.

'Yes, of course. Young Tony is a good boy, an idealist, and that's good. We need our saints, Carlo, they make us rather more acceptable to the rest of the world.' He snapped a finger and a white-coated houseboy came forward.

'Zibibbo, Alfredo.'

'At once, Don Giovanni.'

'You will like this, Asta. A wine from the island of Pantelleria, flavoured with anis.' He turned to Morgan. 'Marco took me for a run into the country the other day to that farmhouse of yours at Valdini.'

'How was it?'

'The caretaker and his wife seemed to be behaving themselves. Very peaceful. You should do something with it.'

'Grandfather was born there, Uncle; it's a piece of the real Sicily. How could I change that?'

'You're a good boy, Carlo; you may be half American, but you have a Sicilian heart.'

As Alfredo opened the bottle, Morgan said, 'So, to the Chungking Covenant. What do you think?'

'We have billions invested in Hong Kong in hotels and casinos and our holdings will be severely damaged when the Communists take over in ninety-seven. Anything that could delay that would be marvellous.'

'But would the discovery of such a document really have an effect?' Asta asked.

He accepted one of the glasses of Zibibbo from Alfredo. 'The Chinese have taken great care to handle the proposed changes in the status of Hong Kong through the United Nations. These days they want everything from international respectability to the Olympic Games. If the document surfaced with the holy name of Mao Tse-tung attached to it, who knows what the outcome would be.'

'That's true,' Morgan agreed. 'All right, they'd scream forgery.'

'Yes,' Asta put in, 'but there is one important point. It isn't a forgery, it's the real thing; we know that and any experts brought in will have to agree.'

'She's smart, this girl.' Luca patted her knee. 'We've nothing to lose, Carlo. With that document on show we can at least hold the whole proceedings up if nothing else. Even if we still lose millions, I'd like to mess it up for the Chinese and particularly for the Brits. It's their fault they didn't sort the whole mess out years ago.'

'Strange you should say that,' Asta told him. 'I'd have thought that was exactly what Mountbatten was trying to do back in forty-four.'

He roared with laughter and raised his glass. 'More wine, Alfredo.'

'What do you suggest?' Morgan asked.

'Find this silver Bible. When you have that you have the Covenant.'

'And that must be somewhere at the Castle at Loch Dhu, according to what Tanner said,' Asta put in.

'Exactly. There's a problem. I had my London lawyer check on the situation at the Castle the moment I received your fax. It's rented out at the moment to a Sheik from Trucial Oman, a Prince of the Royal Family, so there's nothing to be done there. He's in residence and he won't

63

be leaving for another month. My lawyer has leased it in your name for three months from then.'

'Fine,' Morgan said. 'That gives me plenty of time to clear the decks where business is concerned. That Bible must be there somewhere.'

'I instructed my lawyer to get straight up there and see this Lady Katherine Rose, the sister, to do the lease personally. He raised the question of the Bible, told her he'd heard the legend of how all the lairds carried it into battle. When he phoned me he said she's old and a bit confused and told him she hadn't seen the thing in years.'

'There is one thing,' Asta said. 'According to Tony Jackson, he said to Tanner, "So the Bible went back to Loch Dhu?"'

Morgan cut in, 'And Tanner replied, "You could say that."'

Asta nodded. 'And then Tony said he started to laugh. I'd say that's rather strange.'

'Strange or not, that Bible must be there somewhere,' Luca said. 'You'll find it, Carlo.' He stood up. 'Now we eat.'

Marco Russo was standing by the door in the hall and, as they passed him, Luca said, 'You can take Marco with you in case you need a little muscle.' He patted Marco's face. 'The Highlands of Scotland, Marco, you'll have to wrap up.'

'Whatever you say, Capo.'

Marco opened the dining-room door where two waiters were in attendance. Back in the reception room Alfredo cleared the wine bottle and glasses and took them into the kitchen, putting them beside the sink for the maid to wash later. He said to the cook, 'I'm going now,' went out, lit a cigarette and walked down through the gardens to the staff quarters.

Alfredo Ponti was an excellent waiter, but an even better policeman, one of the new dedicated breed imported from mainland Italy. He'd managed to obtain the job with Luca three months previously.

Usually he phoned from outside when he wanted to contact his superiors but the other two houseboys, the cook and the maid were working, so for the moment he was alone. In any case, what he had overheard seemed important so he decided to take a chance, lifted the receiver on the wall phone at the end of the corridor and dialled a number in Palermo. It was answered at once.

'Gagini, it's me, Ponti. I've got something. Carl Morgan appeared tonight with his stepdaughter. I overheard them tell a most curious story to Luca. Have you ever heard of the Chungking Covenant?'

Paolo Gagini, who was a Major in the Italian Secret Intelligence Service based in Rome posing as a businessman in Palermo, said, 'That's a new one. Let me put the tape recorder on. Thank God for that photographic memory of yours. Right, start talking. Tell me everything.'

Which Alfredo did in some detail. When he had finished, Gagini said, 'Good work, though I can't see it helping us much. I'll be in touch. Take care.'

Alfredo replaced the receiver and went to bed.

Gagini, in his apartment in Palermo, sat thinking. He could let them know in Rome, not that anyone would be very interested. Everyone knew what Carl Morgan was, but he was also legitimate. In any case, anything he did in Scotland was the responsibility of the British authorities, which made him think of his oldest friend in British Intelligence. Gagini smiled. He loved this one. He got out his code book and found the number of the Ministry of Defence in London.

When the operator answered he said, 'Give me Brigadier Charles Ferguson; Priority One, please.'

It was perhaps two hours later, when Morgan and Asta had retired, that Alfredo was shaken awake to find Marco bending over him.

'The *Capo* wants you.'

'What is it?'

Marco shrugged. 'Search me. He's on the terrace.'

He went out and Alfredo dressed quickly and went after him. He was not particularly apprehensive. Things had gone so well for three months now and he'd always been so careful, but, as a precaution, he placed a small automatic in his waistband.

He found Luca sitting in a cane chair, Marco leaning against a pillar. The old man said, 'You made a phone call earlier.'

Alfredo's mouth went dry. 'Yes, my cousin in Palermo.'

'You're lying,' Marco said. 'We have an electronic tracking machine. It registered the no-return bar code, so the number can't be traced.'

'And that only applies to the security services,' Luca said.

Alfredo turned and ran through the garden for the fence and Marco drew a silenced pistol.

'Don't kill him,' Luca cried.

Marco shot him in the leg and the young man went down, but turned on the ground, pulling the automatic from his waistband. Marco, with little choice in the matter, shot him between the eyes.

Luca went forward, leaning on his cane. 'Poor boy, so young. They will keep trying. Get rid of him Marco.'

He turned and walked away.

FOUR

Ferguson was at his desk when Hannah Bernstein came in and put a file on his desk. 'Everything there is on Carl Morgan.'

Ferguson sat back. 'Tell me.'

'His father is a retired Brigadier General, but his mother is the niece of Giovanni Luca, which means that, in spite of Yale and all the war hero stuff in Vietnam and his hotels and construction business, he's fronting for the Mafia.'

'Some people would say he was the new, legitimate face of the Mafia.'

'With the greatest respect, Brigadier, that's a load of crap.'

'Why, Chief Inspector, you said a rude word. How encouraging.'

'A thug is a thug even if he does wear suits by Brioni and plays polo with Prince Charles.'

'I couldn't agree more. Have you checked on Loch Dhu Castle and the situation there?'

'Yes, sir, it's at present leased to Prince Ali ben Yusef from Oman. He'll be there for another month.'

'Not much joy there. Arab royal families are always the very devil to deal with.'

'Something else, sir. Carl Morgan has already taken a lease on the place for three months when the Prince leaves.'

'Now why would he do that?' Ferguson frowned and then nodded. 'The Bible. It's got to be.'

'You mean he needs to search for it, sir?'

'Something like that. What else can you tell me about the estate?'

'It's owned by a Lady Rose, Campbell's sister. He was never married. She lives in the gate lodge. She's eighty years of age and in poor health.' Hannah looked in the file. 'I see there's also a small hunting lodge to rent. Ardnamurchan Lodge, it's called. About ten miles from the main house in the deer forest.'

Ferguson nodded. 'Look, let's try the simple approach. Book the Lear out of Gatwick as soon as you like and fly up there and descend on Lady Rose. Express an interest in this shooting lodge on my behalf. Tell her you've always had an interest in the area because your grandfather served with Campbell in the war. Then raise the question of the Bible. For all we know it could be lying on a coffee table.'

'All right, sir, I'll do as you say.' The phone on his desk rang and she picked it up, listened and put it down again. 'Dillon is having his final check at the hospital.'

'I know,' Ferguson said.

'About the Bible, sir? Do you really think it could be just lying around?'

'Somehow I don't think so. Luca and Morgan would have thought of that. The fact that they are going ahead with a lease on the place would seem to indicate that they know damn well it isn't.'

'That's logical.' She put another file on his desk. 'Dillon's medical report. Not good.'

'Yes. Professor Bellamy spoke to me about it. That's why he's giving him a final examination this morning, then Dillon is coming round to see me.'

'Is he finished, sir?'

'Looks like it, but that's not your worry, it's mine, so off you go to Scotland and see what you can find. In the meantime I'll speak to the Prime Minister. A phone call at this stage will be enough, but I do think he should know what's going on sooner rather than later.'

'You can dress now, Sean,' Bellamy told him. 'I'll see you in my office.'

Dillon got off the operating table on which the professor had examined him. The flesh seemed to have shrunk on his bones, there were what appeared to be bruises under his eyes. When he glanced over his shoulder he could see, in the mirror, the angry raised weal of the scar left by the two operations that had saved his life after Norah Bell had gutted him.

He dressed slowly, feeling unaccountably weak, and when he put on his jacket the Walther in the special left pocket seemed to weigh a ton. He went out to the office where Bellamy sat behind his desk.

'How do you feel generally?'

Dillon slumped down. 'Bloody awful. Weak, no energy and then there's the pain.' He shook his head. 'How long does this go on?'

'It takes time,' Bellamy said. 'She chipped your spine, damaged the stomach, kidneys, bladder. Have you any idea how close to death you were?'

'I know, I know,' Dillon said. 'But what do I do?'

'A holiday, a long one, preferably in the sun. Ferguson will take care of it. As for the pain . . .' He pushed a pill bottle forward. 'I've increased your morphine dose to a quarter grain.'

'Thanks very much, I'll be a junkie before you know it.' Dillon got up slowly. 'I'll be on my way. Better see Ferguson and get it over with.'

As he got to the door Bellamy said, 'I'm always here, Sean.'

Hannah, due at Gatwick in an hour, was checking the final details of her trip in the outer office. Loch Dhu was situated in a place called Moidart on the north-west coast of Scotland and not far from the sea, about one hundred and twenty square miles of mountain and moorland with few inhabitants. One good thing. Only five miles from Loch Dhu was an old abandoned airstrip called Ardnamurchan, used by the RAF as an air-sea rescue base during the war. It could comfortably accommodate the Lear. Four hundred and fifty miles, so the trip would take, say, an hour-and-a-half. Then she would need transport to the Castle. She found the telephone number of the gate lodge and called Lady Rose.

The first person to answer was a woman with a robust Scottish voice, but after a while her mistress replaced her. Her voice was different, tired somehow and a slight quaver in it. 'Katherine Rose here.'

'Lady Rose? I wonder if I could come and see you on behalf of a client of mine?' and she went on to explain.

'Certainly, my dear, I'll send my gardener, Angus, to pick you up. I look forward to seeing you. By the way, just call me Lady Katherine. It's customary here.'

Hannah put down the receiver and pulled on her coat. The door opened and Dillon entered. He looked dreadful and her heart sank.

'Why, Dillon, it's good to see you.'

'I doubt that, girl dear. On the other hand, I must say you look good enough to eat. Is the great man in?'

'He's expecting you. Listen, I'll have to dash, the Lear's waiting for me at Gatwick and I've a fast trip to make to Scotland.'

'Then I won't detain you. Happy landings,' and he knocked on Ferguson's door and went in.

'God save all here,' Dillon said.

Ferguson glanced up. 'You look bloody awful.'

'God save you kindly, was the reply to that one,' Dillon told him. 'And, as I see the brandy over there, I'll help myself.'

He did, taking it down in one swallow, then lit a cigarette. Ferguson said, 'Remarkably bad habits for a sick man.'

'Don't let's waste time. Are you putting me out to grass?'

'I'm afraid so. Your appointment was never exactly official, you see. Makes things awkward.'

'Ah, well, all good things come to an end.'

He helped himself to more brandy and Ferguson said, 'Normally there would have been a pension, but in your circumstances I'm afraid not.'

Dillon smiled. 'Remember Michael Aroun, the bastard I did away with in Brittany in ninety-one after the Downing Street affair? He was supposed to put two million into my bank account and screwed me.'

'I remember,' Ferguson said.

'I cleaned out his safe before I left. Assorted currencies, but it came to around six hundred thousand pounds. I'll be

71

all right.' He finished the brandy. 'Well, working with you has been a sincere sensation, I'll say that, but I'd better be on my way.'

As he put his hand to the door, Ferguson said formally, 'One more thing, Dillon; I presume you're carrying the usual Walther. I'd be obliged if you'd leave it on my desk.'

'Screw you, Brigadier,' Sean Dillon said and went out.

The flight to Moidart was spectacular, straight over the English Lake District at thirty thousand feet, then Scotland and the Firth of Forth, the Grampian Mountains on the right and soon the islands Eigg and Rhum and the Isle of Skye to the North. The Lear turned east towards the great shining expanse of Loch Shiel, but before it was the deer forest, Loch Dhu Castle and the loch itself, black and forbidding. The co-pilot was navigating and he pointed as they descended, and there was the airfield, decaying Nissen huts, two hangars and an old control tower.

'Ardnamurchan field. Air-sea rescue during the big war.'

It was on the far side of the loch from the Castle and, as they turned to land, Hannah saw an old station wagon approaching. The Lear rolled to a halt. Both the pilots, who were RAF on secondment, got out with her to stretch their legs. The skipper, a Flight Lieutenant Lacey, said, 'Back of beyond this, Chief Inspector, and no mistake.'

'Better get used to it, Flight Lieutenant. I suspect we'll be up here again,' she said and walked towards the station wagon.

The driver was a man in a tweed cap and jacket with a red face, blotched from too much whisky drinking. 'Angus, Miss; her ladyship sent me to find you.'

'My name's Bernstein,' she said and got into the passenger seat. As they drove away she said, 'You've no idea how excited I am to be here.'

'Why would that be, Miss?' he enquired.

'Oh, my grandfather knew the old Laird during the war, Major Campbell. They served in the Far East together with Lord Mountbatten.'

'Ah, well I wouldn't know about that, Miss. I'm only sixty-four so all I did was National Service and that was in nineteen-forty-eight.'

'I see. I remember my grandfather saying the Laird had a batman from the estate, a Corporal Tanner. Did you know him?'

'Indeed I did, Miss; he was estate manager here for years. Went on a visit to his daughter in New York and died there. Only the other day that happened.'

'What a shame.'

'Death comes to us all,' he intoned.

It was like a line from a bad play, especially when delivered in that Highland Scots accent, and she lapsed into silence as he turned the station wagon into huge old-fashioned iron gates and stopped beside the lodge.

Lady Katherine Rose was old and tired and it showed on her wizened face as she sat there in the wing-backed chair, a rug over her knees. The drawing room in which she greeted Hannah was pleasantly furnished, most of the stuff obviously antique. There was a fire in the hearth but she had a french window open.

'I hope you don't mind, my dear,' she said to Hannah. 'I need the air, you see. My chest isn't what it used to be.'

A pleasant, rather overweight woman in her fifties bustled in with tea and scones on a tray which she placed on a mahogany table. 'Shall I pour?' she said and, like Angus, her accent was Highland.

'Don't fuss, Jean, I'm sure Miss Bernstein is quite capable. Off you go.'

Jean smiled, picked up a shawl which had slipped to the

floor and put it around the old woman's shoulders. Hannah poured the tea.

'So,' Lady Katherine said, 'your employer is Brigadier Charles Ferguson; is that what you said?'

'Yes. He was wondering whether there might be a chance of renting Ardnamurchan Lodge for the shooting. I did contact your agents in London, but was given to understand that the big house was leased.'

'Indeed it is, an Arab prince no less, a dear man with several children who keep descending on me. Far too generous. He sends me food I can't eat and bottles of Dom Perignon I can't drink.'

Hannah put her cup of tea on a side table. 'Yes. I heard he was in residence for another month and after that an American gentleman.'

'Yes, a Mr Morgan. Scandalously wealthy. I've seen his picture in the *Tatler* magazine playing polo with Prince Charles. His lawyer flew up to see me, just like you, in a jet plane. He's taken the place for three months.' She didn't bother with the tea. 'There are some cigarettes in the silver box. Get one for me, there's a dear, and help yourself if you indulge.' She held it in a hand that shook slightly. 'That's better,' she said as she inhaled. 'Clears my chest. Anyway, to business. Ardnamurchan Lodge is free and has full sporting rights. Deer, grouse next month, the fishing. There are two bathrooms, five bedrooms. I could arrange servants.'

'No need for that. The Brigadier has a manservant who also cooks.'

'How very convenient. And you'd come too?'

'Some of the time at least.'

'The Brigadier must be as wealthy as this American, what with private aeroplanes and so forth. What does he do?'

'Various things on the international scene.' Hannah

74

hurried on. 'I was telling your gardener what a thrill it was for me to be here. I first heard of Loch Dhu when I was a young girl from my mother's father. He was an army officer during the Second World War and served on Lord Louis Mountbatten's staff in the Far East.' She was making it up as she went along. 'Gort was his name, Colonel Edward Gort. Perhaps your brother spoke of him?'

'I'm afraid not, my dear. You see Ian was involved in a dreadful air crash in India in forty-four. He was only saved by the courage of his batman, Jack Tanner, a man who'd grown up with him on the estate here. My brother was hospitalised on and off for years. Brain damage, you see. He was never the same. He never talked about the war. To be frank, the poor dear never talked much about anything. He wasn't capable.'

'How tragic,' Hannah said. 'My grandfather never mentioned that. I believe the last time he saw him was in China.'

'That must have been before the crash.'

Hannah got up and poured more tea into her cup. 'Can I get you anything?'

'Another cigarette, my dear; my only vice and, at my age, what does it matter?'

Hannah did as she was told then walked to the french window and looked out from the terrace at the great house in the distance. 'It looks wonderful. Battlements and turrets, just as I imagined it would be.' She turned. 'I'm a hopeless romantic. It was the idea of the Laird of the Clan, as my grandfather described it, that intrigued me. Bagpipes and kilts and all that sort of thing.' She came back. 'Oh, and there was another rather romantic side to it. He told me that Major Campbell always carried a silver Bible with him that was a family heirloom. He'd had it at Dunkirk, but the story was that all the Campbells had carried it into battle for centuries.'

'You're right,' she said. 'It was certainly in Rory Campbell's pocket when he died at the Battle of Culloden fighting for Bonnie Prince Charlie. It's interesting that you should mention it. I haven't thought about that Bible in years. I suppose it must have been lost in the plane crash.'

'I see,' Hannah said carefully.

'Certainly nothing survived except poor Ian and Jack Tanner, of course.' She sighed. 'I just heard the other day that Jack died in New York on a visit to see his daughter. A good man. He ran things on the estate for me for years. The new man, Murdoch, is a pain. You know the kind. College degree in estate management so he thinks he knows everything.'

Hannah nodded and got up. 'So, we can have Ardnamurchan Lodge?'

'Whenever you like. Leave me the details and I'll have Murdoch send you a contract.'

Hannah was already prepared for that and took an envelope from her handbag which she placed on the table. 'There you are. The Brigadier's office is in Cavendish Square. I'll find Angus, shall I, and get him to run me back to the plane?'

'You'll find him in the garden.'

Hannah took her hand which was cool and weightless. 'Goodbye, Lady Katherine.'

'Goodbye, my dear, you're a very lovely young woman.'

'Thank you.'

She turned to the french window and Lady Katherine said, 'A strange coincidence. When that lawyer was here he asked about the Bible, too. Said Mr Morgan had mentioned reading about it in an article on Highland legends in some American magazine. Isn't that extraordinary?'

'It certainly is,' Hannah said. 'He must have been disappointed it wasn't on show.'

'That was the impression I received.' The old woman smiled. 'Goodbye, my dear.'

Hannah found Angus digging in the garden. 'Ready to go, Miss?'

'That's right,' she said.

As they walked round to the front a Range Rover drew up and a tall, saturnine young man in a hunting jacket and a deerstalker cap got out. He looked at her enquiringly.

'This is Miss Bernstein,' Angus told him. 'She's been seeing the Mistress.'

'On behalf of my employer, Brigadier Charles Ferguson,' she said. 'Lady Katherine has agreed to rent the Ardnamurchan Lodge to us.'

He frowned. 'She didn't mention anything to me about it.' He hesitated then put out his hand. 'Stewart Murdoch. I'm the estate factor.'

'I only spoke to her this morning.'

'Then that explains it. I've been at Fort William for two days.'

'I've left her full details and look forward to receiving the contract.' She smiled and got into the station wagon. 'I must rush, there's a plane waiting for me at Ardnamurchan. We'll meet again, I'm sure.'

Angus got behind the wheel and drove away. Murdoch watched them go, frowning, then went inside.

The Lear took off, climbing steeply, rapidly rising to thirty thousand feet. Hannah checked her watch. It was only just after two. With luck she'd be at Gatwick by three-thirty, sooner with a tail-wind. Another hour to reach the Ministry of Defence. She picked up the phone and told the co-pilot to patch her in to Ferguson.

His voice was clear and sharp. 'Had a good trip?'

'Excellent, sir, and the lease on Ardnamurchan Lodge is in the bag. No luck with the Bible. The Lady hasn't seen it in years. Always presumed it was lost in the plane crash.'

'Yes, well we know it wasn't, don't we?'

'Looks like we're in for a sort of country house weekend treasure hunt, sir.'

'You mean Morgan is, Chief Inspector.'

'So how do we handle it?'

'I don't know, I'll think of something. Come home, Chief Inspector; I'll wait for you at the office.'

She put down the phone, made herself a cup of instant coffee and settled back to read a magazine.

When she reached the Ministry she found Ferguson pacing up and down in his office. 'Ah, there you are, I was beginning to despair,' he said unreasonably. 'And don't bother to take your coat off, we can't keep the Prime Minister waiting.'

He took down his coat from the stand, picked up his Malacca cane and went out, and she hurried after him, slightly bewildered.

'But what's going on, sir?'

'I spoke to the Prime Minister earlier and he told me he wished to see us the moment you got back, so let's get cracking.'

The Daimler was admitted at the security gates at the end of Downing Street with no delay. In fact the most famous door in the world opened the second they got out of the car and an aide took their coats and ushered them up the stairs, past all the portraits of previous Prime Ministers, and along the corridor, knocking gently on the door of the great man's study.

They went in, the door closed behind them, the Prime Minister looked up from his desk. 'Brigadier.'

'May I introduce Detective Chief Inspector Hannah Bernstein, Prime Minister, my assistant?'

'Chief Inspector.' The Prime Minister nodded. 'I was naturally more than intrigued by your telephone call this morning. Now tell me everything you've discovered about this affair so far.'

So Ferguson told him, leaving nothing out.

When he was finished, the Prime Minister turned to Hannah. 'Tell me about your visit to this place.'

'Of course, Prime Minister.'

As she ended, he said, 'No question that Lady Katherine could be wrong?'

'Absolutely not, Prime Minister, she was adamant that she hadn't seen it, the Bible I mean, in years.'

There was silence while the Prime Minister brooded. Ferguson said, 'What would you like us to do?'

'Find the damn thing before they do, Brigadier; we've had enough trouble with Hong Kong. It's over, we're coming out and that's it, so if this thing exists, you find it and burn it. And I don't want the Chinese involved. There would be hell to pay, and keep our American cousins out of it too.'

It was Hannah who had the temerity to cut in. 'You really think all this is true, Prime Minister, that it exists?'

'I'm afraid I do. After the Brigadier phoned me this morning I spoke with a certain very distinguished gentleman, now in his nineties, who was once a power at the Colonial Office during the war. He tells me that, many years ago, he recalls rumours about this Chungking Covenant. Apparently it was always dismissed as a myth.'

'So what do you wish us to do, Prime Minister?'

'We can hardly ask Prince Ali ben Yusef for permission to ransack the house and we can hardly send the burglars in.'

'He leaves in four weeks and Morgan moves straight in,' Hannah said.

'Well, he would, wouldn't he? Once he's in he can take

his time and do anything he wants.' The Prime Minister looked up at Ferguson. 'But you'll be there at this Ardnamurchan Lodge to keep an eye on things. What do you intend to do?'

'Improvise, sir.' Ferguson smiled.

The Prime Minister smiled back. 'You're usually rather good at that. See to it, Brigadier; don't let me down. Now you must excuse me.'

As they settled in the back of the Daimler, Hannah said, 'What now?'

'We'll go up to Ardnamurchan Lodge just before Morgan in three to four weeks. In the meantime I want a check on him. Use all international police contacts. I want to know where he goes and what he does.'

'Fine.'

'Good, now let me give you dinner. Blooms I think, in Whitechapel. You can't say no to that, Chief Inspector; the finest Jewish restaurant in London.'

After leaving the Ministry of Defence Dillon had simply caught a taxi to Stable Mews, not far from Ferguson's flat in Cavendish Square. He had a two-bedroomed cottage there at the end of the cobbled yard. By the time he reached it the pain had come again quite badly so he took one of the morphine capsules Bellamy had prescribed and went and lay down on the bed.

It obviously knocked him out and when he came awake quite suddenly it was dark. He got up, visited the toilet and splashed water over his face. In the mirror he looked truly awful and he shuddered and went downstairs. He checked his watch. It was seven-thirty. He really needed something to eat, he knew that, and yet the prospect of food was repugnant to him.

Perhaps a walk would clear his head and then he could find a café. He opened the front door. Rain fell gently in a fine mist through the light of the street lamp on the corner. He pulled on his jacket, aware of the weight of the Walther and paused, wondering whether to leave it, but the damn thing had been a part of him for so long. He found an old Burberry trenchcoat and a black umbrella and ventured out.

He walked from street to street, pausing only once to go into a corner pub where he had a large brandy and a pork pie which was so disgusting that just one bite made him want to throw up.

He continued to walk aimlessly. There was a certain amount of fog now, crouching at the end of the street, and it gave a closed-in feeling to things as if he was in his own private world. He felt a vague sense of alarm, probably drug paranoia, and somewhere in the distance Big Ben struck eleven, the sound curiously muffled by the fog. There was silence now and then the unmistakable sound of a ship's foghorn as it moved down river and he realized the Thames was close at hand.

He turned into another street and found himself beside the river. There was a corner shop still open. He went in and bought a packet of cigarettes and was served by a young Pakistani youth.

'Would there be a café anywhere near at hand?' Dillon asked.

'Plenty up on the High Street, but if you like Chinese, there's the Red Dragon round the corner on China Wharf.'

'An interesting name,' Dillon said, lighting a cigarette, hand shaking.

'The tea clippers used to dock there in the old days of the China run.' The youth hesitated. 'Are you all right?'

'Nothing to worry about, just out of hospital,' Dillon said. 'But it's kind of you to ask.'

He walked along the street past towering warehouses. It

was raining heavily now and then he turned the corner and saw a ten-foot dragon in red neon shining through the rain. He put down his umbrella, opened the door and went in.

It was a long, narrow room with dark panelled walls, a bar of polished mahogany and a couple of dozen tables each covered with a neat white linen cloth. There were a number of artefacts on display and Chinese watercolours on the wall.

There was only one customer, a Chinese of at least sixty with a bald head and round, enigmatic face. He was no more than five feet tall and very fat and, in spite of his tan gabardine suit, bore a striking resemblance to a bronze statue of Buddha which stood in one corner. He was eating a dish of cuttle fish and chopped vegetables with a very Western fork and ignored Dillon completely.

There was a Chinese girl behind the bar. She had a flower in her hair and wore a *Cheongsam* in black silk, embroidered with a red dragon which was twin to the one outside.

'I'm sorry,' she said in perfect English. 'We've just closed.'

'Any chance of a quick drink?' Dillon asked.

'I'm afraid we only have a table licence.'

She was very beautiful, with her black hair and pale skin, dark watchful eyes and high cheekbones, and Dillon felt like reaching out to touch her and then the red dragon on her dark dress seemed to come alive, undulating, and he closed his eyes and clutched at the bar.

Once in the Mediterranean on a diving job for the Israelis that had involved taking out two PLO high-speed boats that had been involved in landing terrorists by night in Israel, he had run out of air at fifty feet. Surfacing half-dead he'd had the same sensation as now of drifting up from the dark places into light.

The fat man had him in a grip of surprising strength and put him into a chair. Dillon took several deep breaths and smiled. 'Sorry about this. I've been ill for some time and I probably walked too far tonight.'

The expression on the fat man's face did not alter and the girl said in Cantonese, 'I'll handle this, Uncle; finish your meal.'

Dillon, who spoke Cantonese rather well, listened with interest as the man replied, 'Do you think they will still come, Niece?'

'Who knows? The worst kind of foreign devils, pus from an infected wound. Still, I'll leave the door open a little longer.' She smiled at Dillon. 'Please excuse us. My uncle speaks very little English.'

'That's fine. If I could just sit here for a moment.'

'Coffee,' the girl said. 'Very black and with a large brandy.'

'God save us, the brandy is fine, but would you happen to have a cup of tea, love? It's what I was raised on.'

'Something we have in common.'

She smiled and went behind the bar and took down a bottle of brandy and a glass. At that moment a car drew up outside. She paused, then moved to the end of the bar and peered out through the window.

'They are here, Uncle.'

As she came round the end of the bar the door opened and four men entered. The leader was six feet tall with a hard, raw-boned face. He wore a cavalry twill car coat that looked very expensive.

He smiled quite pleasantly. 'Here we are again then,' he said. 'Have you got it for me?'

The accent was unmistakably Belfast. The girl said, 'A waste of your time, Mr McGuire, there is nothing for you here.'

Two of his companions were black, the third an albino

83

with lashes so fair they were almost transparent. He said, 'Don't give us any trouble, darlin', we've been good to you. A grand a week for a place like this? I'd say you were getting off lightly.'

She shook her head. 'Not a penny.'

McGuire sighed, plucked the bottle of brandy from her hand and threw it into the bar mirror, splintering the glass. 'That's just for openers. Now you, Terry.'

The albino moved fast, his right hand finding the high neck of the silk dress, ripping it to the waist, baring one of her breasts. He pulled her close, cupping the breast in one hand.

'Now then, what have we here?'

The fat man was on his feet and Dillon kicked a chair across to block his way. 'Stay out of this, Uncle, I'll handle it,' he called in Cantonese.

The four men turned quickly to face Dillon and McGuire was still smiling. 'What have we got here then, a hero?'

'Let her go,' Dillon said.

Terry smiled and pulled the girl closer. 'No, I like it too much.' All the frustration, the anger and the pain of the last few weeks rose like bile in Dillon's mouth and he pulled out the Walther and fired blindly, finishing off the bar mirror.

Terry sent the girl staggering. 'Look at his hand,' he whispered. 'He's shaking all over the place.'

McGuire showed no sign of fear. 'The accent makes me feel at home,' he said.

'I mind yours too, old son,' Dillon told him. 'The Shankill or the Falls Road, it's no difference to me. Now toss your wallet across.'

McGuire didn't even hesitate and threw it on the table. It was stuffed with notes. 'I see you've been on your rounds,' Dillon said. 'It should take care of the damage.'

'Here, there's nearly two grand there,' Terry said.

'Anything over can go to the widows and orphans.' Dillon glanced at the girl. 'No police, right?'

'No police.'

Behind her the kitchen door opened and two waiters and a chef emerged. The waiters carried butchers' knives, the chef a meat cleaver.

'I'd go, if I were you,' Dillon said. 'These people have rather violent ways when roused.'

McGuire smiled. 'I'll remember you, friend. Come on boys,' and he turned and went out.

They heard the car start up and drive away. With what little strength Dillon had left in him, he sagged back in the chair and replaced the Walther. 'I could do with that brandy now.'

And she was angry, that was the strange thing. She turned on her heel and pushed past the waiters into the kitchen.

'What did I do wrong?' Dillon asked as the staff followed her through.

'It is nothing,' the fat man said. 'She is upset. Let me get you your brandy.'

He went to the bar, got a fresh bottle and two glasses, came back and sat down. 'You spoke to me in Cantonese. You have visited China often?'

'A few times, but not often. Hong Kong mainly.'

'Fascinating. I am from Hong Kong and so is my niece. My name is Yuan Tao.'

'Sean Dillon.'

'You're Irish and visit Hong Kong only now and then and yet your Cantonese is excellent. How can this be?'

'Well, it's like this. Some people can do complicated mathematics in their head quicker than a computer.'

'So?'

'I'm like that with languages. I just soak them up.' Dillon drank a little brandy. 'I presume that lot have been here before?'

'I understand so. I only flew in yesterday. I believe they have been pressing their demands here and elsewhere for some weeks.'

The girl returned wearing slacks and a sweater. She was still angry and ignored her uncle, glaring at Dillon. 'What do you want here?'

Yuan Tao cut in. 'We owe Mr Dillon a great deal.'

'We owe him nothing and he has ruined everything. Is it just coincidence that he walks in here?'

'Strangely enough, it was,' Dillon said. 'Girl dear, life's full of them.'

'And what kind of man carries a gun in London? Another criminal.'

'Jesus,' Dillon told Yuan Tao, 'the logic on her. I could be a copper or the last of the vigilantes doing a Charles Bronson eradicating the evildoers.' The brandy had gone to his head and he got up. 'I'll be on my way. It's been fun,' and he was out of the door before they could stop him.

FIVE

Dᴵˡˡᴼᴺ ᴡᴬˢ ᵀᴵᴿᴱᴰ, very tired, and the pavement seemed to move beneath his feet. He followed the road and it brought him alongside the Thames. He stood at some railings, staring into the fog, aware of another ship moving out there. He was confused, things happening in slow motion, not aware that someone was behind him until an arm wrapped round his neck, cutting off his air. A hand slipped inside his jacket and found the Walther. Dillon was shoved into the railings, stayed there for a moment then turned and moved forward.

The albino, Terry, stood there holding the Walther. 'Here we are again, then.'

A black limousine pulled into the kerb. Dillon was aware of someone else at his back, took a deep breath and brought up all his resources. He swung his right foot up, caught Terry's hand and the Walther soared over the railings into the Thames. He jerked his head back, crunching the nose of the man behind, then ran along the pavement. He turned the corner and found himself on a deserted wharf blocked by high gates, securely padlocked.

As he turned, the limousine arrived and they all seemed to come at him together, the first man with an iron bar which clanged against the gate as Dillon lost his footing and fell, rolling desperately to avoid the swinging kicks. And then they had him up, one of them pinning him against the gates.

McGuire, lighting a cigarette, stood by the limousine. He said, 'You asked for this, friend, you really did. OK, Terry, slice him up.'

Terry's hand came out of his pocket holding an old-fashioned cut-throat razor which he opened as he came forward. He was quite calm and the blade of the razor flashed dully in the light of a street lamp and somewhere a cry echoed flatly on the damp air. Terry and McGuire swung round and Yuan Tao came walking out of the rain.

The jacket of his gabardine suit was soaked and somehow he was different, moving with a kind of strange relentlessness, as if nothing could ever stop him, and McGuire said, 'For God's sake, put him out of his misery.'

The man with the iron bar darted round the limousine and ran at Yuan Tao, the bar swinging, and the Chinese actually took the blow on his left forearm with no apparent effect. In the same moment his right fist jabbed in a short screwing motion that landed under the man's breast bone. He went down like a stone without a sound.

Yuan Tao leaned over him for a second and McGuire ran round the limousine and kicked out at him. The older

88

man caught the foot with effortless ease and twisted, so that Dillon could have sworn he heard bone crack, then he lifted, hurling McGuire across the bonnet of the car. He lay on the pavement, moaning. Yuan Tao came round the limousine, his face very calm, and the man holding Dillon from the rear released him and ran away.

Terry held up the razor. 'All right, fatty, let's be having you.'

'What about me, then, you bastard,' Dillon said and, as Terry turned, gave him a punch in the mouth, summoning all his remaining strength.

Terry lay on the pavement, cursing, blood on his mouth, and Yuan Tao stamped on his hand and kicked the razor away. A van turned into the street and braked to a halt. As the chef got out, the two waiters came round the corner holding the man who had run away.

'I'd tell them to leave him in one piece,' Dillon said in Cantonese. 'You'll need him to drive this lot away.'

'An excellent point,' Yuan Tao said. 'At least you are still in one piece.'

'Only just. I'm beginning to see why your niece was annoyed. Presumably you were actually hoping McGuire would show up?'

'I flew in especially from Hong Kong for the pleasure. My niece Su Yin cabled for my help. A matter of family. It was difficult for me to get away. I was at a retreat at one of our monasteries.'

'Monasteries?' Dillon said.

'I should explain, Mr Dillon; I am a Shaolin monk, if you know what that is.'

Dillon laughed shakily. 'I certainly do. If only McGuire had. It means, I suspect, that you're an expert in *kung fu*?'

'Darkmaster, Mr Dillon; our most extreme grade. I have studied all my life. I think I shall stay for two or three weeks to make sure there is no more trouble.'

'I shouldn't worry, I think they'll have got the point.'

McGuire, Terry and one of the blacks still lay on the pavement and the chef and two waiters brought the fourth man forward. Yuan Tao went and spoke to them in Cantonese and then returned. 'They'll deal with things here. Su Yin is waiting in her car at the restaurant.'

They walked back, turned the corner and found a dark saloon parked under the Red Dragon. As they approached she got out and, ignoring her uncle, said to Dillon in Cantonese, 'Are you all right?'

'I am now.'

'I am sorry for my behaviour.' She bowed. 'I deserve punishment, as my honourable uncle pointed out. Please forgive me.'

'There's nothing to forgive,' Dillon told her and from the direction of the river a scream sounded.

She turned to her uncle. 'What was that?'

'The little worm with the white hair, the one who shamed you before us, I told them to cut off his right ear.'

Su Yin's face didn't alter. 'I thank you, Uncle.' She bowed again then turned to Dillon. 'You will come with us now, Mr Dillon,' and this time she spoke in English.

'Girl dear, I wouldn't miss it for the world,' he said and got in the back of the car.

'If you have studied *judo* or *karate* you will have heard of *kiai*, the power that makes a man perform miracles of strength and force. Only the greatest of masters acquire this and only after years of training and discipline, both mental and physical.'

'Well, you certainly have it,' Dillon said. 'I can still see that steel bar bouncing off your arm.'

He was immersed to his neck in a bath of water so hot that sweat ran down his face. Yuan Tao squatted against the wall in an old robe and peered at him through the steam.

Dillon carried on, 'Once in Japan I was taken to see an old man of eighty, a Zen priest with arms like sticks. I think he might have weighed seven stone. He remained seated while two *karate* black belts repeatedly attacked him.'

'And?'

'He threw them effortlessly. I was told later that his power sprang from what they called the *tanden* or second brain.'

'Which can only be developed by years of meditation. All this is a development of the ancient Chinese art of Shaolin Temple Boxing. It came from India in the sixth century with Zen Buddhism and was developed by the monks of Shaolin Temple in Hohan Province.'

'Isn't that a rough game for priests? I mean, I had an uncle, a Catholic priest, who taught me bare-knuckle boxing as a boy and him a prize fighter as a younger man, but this . . .'

'We have a saying. A man avoids warfare only by being prepared for it. The monks learned that lesson. Centuries ago members of my family learned the art and passed it down. Over the centuries my ancestors fought evildoers on behalf of the poor, even the forces of the Emperor when necessary. We served our society.'

'Are you talking of the Triad Society here?' Dillon asked. 'I thought they were simply a kind of Chinese version of the Mafia?'

'Like the Mafia, they started as secret societies to protect the poor against the rich landowners and, like the Mafia, they have become corrupted over the years, but not all.'

'I've read something about this,' Dillon said. 'Are you telling me you are a Triad?'

'Like my forefathers before me, I am a member of the Secret Breath, the oldest of all, founded in Hohan in the sixteenth century. Unlike others, my society has not been corrupted. I am a Shaolin monk, I also have business interests, there is nothing wrong in that, but I will stand aside for no man.'

'So all this and your fighting ability has been handed down?'

'Of course. There are many methods, many schools, but without *ch'i* they are nothing.'

'And what would that be?'

'A special energy. When accumulated just below the navel, it has an elemental force which is infinitely greater than physical force alone. It means that a fist is simply a focusing agent. There is no need for the tremendous punches used by Western boxers. I strike from only a few inches away, screwing my fist on impact. The result may be a ruptured spleen or broken bones.'

'I can believe that, but deflecting that steel bar with your arm. How do you do that?'

'Practice, Mr Dillon, fifty years of practice.'

'I haven't got that long.' Dillon stood up and Yuan Tao passed him a towel.

'One may accomplish miracles in a matter of weeks with discipline and application and, with a man like you, I doubt whether one would be starting from scratch. There are scars from knife wounds in your back and that is an old bullet wound in the left shoulder and then there was the gun.' He shrugged. 'No ordinary man.'

'I was stabbed in the back fairly recently,' Dillon told him. 'They saved me with two operations, but it poisoned my system.'

'And your occupation?'

'I worked for British Intelligence. They threw me out this morning, said I wasn't up to it any more.'

'Then they are wrong.'

There was a pause and Dillon said, 'Are you saying you'll take me on?'

'I owe you a debt, Mr Dillon.'

'Come off it, you didn't need me. I interfered.'

'But you didn't know you were interfering and that makes a difference. It is a man's intentions which are important.' Yuan Tao smiled. 'Wouldn't you like to prove your people wrong?'

'By God and I would so,' Dillon said and then he hesitated as Yuan Tao handed him a robe. 'I'd prefer honesty between us from the beginning.'

'So?'

Dillon stood up and pulled on the robe. 'I was for years a member of the Provisional IRA and high on the most-wanted list of the Royal Ulster Constabulary and British Intelligence.'

'And yet you worked for the British?'

'Yes, well I didn't have much choice at first.'

'But now something has changed inside your head?'

Dillon grinned. 'Is there nothing you don't know? Anyway, does it make a difference?'

'Why should it? From the way you struck one of those men tonight I think you have studied *karate*.'

'Some, but no big deal. Brown belt and working for black, then I ran out of time.'

'This is good. I think we can accomplish a great deal. But now we will eat. Flesh on your bones again.'

He led the way along a corridor to a sitting room furnished in a mixture of European and Chinese styles. Su Yin sat by the fire reading a book and wearing a black silk trouser suit.

'I have news, Niece,' Yuan Tao said as she got up. 'Mr Dillon is to spend three weeks as our guest. This will not inconvenience you?'

'Of course not, Uncle; I will get the supper now.'

She moved to the door, opened it and glanced back at Dillon over her shoulder and, for the first time since they had met, she smiled.

★

93

It was the morning of 4 July that Morgan and Asta flew into London. They were picked up at Heathrow by a Rolls laid on by his London head office.

'The Berkeley?' she said.

'Where else, the best hotel in town. I've got us the Wellington Suite up on the roof, with the two bedrooms and that wonderful conservatory.'

'And so convenient for Harrods,' she said.

He squeezed her hand. 'When did I ever tell you not to spend my money? I'll just drop you off; I've business at the office, but I'll be back. Don't forget we have the Fourth of July party at the American Embassy tonight. Wear something really nice.'

'I'll knock their eyes out.'

'You always do, sweetheart; your mother would have been real proud of you,' and he took her hand as the Rolls moved away.

Hannah Bernstein knocked and went into Ferguson's office and found him working hard at his desk. 'Paper and even more paper.' He sat back. 'What is it?'

'I've had a phone call from Kim at Ardnamurchan Lodge. He arrived there safely last night in the Range Rover you appropriated. He said the journey was very strenuous, that the mountains reminded him of Nepal, but that the lodge is very nice. Apparently Lady Katherine's cook, Jeannie, appeared with a meat and potato pie to make sure he was all right.'

'Good, and Morgan?'

'The Prince moves out on Sunday morning. He has slots arranged from Air Traffic Control from Ardnamurchan Airfield. I've checked and Morgan has booked a slot to fly in that lunchtime in his Company Citation. No time for breaking and entering, I'm afraid.'

'And where is he now?'

'Arrived at Heathrow an hour ago with his stepdaughter; booked into the Wellington Suite at the Berkeley.'

'Good God, the Duke must be turning in his grave.'

'Appearance at the American Embassy tonight, sir.'

'Which means I'll have to skip that Fourth of July junket. Never mind. Is the other business in hand?'

'Yes, sir.'

'Excellent. I'll see you later, then.'

He returned to his work and she went out.

Dillon came awake early from a deep sleep, aware at once of pale evening light filtering in through the curtained window. He was alone. He turned to look at the pillow beside him, at the indentation where her head had been, and then he got up, walked to the window and looked out through the half-drawn curtains to the cobbled street of Stable Mews.

It was a fine evening and he turned and went to the wardrobe feeling relaxed and alive, but more important, whole again. His eyes were calm, his head clear and the ache in his stomach was honest hunger. He stood in front of the mirror and examined himself. He looked younger, fitter in every way. When he turned to examine his back in the mirror, the angry weal of the operation scars from the knife wounds were already fading into white lines. It was extraordinary. Barely four weeks since that night in Wapping. What Yuan Tao had achieved was a miracle. He pulled on a track suit then followed the sound of running water to the bathroom. When he opened the door Su Yin was in the shower.

'It's me,' he called. 'Are we having dinner tonight?'

'I have a business to run,' she called. 'You keep forgetting.'

'We could eat late.'

'All right, we'll see, now go and do your exercises.'

He closed the door and returned to the bedroom. It was

cool in there and quiet, only the faint traffic sounds in the distance. He could almost hear the silence and stood there, relaxing completely, remembering the lines of the ancient Taoist verse that Yuan Tao had taught him.

> In motion, be like water
> At rest, like a mirror
> Respond, like the echo
> Be subtle as though non-existent

The ability to relax completely, the most important gift of all, a faculty retained by all other animals except man. Cultivated, it could provide a power that was positively superhuman, created by vigorous discipline and a system of training at least a thousand years old. Out of it sprang the intrinsic energy *ch'i*, the life force which in repose gave a man the pliability of a child and in action the power of the tiger.

He sat on the floor cross-legged, relaxing totally, breathing in through his nose and out through his mouth. He closed his eyes and covered his left ear with his right hand. He varied this after five minutes by covering his right ear with his left hand, still breathing deeply and steadily. Then he covered both ears, arms crossed.

Darkness enfolded him and, when he finally opened his eyes, his mouth was sharply cool. He took a long shuddering breath and, when he got to his feet, his limbs seemed to be filled with power. He wondered how Bellamy would react and yet the results were there for all to see. A hand that no longer trembled, a clear eye and a strength he would never have believed possible.

Su Yin came in at that moment wearing cream slacks and a Spanish shirt in vivid orange. She was combing her hair. 'You look pleased with yourself.'

'And why wouldn't I? I've spent the afternoon in bed

with a supremely beautiful woman and I still feel like Samson.'

She laughed. 'You're hopeless, Sean. Get me a taxi.'

He phoned the usual number then turned. 'What about tonight? We could eat late at the Ritz and catch the cabaret.'

'It's not possible.' She put a hand to her face. 'I know how good you feel these days, but you can't have everything in this life.' She hesitated. 'You miss Yuan Tao, don't you?'

'Very much, which is strange considering he only left five days ago.'

'Would you miss me as much?'

'Of course. Why do you ask?'

'I'm going home, Sean. My sister and her husband are opening a new night club in Hong Kong. My uncle phoned me last night. They need me.'

'And the Red Dragon?'

'Will continue quite happily with my head waiter promoted to manager.'

'And me?' he said. 'What about me?'

'Are you trying to say you love me?' He hesitated before replying and it was enough. 'No, Sean, we've had as good a time together as any two people could hope for in this life, but everything passes and it's time for me to go home.'

'How soon?'

'Probably the weekend.' As the doorbell rang, she picked up her briefcase. 'There's my taxi. I must go. I've lots to do.'

He went with her to the door and opened it. The taxi was waiting, engine running. She paused on the step. 'This isn't the end, Sean. You'll call me?'

He kissed her lightly on both cheeks. 'Of course.'

But he wouldn't, he knew that and she knew it too; he could tell that by the way she paused before getting into the taxi, glancing back as if aware that it was the last time and then the door slammed and she was gone.

He was in the shower for a good fifteen minutes, thinking about it, when the front-door bell rang. Perhaps she'd come back? He found a bathrobe and went out, drying his hair with a towel. When he opened the door a man in brown overalls stood there, a clipboard in his hand, a British Telecom van parked behind him.

'Sorry to bother you, sir, we've had four telephone breakdowns already this morning in the mews. Could I check your box?' He held up a British Telecom identity pass with his photo on it above the name J. Smith.

'Sure and why not?' Dillon turned and led the way along the corridor. 'The junction box is under the stairs. I'll just go and change.'

He went upstairs, finished drying his hair, combed it and pulled on an old track suit and trainers then went downstairs. The telephone engineer was under the stairs.

'Everything all right?' Dillon asked.

'I think so, sir.'

Dillon turned to go through the living room to the kitchen and saw a large laundry basket in the middle of the room. 'What in the hell is this?' he demanded.

'Oh, that's for you.'

A second telephone engineer in the same uniform overalls stepped from behind the door, holding an Italian Beretta automatic pistol. He was getting on a little and had a wrinkled and kindly face.

'Jesus, son, there's no need for that thing, just tell me what you want,' Dillon said and moved to the wide Victorian fireplace and stood with his hand on the mantelpiece.

'I wouldn't try to grab for the Walther you keep hanging

from a nail just into the chimney, sir, we've already removed it,' the older man said. 'So just lie on the floor, hands behind your neck.'

Dillon did as he was told as Smith joined them. 'Steady does it, Mr Dillon,' he said and Dillon was aware of a needle jabbing into his right buttock.

Whatever it was, it was good. One moment he was there, the next he was gone, it was as simple as that.

He came back to life as quickly as he had left it. It was night now and the only illumination in the room was from a kind of night light on the locker beside the single bed on which he lay. He still wore his track suit, they hadn't even taken off his trainers. He swung his legs to the floor, took a couple of deep breaths then heard voices and a key rattled in the lock. He hurriedly lay back and closed his eyes.

'Still out. Is that all right, Doc?' It was Smith speaking; Dillon recognized his voice.

. Someone else said, 'Let me see.' A finger checked his pulse on the right wrist and then his track-suit top was unzipped and a stethoscope applied. 'Pulse fine, heart fine,' the doctor said and rolled back Dillon's eyelids one after the other and probed with a light. He was a tall, cadaverous Indian in a white coat and Dillon, by an act of supreme will, stayed rigid, staring. 'No, he'll be awake soon. One cannot be certain of the time element with these drug dosages. There are individual variations in response. We'll come back in an hour.'

The door closed, the key turned. Two bolts were also rammed home. Dillon was on his feet now, moved to the door and stood there listening. There was little point in wasting time on the door, that was obvious. He moved to the window and drew the curtain and was immediately presented with solid bars. He peered out. Rain fell steadily, dripping through a leak from the gutter which was just above his head. There was a garden outside, a high wall about fifty yards away.

If that was the gutter that meant there was only roof space above him. It could be an attic, but only one way to find out.

There was a small wooden table and a chair against the wall. He dragged the table into the corner by the window and climbed on to it. The plaster of the ceiling was so old and soft that when he put his elbow into it it broke at once, shards of plaster crumbling, dropping into the room. He enlarged the hole quickly, tearing wooden lathing away with his bare hands. When it was large enough, he got down, placed the chair on the table, then clambered up on it, pulling himself up to find a dark echoing roof space, a chink of light drifting through a crack here and there.

He moved cautiously, walking on beams. The roof space was extensive and obviously covered the whole house, a rabbit warren of half-walls and eaves. He finally came to a trapdoor which he opened cautiously. Below was a small landing in darkness, stairs leading down to where there was diffused light.

Dillon dropped to the landing, paused to listen and then went down the stairs. He found himself at one end of a long corridor which was fully lit. He hesitated and, at that moment, a door opened on his left and Smith and the Indian doctor walked out. And Smith was fast, Dillon had to give him that, pulling a Walther from his pocket even as Dillon moved in, smashing a fist into his stomach and raising a knee into the man's face as he keeled over. Smith dropped the Walther as he fell and Dillon picked it up.

'All right, old son,' he said to the doctor. 'Answers. Where am I?'

The Indian was hugely alarmed. 'St Mark's Nursing Home, Holland Park, Mr Dillon. Please.' His hands fluttered. 'I loathe guns.'

'You'll loathe them even more when I've finished with you. What's going on here? Who am I up against?'

'Please Mr Dillon.' The man was pleading now. 'I just work here.'

There was a sudden shout and Dillon turned to see the second of his kidnappers standing at the end of the corridor. He drew his Beretta, Dillon took a quick snap-shot with the Walther, the man went over backwards. Dillon shoved the Indian into the room, turned and went headlong down the stairs. Before he reached the bottom a shrill alarm bell sounded monotonously over and over again. Dillon didn't hesitate, reaching the corridor on the ground floor in seconds, running straight for the door at the far end. He unlocked it hurriedly and plunged out into the garden.

It was raining hard. He seemed to be at the rear of the house and somewhere on the other side he heard voices calling and the bark of a dog. He ran across a piece of lawn and carried on through bushes, a hand raised to protect his face from flailing branches until he reached the wall. It was about fifteen feet high, festooned with barbed wire. Possible to climb a nearby tree perhaps and leap across, but the black wire strung at that level looked ominous. He picked up a large branch lying on the ground and reached up. When he touched the wire there was an immediate flash.

He turned and ran on, parallel to the wall. There was more than one dog barking now, but the rain would help kill his scent and then he came to the edge of trees and the drive to the gates leading to the outside world. They were closed and two men stood there wearing berets and camouflage uniforms and holding assault rifles.

A Land Rover drew up and someone got out to speak to them, a man in civilian clothes. Dillon turned and hurried back towards the house. The alarm stopped abruptly. He paused by the rear entrance he had exited from earlier, then opened it. The corridor was silent and he moved along it cautiously and stood at the bottom of the stairs.

There were voices in the distance. He listened for a moment then went cautiously back up the stairs. The last place they'd look for him, or so he hoped. He reached the corridor on the top floor. Smith and the other man had gone, but, as Dillon paused there, considering his next move, the door opened on his right and, for the second time that night, the Indian doctor emerged.

His distress was almost comical. 'Oh, my God, Mr Dillon, I thought you well away by now.'

'I've returned to haunt you,' Dillon told him. 'You didn't tell me your name.'

'Chowdray – Dr Emas Chowdray.'

'Good. I'll tell you what we're going to do. Somewhere in this place is the person in charge. You're going to take me to where he is. If you don't,' he tucked Chowdray under the chin with the Walther, 'you'll loathe guns even more.'

'No need for this violence, I assure you, Mr Dillon. I will comply.'

He led the way down the stairs, turning along a corridor on the first floor, reaching a carpeted landing. A curving Regency staircase led to a magnificent hall. The dogs were still barking in the garden outside, but it was so quiet in the hall they could hear the ticking of the grandfather clock in the corner.

'Where are we going?' Dillon whispered.

'Down there, the mahogany door,' Chowdray told him.

'Down we go, then.'

They descended the carpeted stairs; moved across the hall to the door. 'The library, Mr Dillon.'

'Nice and easy,' Dillon said. 'Open it.'

Chowdray did so and Dillon pushed him inside. The walls were lined with books, a fire burned brightly in an

Adam fireplace. Detective Chief Inspector Hannah Bernstein stood by the fire, talking to the two fake telephone engineers.

She turned and smiled. 'Come in, Mr Dillon, do. You've
just won me five pounds. I told these two this is exactly
where you would end up.'

SIX

THE CAR WHICH DROPPED Dillon at his cottage in Stable Mews waited while he went in. He changed into grey slacks, a silk navy blue polo neck sweater and a Donegal tweed jacket. He got his wallet, cigarette case and lighter and was outside and into the car again in a matter of minutes. It was not long afterwards that they reached Cavendish Square and he rang the bell of Ferguson's flat. It was Hannah Bernstein who answered.

'Do you handle the domestic chores as well now?' he asked. 'Where's Kim?'

'In Scotland,' she told him. 'You'll find out why. He's waiting.'

She led the way along the corridor into the sitting room where they found Ferguson sitting beside the fire reading the evening paper. He looked up calmly. 'There you are, Dillon. I must say, you look remarkably fit.'

'More bloody games,' Dillon said.

'A practical test which I thought would save me a great deal of time and indicate just how true the reports I've been getting on you were.' He looked at Hannah. 'You've got it all on video?'

'Yes, sir.'

He returned to Dillon. 'You certainly gave poor old Smith a working over and, as for his colleague, it's a good job you only had blanks in that Walther.' He shook his head. 'My God, Dillon, you really are a bastard when you get going.'

'God bless your honour for the pat on the head,' Dillon said. 'And is there just the slightest chance you could be telling me what in the hell this is all about?'

'Certainly,' Ferguson said. 'There's a bottle of Bushmills on the sideboard. You get the file out, Chief Inspector.'

'Thank you,' Dillon said with irony and went and helped himself.

Ferguson said, 'If I hadn't seen it with my own eyes I wouldn't have believed it. Remarkable fellow this Yuan Tao. Wish he could work for me.'

'I suppose you could always try to buy him,' Dillon said.

'Not really,' Ferguson said. 'He owns three factories in Hong Kong and one of the largest shipping lines in the Far East, besides a number of minor interests – restaurants, that sort of thing. Didn't he tell you?'

'No,' Dillon said and then he smiled. 'He wouldn't have. He's not that sort of bloke, Brigadier.'

'His niece seems an attractive girl.'

'She is. She's also returning to Hong Kong this weekend. I bet you didn't know that.'

'What a pity. We'll have to find another way of filling your time.'

'I'm sure you won't have the slightest difficulty,' Dillon told him.

'As usual, you've hit the nail on the head. I obviously wanted you back anyway, but as it happens something special has come up, something that I think requires the Dillon touch. For one thing there's a rather attractive young lady involved, but we'll come to that later. Chief Inspector, the file.'

'Here, sir,' she said and handed it to him.

'Have you heard of a man called Carl Morgan?'

'Billionaire hotel owner, financier, amongst other things,' Dillon said. 'Never out of the society pages in the magazines. He's also closely linked with the Mafia. His uncle is a man called Don Giovanni Luca. In Sicily he's *Capo di tutti Capi*, Boss of all the Bosses.'

Ferguson was genuinely impressed. 'How on earth do you know all this?'

'Oh, about a thousand years ago when I worked with a certain illegal organisation called the IRA, the Sicilian Mafia was one of the sources from which we obtained arms.'

'Really,' Hannah Bernstein said drily. 'It might be useful to have you sit down and commit everything you remember about how that worked to paper.'

'It's a thought,' Dillon told her.

She handed him a file. 'Have a look at that.'

'Delighted.'

'I'll make some tea, sir.'

She went out and Dillon sat on the window seat, smoking a cigarette. As he finished, she returned with a tray and he joined them by the fire.

'Fascinating stuff this Chungking Covenant business.' There were some photos clipped to the back of the file, one of them of Morgan in polo kit. 'The man himself. Looks like an advert for some manly aftershave.'

'He's a dangerous man,' Hannah said as she poured tea. 'Don't kid yourself.'

'I know, girl dear,' he said. There were other photos, some showing Morgan with the great and good and a couple with Luca. 'He certainly knows everybody.'

'You could say that.'

'And this?' Dillon asked.

The last photo showed Morgan on his yacht at Cannes Harbour, reclining in a deck chair, a glass of champagne in hand, gazing up at a young girl who leaned on the rail. She looked about sixteen and wore a bikini, blonde hair to her shoulders.

'His stepdaughter, Asta, though she uses his name,' Hannah told him.

'Swedish?'

'Yes. Taken more than four years ago. She's twenty-one in three weeks or so. We have a photo of her in *Tatler* somewhere, taken with Morgan at Goodwood races. Very, very attractive.'

'I'd say Morgan would agree with you, to judge from the way he's looking at her in that picture.'

'Why do you say that particularly?' Ferguson asked.

'He smiles a lot usually, he's smiling on all the other photos, but not on this one. It's as if he's saying, "I take you seriously". Where does the mother fit in? You haven't indicated her on any photos.'

'She was drowned a year ago while diving off a Greek island called Hydra,' said Hannah.

'An accident?'

'Faulty air tank, that's what the autopsy said, but there's a copy of an investigation mounted by the Athens police here.' Hannah produced it from the file. 'The Brigadier tells me you're an expert diver. You'll find it interesting.'

107

Dillon read it quickly then looked up, frowning. 'No accident, this. That valve must have been tampered with. Did it end at that?'

'The police didn't even raise the matter with Morgan. I got this from their dead-file courtesy of a friend in Greek Intelligence,' Ferguson told him. 'Morgan has huge interests in Greek shipping, casinos, hotels. There an order from the top to kill the investigation.'

'They'd never have got anywhere,' Hannah said. 'Not with the kind of money he has and all that power and influence.'

'But what we're saying is he killed his wife or arranged to have it done,' Dillon said. 'Why would he do that? Was she wealthy?'

'Yes, but nothing like as rich as he is,' Ferguson said. 'My hunch is that perhaps she'd got to know too much.'

'And that's your opinion?' Dillon asked Hannah Bernstein.

'Possibly.' She picked up the photo taken on the yacht. 'But maybe it was something else. Perhaps he wanted Asta.'

Dillon nodded. 'That's what I was thinking.' He turned to Ferguson. 'So what are we going to do on this one?'

Ferguson nodded to Hannah who took charge. 'The house at Loch Dhu – Morgan goes in this coming Monday. The Brigadier and I are going up on Friday, flying to this old RAF station at Ardnamurchan, and we move into Ardnamurchan Lodge where Kim is already in residence.'

'And what about me?'

'You're my nephew,' Ferguson said. 'My mother was Irish, remember? You'll join us a few days later.'

'Why?'

'Our information is that Asta isn't going with Morgan. She's attending a ball at the Dorchester which is being given by the Brazilian Embassy on Monday night. Morgan was supposed to go and she's standing in for him,' Hannah said. 'We've discovered that she flies to Glasgow on Tuesday and then intends to take the train to Fort William and from there to Arisaig where she'll be picked up by car.'

'How do you know this?' Dillon asked.

'Oh, let's say we have a friend on the staff at the Berkeley,' she said.

'Why take the train from Glasgow when she could fly direct to Ardnamurchan in Morgan's Citation?'

'God knows,' Ferguson said. 'Perhaps she fancies the scenic route. That train goes through some of the most spectacular scenery in Europe.'

'So what am I supposed to do?'

'The Chief Inspector has a gold-edged invitation for one Sean Dillon to attend the Brazilian Embassy Ball on Monday night,' Ferguson told him. 'It's black tie for you, Dillon; you do have one?'

'Sure, and don't I need it for those spare nights I'm a waiter at the Savoy? And what do I do when I'm there?'

For the first time Hannah Bernstein looked unsure. 'Well, try and get to know her.'

'Pick her up, you mean? Won't that look something of a coincidence when I turn up at Ardnamurchan Lodge later?'

'Quite deliberate on my part, dear boy. Remember our little adventure in the American Virgins?' Ferguson turned to Hannah. 'I'm sure you've read the file, Chief Inspector. The late lamented *Señor* Santiago and his motley crew knew who we were just as we knew who they were and what they were up to. It was what I call a we-know-that-you-know-that-you-know-that-we-know situation.'

'So?' Dillon said.

'Morgan at Loch Dhu for nefarious purposes, an isolated estate miles from anywhere in the Highlands of Scotland, discovers he's got neighbours up for the shooting staying on the other side of the Loch at Ardnamurchan Lodge.

He'll be checking us out the minute he knows we're there, dear boy, and don't tell me we could all use false names. With the kind of company he keeps, especially his Mafia contacts in London, he'll not have the slightest difficulty in sorting us out.'

'All right, point taken, but I know you, you old bugger, and there's more to it.'

'Hasn't he an elegant turn of phrase, Chief Inspector?' Ferguson smiled. 'Yes, of course, there is. As I've indicated, I want him to know we're there, I want him to know we're breathing down his bloody neck. Of course I'll also see that the story, Morgan taking Loch Dhu and Asta standing in for him at the Brazilian Embassy affair, is leaked to the *Daily Mail*'s gossip column. You could always say later that you read that, were intrigued because you were going to the same spot, so you went out of your way to meet her. It won't make the slightest difference. Morgan will still smell stinking fish.'

'Won't that be dangerous, Brigadier?' Hannah Bernstein commented.

'Yes it will, Chief Inspector, that's why we have Dillon.' He smiled and stood up. 'It's getting late and dinner is indicated. You must be famished, both of you. I'll take you to the River Room at the Savoy. Excellent dance band, Chief Inspector, you can have a turn round the floor with the desperado here. He may surprise you.'

When Monday night came, Dillon arrived early at the Dorchester. He wore a dark blue Burberry trenchcoat which he left at the cloakroom. His dinner jacket was a totally conventional piece of immaculate tailoring by Armani, single breasted with lapels of raw silk, black studs vivid against the white shirt. He was really rather pleased with his general appearance and hoped that Asta Morgan would feel the same. He fortified himself with a glass of champagne in the Piano Bar and went down to the grand ballroom, where he presented his card and was admitted to discover the Brazilian Ambassador and his wife greeting their guests.

His name was called and he went forward. 'Mr Dillon?' the Ambassador said, a slight query in his voice.

'Ministry of Defence,' Dillon said. 'So good of you to invite me.' He turned to the Ambassador's wife and kissed her hand gallantly. 'My compliments on the dress, most becoming.'

She flushed with pleasure and, as he walked away, he heard her say in Portuguese to her husband, 'What a charming man.'

The ballroom was already busy, a dance band playing, exquisitely gowned women, most men in black tie, although there was a sprinkling of military dress uniforms and here and there a church dignitary. With the crystal chandeliers, the mirrors, it was really quite a splendid scene and he took a glass of champagne from a passing waiter and worked his way through the crowd, looking for Asta Morgan and seeing no sign of her. Finally he went back to the entrance, lit a cigarette and waited.

It was almost an hour later that he heard her name called. She wore her hair up, revealing her entire face, the high Scandinavian cheek bones, and an expression that seemed to say that she didn't give a damn about anyone, or anything, for that matter. She wore an absurdly simple dress of black silk, banded at the waist, the hem well above the knee, black stockings, and carried an evening purse in a sort of black chain mail. Heads turned to watch as she stood talking to the Ambassador and his wife for quite some time.

'Probably making Morgan's excuses,' Dillon said softly.

Finally, she came down the stairs, pausing to open her purse. She took out a gold cigarette case, selected one, then searched for a lighter. 'Damn!' she said.

Dillon stepped forward, the Zippo flaring in his right hand. 'Sure and nothing's ever there when you want it, isn't that the truth?'

She looked him over calmly, then held his wrist and took the light. 'Thank you.'

As she turned to go, Dillon said cheerfully, 'Six inches at least, those heels; mind how you go, dear girl, a plaster cast wouldn't go well with that slip of a dress.'

Her eyes widened in astonishment, then she laughed and walked away.

She seemed to know a vast number of people, working her way from group to group, occasionally posing for society photographers, and she was certainly popular. Dillon stayed close enough to observe her and simply waited to see what the night would bring.

She danced on a number of occasions, with a variety of men, including the Ambassador himself and two Government ministers and an actor or two. Dillon's opportunity came about an hour later when he saw her dancing with a Member of Parliament notorious for his womanising. As the dance finished he kept his arm round her waist as they left the floor. They were standing by the buffet and she was trying to get away, but he had her by the wrist now.

Dillon moved in fast. 'Jesus, Asta, I'm sorry I'm so late. Business.' The other man released her, frowning, and Dillon kissed her on the mouth. 'Sean Dillon,' he murmured.

She pushed him away and said petulantly, 'You really are a swine, Sean; nothing but excuses. Business. Is that the best you can do?'

Dillon took her hand, totally ignoring the MP. 'Well, I'll think of something. Let's take a turn round the floor.'

The band played a foxtrot and she was light in his arms. 'By God, girl, but you do this well,' he said.

'I learned at boarding school. Twice a week we had

ballroom dancing in the hall. Girls dancing together, of course. Always a row over who was to lead.'

'I can imagine. You know, when I was a boy back home in Belfast we used to club together so one of the crowd could pay to get in at the dance hall then he'd open a fire door so the rest got in for free.'

'You dogs,' she said.

'Well, at sixteen you didn't have the cash, but once in it was fantasy time. All those girls in cotton frocks smelling of talcum powder.' She grinned. 'We lived in a very working-class area. Perfume was far too expensive.'

'And that's where you perfected your performance?'

'And what performance would that be?'

'Oh, come off it,' she said. 'The smooth act you pulled back there. Now I'm supposed to be grateful, isn't that how it goes?'

'You mean we vanish into the night so that I can have my wicked way with you?' He smiled. 'I'm sorry, my love, but I've other things planned and I'm sure you do.' He stopped on the edge of the floor and kissed her hand. 'It's been fun, but try and keep better company.'

He turned and walked away and Asta Morgan watched him go, a look of astonishment on her face.

The pianist in the Piano Bar at the Dorchester was Dillon's personal favourite in the whole of London. When the Irishman appeared, he waved and Dillon joined him, leaning on the piano.

'Heh, you look great, man; something special tonight?'

'Ball for the Brazilian Embassy, the great and the good sometimes making fools of themselves.'

'Takes all sorts. You want to fill in? I could do with a visit to the men's room.'

'My pleasure.'

Dillon slipped behind the piano and sat down as the

pianist stood. A waitress approached, smiling. 'The usual, Mr Dillon?'

'Krug, my love, non-vintage.' Dillon took a cigarette from his old silver case, lit it and moved into 'A Foggy Day in London Town', a personal favourite.

He sat there, the cigarette dangling from the side of his mouth, smoke drifting up, immersed in the music and yet still perfectly aware of Asta Morgan's approach.

'A man of talent, I see.'

'As an old enemy of mine once said, a passable bar-room piano, that's all, fruits of a misspent youth.'

'Enemy you say?'

'We supported the same cause, but had different attitudes on how to go about it, let's put it that way.'

'A cause, Mr Dillon? That sounds serious.'

'A heavy burden.' The waitress arrived with the Krug in a bucket and he nodded. 'A glass for the lady; we'll sit in the booth over there.'

'"I was a stranger in the city,"' she said, giving him some of the verse.

'"Out of town were the people I knew,"' he replied. 'Thank the Gershwins for it, George and Ira. They must have loved this old town. Wrote it for a movie called *A Damsel in Distress*. Fred Astaire sang it.'

'I hear he could dance a little too,' she said.

The black pianist returned at that moment. 'Heh, man, that's nice.'

'But not as good as you. Take over.' Dillon got out of the way as the pianist sat beside him.

They sat in the booth and Dillon lit a cigarette for her and gave her a glass of champagne.

'I'd judge you to be a man of accomplishment and high standards and yet you drink non-vintage,' she said as she sampled the Krug.

'The greatest champagne of all, the non-vintage,' he

said. 'It's quite unique. It's the grape mix, and not many people know that. They go by what's printed on the label, the surface of things.'

'A philosopher too. What do you do, Mr Dillon?'

'As little as possible.'

'Don't we all? You spoke of a cause, not a job or a profession, a cause. Now that I do find interesting.'

'Jesus, Asta Morgan, here we are in the best bar in London drinking Krug champagne and you're turning serious on me.'

'How do you know my name?'

'Well, the *Tatler* know it and *Hello* and all those other society magazines you keep appearing in. Hardly a secret, you and your father keeping such high-class company. Why, they even had you in the Royal Enclosure at Ascot last month with the Queen Mother, God save her, and me just a poor Irish peasant boy with his nose to the window.'

'I was in the Enclosure because my father had a horse running and I doubt whether you've ever put your nose to a window in your life, Mr Dillon; I've a strong suspicion you'd be much more likely to kick it in.' She stood up. 'My turn to leave now. It's been nice and I'm grateful for you intervening back there. Hamish Hunt is a pig when he's been drinking.'

'A girl like you, my love, would tempt a cardinal from Rome and no drink taken,' Dillon told her.

For a moment she changed, the hard edge gone, flushed, looking slightly uncertain. 'Why, Mr Dillon, compliments and at this time of night? Whatever next.'

Dillon watched her go, then got up and followed. He paid his bill quickly, retrieved his Burberry and pulled it on, walking out into the magnificent foyer of the Dorchester. There was no sign of her at the entrance and the doorman approached.

'Cab, sir?'

'I was looking for Miss Asta Morgan,' Dillon told him. 'But I seem to have missed her.'

'I know Miss Morgan well, sir. She's been at the ball tonight. I'd say her driver will be picking her up at the side entrance.'

'Thanks.'

Dillon walked round and followed the pavement, the Park Lane traffic flashing by. There were a number of limousines parked, waiting for their passengers, and, as he approached, Asta Morgan emerged wearing a rather dramatic black cloak, the hood pulled up. She paused, looking up and down the line of limousines, obviously not finding what she was looking for, and started along the pavement. At the same moment the MP, Hamish Hunt, emerged from the hotel and went after her.

Dillon moved in fast, but Hunt had her by the arm and up against the wall, his hands under her cloak. His voice was loud, slurred with the drink. 'Come on, Asta, just a kiss.'

She turned her face away and Dillon tapped him on the shoulder. Hunt turned in surprise and Dillon ran a foot down his shin, stamping hard on Hunt's instep then head-butted him sharply and savagely and with total economy. Hunt staggered back and slid down the wall.

'Drunk again,' Dillon said. 'I wonder what the voters will say,' and he took Asta's hand and pulled her away.

A Mercedes limousine slid up the kerb and a uniformed chauffeur jumped out. 'I hope I haven't kept you waiting, Miss Asta; the police were moving us on earlier, I had to go round.'

'That's all right, Henry.'

A uniformed police officer moved along the pavement towards Hunt, who was sitting against the wall, and Asta opened the rear door of the Mercedes and pulled Dillon by the hand.

'Come on, we'd better get out of here.'

He followed her in, the chauffeur got behind the wheel and eased into the traffic. 'Jesus, ma'am, the grand car you've got here and me just a poor Irish boy up from the country and hoping to make a pound or two.'

She laughed out loud. 'Poor Irish boy, Mr Dillon, I've never heard such rot. If you are it's the first one I've heard of who wears clothes by Armani.'

'Ah, you noticed?'

'If there's one thing I'm an expert on it's fashion, that's *my* fruits of a misspent youth.'

'Sure, and it's the terrible old woman you are already, Asta Morgan.'

'All right,' she said. 'Where can we take you?'

'Anywhere?'

'The least I can do.'

He pressed the button that lowered the glass window separating them from the chauffeur. 'Take us to the Embankment, driver,' he said and raised the window again.

'The Embankment?' she said. 'What for?'

He offered her a cigarette. 'Didn't you ever see those old movies where the fella and his girl walked along the pavement by the Embankment overlooking the Thames?'

'Before my time, Mr Dillon,' she said and leaned forward for a light. 'But I'm willing to try anything once.'

When they reached the Embankment it was raining. 'Would you look at that now,' Dillon said.

She put the partition window down. 'We're going to walk, Henry; pick us up at Lambeth Bridge. Have you an umbrella?'

'Certainly, Miss Asta.'

He got out to open the doors and put up a large black umbrella which Dillon took. Asta slipped a hand in his arm and they started to walk. 'Is this romantic enough for you?' he demanded.

'I wouldn't have thought you the romantic type,' she said. 'But if you mean do I like it, yes. I love the rain, the city by night, the feeling that anything could be waiting just up around the next corner.'

'Probably a mugger these days.'

'Now I know you're not a romantic.'

He paused to get out his cigarettes and gave her one. 'No, I take your point. When I was young and foolish a thousand years ago, life seemed to have infinite possibilities.'

'And what happened?'

'Life.' He laughed.

'You don't mess about, do you? I mean, back there with that creep Hamish Hunt, you went in hard.'

'And what does that tell you?'

'That you can take care of yourself and that's unusual in a man who wears an evening suit that cost at least fifteen hundred pounds. What do you do?'

'Well now, let's see. I went to the Royal Academy of Dramatic Art, but that was a long time ago. I played Lyngstrand in Ibsen's *Lady from the Sea* at the National Theatre. He was the one who coughed a lot.'

'And afterwards? I mean you obviously gave up acting or I'd have heard of you.'

'Not entirely. You might say I took a considerable interest in what might be termed the theatre of the street, back home in the old country.'

'Strange,' she said. 'If I had to guess I'd say you'd been a soldier.'

'And who's the clever girl then?'

'Damn you, Dillon,' she said. 'Mystery piles on mystery with you.'

'You'll just have to unpeel me layer by layer like an onion, but that would take time.'

'And that's exactly what I don't have,' she said. 'I'm going up to Scotland tomorrow.'

'I know,' Dillon said. 'There was a mention in Nigel Dempster's gossip column in the *Mail* this morning. "Carl Morgan takes the lease on a Highland Estate for the shooting"; that was the byline. It also said you were standing in for him tonight at the Brazilian Embassy Ball.'

'You *are* well informed.'

They had reached Lambeth Bridge by now and found the Mercedes waiting. Dillon handed her in. 'I enjoyed that.'

'I'll drop you off,' she said.

'No need.'

'Don't be silly, I'm curious to see where you live.'

'Anything to oblige.' He got in beside her. 'Stable Mews, Henry; that's close to Cavendish Square. I'll show you where when we get there.'

When they turned into the cobbled street, it was still raining. He got out and closed the door. Asta put the window down and looked out at the cottage.

'All in darkness. No lady friend, Dillon?'

'Alas no, but you can come in for a cup of tea if you like.'

She laughed. 'Oh, no, I've had enough excitement for one night.'

'Another time, perhaps.'

'I don't think so. In fact, I doubt whether we'll ever see each other again.'

'Ships that pass in the night?'

'Something like that. Home, Henry,' and, as she put up the window, the Mercedes pulled away.

Dillon watched it go and, as he turned to open the door, he was smiling.

SEVEN

It was peaceful in the small railway station by the lochside and Dillon peered out of the rear compartment, keeping out of sight. Following her had been easy. The Lear had taken him to Glasgow Airport at breakfast time and he had waited until Asta had arrived on the morning shuttle from London; had followed her down to the central railway station. Keeping out of the way from Glasgow to Fort William had been easy, for the train was busy with many tourists here to see Loch Lomond and afterwards the spectacular mountain scenery of the Highlands.

The smaller, local train from Fort William to Arisaig had been more difficult, for there were only a handful of passengers and he'd kept out of sight, leaping into the rear compartment at the last moment. The station they had stopped at now was named Shiel, according to the board at one side of the ticket office. They seemed to be standing there for quite some time. It was very pleasant, a mountain above them rearing three thousand feet into the clear blue sky, sunlight glinting on a waterfall that spilled over granite into birch trees.

Asta Morgan suddenly stepped on to the platform. She wore a leather jacket and linen slacks and leather brogues. She made an attractive sight in the quiet setting. She moved across to the ticket collector, who stood at the barrier. There was some conversation, a burst of laughter and she went through the barrier.

The ticket collector moved to join the guard who was standing by the open door beside Dillon. 'You've lost a passenger, Tom.'

'Do you tell me?'

'A bonny lass, a Miss Morgan, hair of corn and a face to thank God for. Her father is yon fella Morgan that's just leased Loch Dhu Castle. She's away over the mountain. You'll put her luggage down at Arisaig and leave a message.'

Dillon grabbed his Burberry trenchcoat and brushed past the guard. 'Do you mean there's a shortcut over the mountain?'

'Well, that would depend where you want to be?'

'Ardnamurchan Lodge.'

The guard nodded. 'Over the top of Ben Breac and a twelve-mile walk on the other side. You'll be staying with Brigadier Ferguson, the new tenant?'

'My uncle; he'll be waiting at Arisaig. Perhaps you could tell him where I am and give him my luggage.' Dillon slipped a five pound note into his hand.

'Leave it to me, sir.'

The guard blew his whistle and boarded the train. Dillon turned to the ticket collector. 'Where do I go?'

'Through the village and over the bridge. There's a path through the birches; hard going, but you can't miss the cairns that mark the way. Once over the top, the track is plain to the glen below.'

'Will the weather hold?'

The man looked up at the mountain. 'A touch of mist and rain in the evening. I'd keep going; don't waste time on top.' He smiled. 'I'd tell the young lady that, sir; no place for a lassie to be on her own.'

Dillon smiled. 'I'll do that; a pity to see her get wet.'

'A thousand pities, sir.'

At the small village store he purchased two packs of cigarettes and two half-pound bars of milk chocolate for sustenance. Twelve miles on the other side of the mountain and that didn't count the miles that stood up on end. Something told him he could be hungry before he reached Ardnamurchan.

He marched down the street and crossed the bridge. The track snaked up through the birch trees, lifting steeply, bracken pressing in on either side. It was cool and dark and remote from the world and Dillon, thanks to his renewed energy, was enjoying every moment of it. There was no sign of Asta, which suited him for now.

The trees grew sparser and he emerged on to a bracken-covered slope. Occasionally grouse or plover lifted out of the heather, disturbed by his presence, and finally he came to a boulder-strewn plain that stretched to the lower slopes of Ben Breac. He saw Asta then, six or seven hundred feet up on the shoulder of the mountain.

She turned to look down and he dropped into the bracken. When he glanced up a few moments later, she had disappeared round the shoulder of the mountain. She was certainly moving fast, but then she was young and healthy and the track was plainly visible.

There was another way, of course, though only a fool would try that, which was straight up the breast of the mountain and the granite cliffs beyond to the summit. He took out an Ordnance Survey map of Moidart and had a look at the situation. Dillon glanced up. What the hell, strong nerves were all that was needed here and, with luck, he might actually get ahead of her. He tied his Burberry around his waist and started up.

The lower slopes were easy going with his new-found strength, but after half an hour he came to a great cascading bank of scree and loose stones that moved beneath his feet alarmingly. He went to his left, found the waterfall he'd noted from the station and followed its trail upwards, moving from boulder to boulder.

Finally, he reached the plateau and the final cliffs were before him and they were not quite as intimidating as they'd looked from the station, fissured with gullies and channels reaching to the top. He looked, checking his route, ate half a bar of chocolate, then made sure his raincoat was secure and started up, climbing strongly, testing each handhold. He looked down once and saw the railway station in the valley below like a child's toy. The next time he looked it had disappeared, blanked out by mist, and a sudden breeze touched him coldly.

He came over the granite edge to the summit a few minutes later to find himself cocooned in mist and he'd spent enough time in hill country in the past to know that there was only one thing to do in such conditions: stay put. He did just that, lighting a cigarette, wondering how Asta Morgan was getting on. It was a good hour later when a sudden current of air dissolved the curtain of the mist and, down there, the valleys lay dark and quiet in the evening sunlight.

In the distance was a cairn of stones marking the ultimate peak, but there was no Asta. He cut across the track and followed it back until he reached a point where he could look down almost three thousand feet to the railway line and there was no sign of her. So, she had beaten him to the summit, hardly surprising for, with the track to follow, the mist would have been no problem.

He turned back, following the track to descend on the other side, and paused suddenly as he stared down at the incredible sight before him. The sea in the distance was calm, the islands of Rhum and Eigg like cardboard cut-outs, and on the dark horizon the Isle of Skye, the final barrier to the Atlantic. It was one of the most beautiful sights he had ever seen and he started down.

Asta was tired and her right ankle was beginning to ache, legacy of an old skiing accident. It had been harder crossing Ben Breac than she had imagined and now she was faced with a twelve-mile hike. What had originally started as an amusing idea was now becoming rather a bore.

The track along the glen was dry and dusty and hard on her feet and, after a while, she came to a five-barred gate with a sign that said LOCH DHU ESTATE – KEEP OUT. It was padlocked and she pulled herself over and limped on. And then she rounded a curve and saw a small hunting lodge by a burn. The door was locked, but, when she went round to the rear, a window stood ajar. She hauled herself through and found herself in a small kitchen area.

It was gloomy now, darkness falling, but there was an oil lamp and kitchen matches. She lit the lamp and went into the other room. It was adequately furnished with whitewashed walls and a wooden floor and a fire was laid in the hearth. She put a match to it and sat in one of the wing-backed chairs, suddenly tired. The warmth from the fire felt good and her ankle didn't hurt now. She added pine logs to the fire and heard a vehicle drive up outside. A key rattled in the lock and the front door opened.

The man who stood there was of medium height with a weak, sullen face that badly needed a shave. He wore a shabby tweed suit and cap, his yellow hair shoulder-length, and he carried a double-barrelled shotgun.

'Would you look at that now?' he said.

Asta said calmly, 'What do you want?'

'That's a good one,' he said, 'and you trespassing. How in the hell did you get in here?'

'Through the kitchen window.'

'I don't think my boss would like that. He's new. Just took over the estate yesterday, did Mr Morgan, but I know a hard man when I see one. I mean, if he knew about this he might make it a police matter.'

'Don't be stupid. I turned my ankle coming over Ben Breac. I needed a rest, that's all. Now that you're here you can give me a lift.'

He moved closer and his hand was shaking as he put it on her shoulder. 'That depends, doesn't it?'

His blotched face, the stink of whisky on his breath, was suddenly repulsive to her. 'What's your name?'

'That's more friendly. It's Fergus – Fergus Munro.'

She pulled away and sent him staggering with a vigorous push. 'Then don't be stupid, Fergus Munro.'

He reached angrily, dropping the shotgun. 'You bitch, I'll teach you.' He grabbed at her, catching the blouse beneath the leather coat, the thin material ripping from her left shoulder to the breast.

She gave a cry of rage, striking out at him, her nails gouging his right cheek and then beyond him she saw a man materialise from the darkness into the doorway.

Dillon punched him in the kidneys very hard and hauled him back by the scruff of the neck and hurled him across

125

the room. Munro hit the wall and fell to one knee. He reached for the shotgun which Dillon kicked out of the way, grabbing for his right wrist, twisting it up, taut and straight, ramming Munro head-first into the wall. He scrambled up, blood on his face and plunged through the open door.

As Dillon went after him Asta cried, 'Let him go!'

Dillon paused, a hand on each side of the door frame, then he closed it and turned. 'Are you all right?'

Outside an engine burst into life. 'Yes, fine, what was that?'

'He had a Shogun.'

She eased herself back in the chair. 'I was really beginning to despair, Dillon; I thought you were never going to catch up with me. What on earth are you doing here?'

'Confession time,' he said. 'I've an uncle, Brigadier Charles Ferguson, who rented a place called Ardnamurchan Lodge, not far from here, for the shooting which it shares with the Loch Dhu Estate.'

'Really? My father will be surprised. He never likes to share anything with anyone.'

'Yes, well when I read that item in the gossip column in the *Daily Mail*, saw your photo, I couldn't resist wangling myself an invitation to the Brazilian Embassy to meet you.'

'Just like that?'

'I'm terribly well connected. You'd be surprised.'

'Nothing would surprise me about you and, for what it's worth, I don't believe a word of it.' She put down her right foot and winced. 'Damn!'

'Trouble?'

'An old injury.'

She pulled up the right leg of her slacks and he eased off the shoe and sock. 'I'd have thought you would have caught up with me.'

'I tried the short route straight up and it proved longer. I had to sit down in the mist.'

'I just kept on walking. I noticed you at the station in Glasgow. I was coming out of the loo and saw you buying a map at the bookstall. I waited till you boarded the train before getting on board myself. Most intriguing, especially when you changed trains as I did at Fort William.'

'So, you left the train to draw me on?'

'Of course.'

'Damn you, Asta, I should put you over my knee.'

'Is that a promise? We Swedes are reputed to be terribly oversexed.'

He laughed out loud. 'I'd better get on with this foot while Fergus Munro hotfoots it to Loch Dhu Castle with his tale of woe. I should think we can expect company soon.'

'I should hope so. I haven't the slightest intention of walking any further.'

Dillon raised her foot. There was a faint puffiness at the ankle and a jagged scar.

'How did you get that?'

'Skiing; there was a time when I was an Olympic possibility.'

'Too bad. I'll take the lamp for a minute.'

He went into the kitchen, checked the drawers and found some kitchen towels. He soaked one in cold water and returned to the living room.

'A cold compress will help.' He bandaged the ankle expertly. 'Tired?'

'Not too much. Hungry, though.'

He got one of the half-pound blocks of chocolate from his Burberry pocket. 'Bad for your figure, but sustaining.'

'You're a magician, Dillon.' She ate the chocolate greedily and he lit a cigarette and sat by the fire. She suddenly paused. 'What about you?'

'I had some.' He stretched. 'The grand place this. Fish in the burn, deer in the forest, a roof over your head and a fine strong girl like yourself to help on the land.'

'Thanks very much. An arid sort of life, I should have thought.'

'Haven't you heard the old Italian saying? One can live well on bread and kisses.'

'Or chocolate.' She held up what was left of the bar and they both laughed.

Dillon got up, went and opened the door. There was a full moon and the only sound was the burn as its waters ran by.

'We could be the last two people left on earth,' she said.

'Not for long, there's a vehicle coming.' He moved out of the porch and stood there waiting.

Two Shoguns braked to a halt. Fergus Munro was driving the first one and Murdoch was sitting next to him. As Munro got out the factor came round from the other side clutching a shotgun. Carl Morgan was at the wheel of the second one and got out, an enormously powerful looking figure in his sheepskin coat.

Murdoch said something to Munro and clicked back the hammers on the shotgun. Munro opened the door of the Shogun and Murdoch whistled softly. There was a sudden scramble inside and a black shadow materialised from the darkness to stand beside him.

'Flush him out, boy.'

As the dog came forward with a rush, Dillon saw that it was a Doberman pinscher, one of the most deadly fighting dogs in the world. He went forward to meet it.

'Good boy,' he said and extended a hand.

The dog froze, a growl starting somewhere at the back of the throat, and Munro said, 'That's him, Mr Morgan. That's the bastard who attacked me, and his fancy woman still inside, no doubt.'

Morgan said, 'Private property, my friend; you should have stayed out.'

The dog growled again, full of menace, and Dillon whistled softly, an eerie sound that set the teeth on edge. The dog's ears went back and Dillon fondled his muzzle and stroked him.

'Good God!' Murdoch said.

'Easy when you know how,' Dillon told him. 'I learned that from a man who was once my friend.' He smiled. 'Later, he regretted teaching me anything, but that's life.'

Morgan said calmly, 'Who in the hell are you?'

It was then that Asta joined the scene. 'Carl, is that you? Thank God you're here.'

She stumbled from the doorway and Morgan, astonishment on his face, moved fast to catch her in his arms. 'Asta, for God's sake, what is this?'

He helped her inside and Fergus Munro said to Murdoch, 'Asta? Who in the hell is Asta?'

'Something tells me you're in for a very unpleasant surprise, my old son,' Dillon told him, and he turned and followed them in, the Doberman at his heels.

Asta was back in the chair and Morgan knelt beside her, holding a hand. 'It was horrible, Carl. I left the train at Lochailort and came over the mountain, turned my ankle and was feeling absolutely foul when I found the lodge and got in through the kitchen window. And then this man came, the man out there. He was horrible.'

Morgan stood up. 'The man out there?' he said and his face was very pale.

'Yes, Carl, he threatened me.' Her hand went to the torn blouse. 'In fact he was thoroughly unpleasant and then Mr Dillon here came and there was a struggle and he threw him out.'

Morgan had murder in his eyes. He turned to Murdoch who stood in the doorway. 'Do you realise who this is?

My daughter, Asta. Where's that bastard Fergus who brought us here?'

The roar of an engine breaking into life answered him and he pushed Murdoch to one side and ran out to see one of the Shoguns drive away.

'Shall I go after him?' Murdoch said.

'No.' Morgan shook his head, hands unclenching. 'We'll deal with him later.' He turned to Dillon and held out a hand. 'I'm Carl Morgan and I would seem to be considerably in your debt.'

'Dillon – Sean Dillon.'

Morgan turned to Asta. 'Are you trying to tell me you walked over that damn mountain this afternoon?'

'It seemed like a good idea at the time. I thought I'd just walk in on you. Surprise you.'

Morgan turned to Dillon who, lighting a cigarette, forestalled him. 'I'm on my way to join my uncle, Brigadier Charles Ferguson, for the shooting. He's leased a place called Ardnamurchan Lodge.'

There was something in Morgan's eyes straight away, but he simply said, 'That makes us neighbours, then. I presume you also thought it was a good idea to walk over the mountain?'

'Not at all, I thought it was a lousy idea and so did the ticket collector when she left the train. To be frank, I'd noticed her destination from her luggage labels. I got out to stretch my legs and saw her make off. When I asked the ticket collector what was going on, he told me she was going to walk over the mountain. As I said, he didn't think much of the idea and neither did I so I decided to follow. Unfortunately I chose another route and was delayed by the mist so I didn't catch up with her until she reached the lodge.'

Asta said weakly, 'I'm afraid I've made something of a fool of myself. Could we go now, Carl?'

She was acting up to the hilt, and Dillon, an actor himself, saw that, but not Morgan, who put an arm round her, instant concern there. 'Of course we will.' He glanced at Dillon. 'We'll drop you off on the way.'

'That would be fine,' Dillon said.

Murdoch took the wheel on the way down the glen and Dillon and Morgan sat on the large bench seat, Asta between them, the Doberman on the floor at their feet. Dillon fondled its ears.

'Guard dog, they said.' Morgan shook his head. 'With you he's more like a big pussy cat.'

'An emotional thing between me and him, Mr Morgan. He likes me.'

'Loves you, more like,' Asta said. 'I've never seen anything like it.'

'I still wouldn't like to be the intruder who comes over the wall and finds him there.'

'So, Brigadier Ferguson is your uncle?' Morgan said. 'I haven't had the pleasure yet, but then I only arrived at Loch Dhu Castle myself yesterday.'

'Yes,' Dillon said; 'so I understand.'

'Is the Brigadier retired or in business or what?'

'Oh, he was in the army for years, but now he's a consultant to a number of businesses worldwide.'

'And you?'

'I help out. A sort of middle man, you might say. I've got this thing for languages, so he finds me useful.'

'I'm sure he does.'

Murdoch changed down and swung in through gates, following a narrow drive to the house beyond, lights at the window. He braked to a halt. 'Ardnamurchan Lodge.'

It was raining again, rattling against the windscreen. Morgan said, 'It does that a lot, six days out of seven, driving in from the Atlantic.'

'Just think,' Asta said, 'we could be in Barbados.'

'Oh, it has its points, I'm sure,' Dillon said.

She took his hand. 'I hope to get a chance to thank you properly. Perhaps tomorrow?'

Morgan said, 'Plenty of time for that, I'll fix something up. You both need a chance to settle in.'

As Dillon got out, Morgan followed him. 'I'll see you to the door.'

At that moment it opened and Ferguson appeared. 'Good God, Sean, is that you? We got your message at Arisaig, but I was beginning to get worried. What happened?'

'A long story, I'll tell you later. Can I introduce our neighbour, Carl Morgan?'

'What a pleasure.' Ferguson took Morgan's hand. 'Your reputation precedes you. Will you have a drink before you go?'

'No, I must get my daughter home,' Morgan said. 'Another time.'

'I believe we'll be sharing the shooting,' Ferguson said genially.

'Yes, they didn't tell me that when I took the lease,' Morgan told him.

'Dear me, I trust there won't be a problem.'

'Oh, I don't see why there should be as long as we're not shooting from opposite sides.' Morgan smiled. 'Good night.' He got back in the Shogun and it drove away.

'He knows,' Dillon said.

'Of course he does,' Ferguson told him. 'Now come in out of this appalling rain and tell me what you've been up to.'

When the Shogun arrived at Loch Dhu Castle, Morgan helped Asta out and said to Murdoch, 'You come too, we need to talk.'

'Very well, Mr Morgan.'

The great iron-banded oak door was opened by Marco

Russo, wearing a black alpaca jacket and striped trousers. 'My God, Marco,' Asta said. 'I can't believe it, a butler now?'

She was probably the only human being he had ever smiled for and he did now. 'A short engagement only, Miss Asta.'

'Tell the maid to run a bath,' Morgan said and turned to Murdoch. 'You wait in the study.'

He took Asta through the magnificent baronial hall and placed her in the great oak chair beside the log fire that crackled in the open hearth.

'Right,' he said, 'Dillon. He followed you over the mountain. Why?'

'He told you.'

'That's a load of tripe.'

'Well, he knew who I was and where I was going, but not because of my luggage labels.'

'Explain.'

Which she did, the Brazilian Embassy Ball, the write-up in the *Daily Mail*'s social column, everything.

'I might have known,' Morgan said when she finished.

'Why do you say that?'

'As soon as I heard about the new tenant at Ardnamurchan Lodge I had him checked. Brigadier Charles Ferguson, Asta, is head of a very élite section of British Intelligence, usually involved with anti-terrorism and responsible to the Prime Minister only.'

'But I don't understand.'

'They know,' he said. 'The Chungking Covenant.'

'My God!' she said. 'And Dillon works for him?' She nodded. 'It makes sense now.'

'What does?'

'Well, I told you Dillon saved me from that beast Hamish Hunt at the ball. What I didn't tell you was that Hunt grabbed me in Park Lane afterwards. He was terribly drunk, Carl, and pretty foul.'

His face was pale again. 'And?

'Dillon appeared and beat him up. I've never seen anything like it. He was so economical.'

'He would be, a real pro. I thought so.' Morgan smiled. 'So I owe him not once, but twice.' He helped her up. 'Off you go and get your bath, we'll have some supper later.' As he walked away, he called, 'Marco?'

The Sicilian appeared from the shadows. '*Signore?*'

'Listen to this.' Very quickly Morgan gave him a résumé of events in Italian.

When he was finished Marco said, 'He sounds hot stuff, this Dillon.'

'Get on to London now. I want answers and they've only got an hour, make that clear.'

'As you say, *signore.*'

He walked away and Morgan went and opened the study door. It was a pleasant room, lined with books, french windows to a terrace, and, as in the hall, a fire burned in the hearth. Murdoch was standing staring down into it and smoking a cigarette.

Morgan sat at the desk, opened a drawer and took out a cheque book. 'Over here.'

'Yes, Mr Morgan.' Murdoch crossed the room and Morgan wrote a cheque and handed it to him. The factor looked at it in astonishment. 'Twenty-five thousand pounds. But what's this for, Mr Morgan?'

'Loyalty, Murdoch; I like greedy people and I've formed the opinion that that's what you are.'

Murdoch was stunned. 'If you say so, sir.'

'Oh, but I do and here's the good news, Murdoch. When I leave you get the same amount, for services rendered, naturally.'

Murdoch had control of himself now, a slight smile on his face. 'Of course, sir, anything you say.'

Morgan said, 'For several hundred years the Lairds of

Loch Dhu took a silver Bible into battle. It was always recovered, even when they died. It was with the old Laird when his plane crashed in India in nineteen-forty-four. I've reason to believe it was returned to the Castle, but where is it, Murdoch, that's the thing?'

'Lady Katherine, sir . . .'

'Knows nothing, hasn't seen it in years. It's here, Murdoch, tucked away somewhere, and we're going to find it. Understand?'

'Yes, sir.'

'Discuss it with the servants. Just tell them it's a valuable family heirloom and there's a reward for whoever finds it.'

'I will, sir.'

'You can go now.' Murdoch had the door open when Morgan called, 'And Murdoch?'

'Yes, sir?'

'Brigadier Ferguson and Dillon, they're not on our side.'

'I understand, sir.'

'Good, and don't forget. I want to know where that bastard Fergus Munro is to be found, preferably tonight.'

'Yes, sir.'

'One more thing. Is there anyone on the estate staff who works at Ardnamurchan Lodge?'

'Ferguson has his own man, sir; this Gurkha body servant. There's Lady Katherine's gardener, Angus. He sees to the garden and the daily wood supply.'

'Can he be bought?'

Murdoch nodded. 'I'd say so.'

'Good. Eyes and ears is what I want. See to it and find Fergus.'

'I will, sir.' Murdoch went out, closing the door.

Morgan sat there for a while then noticed a library ladder. On impulse he got up, pushed it to one end of the shelves on one of the walls and mounted. He climbed to the top and started to remove the books a few at a time, peering behind.

EIGHT

Dillon, having bathed and changed into a comfortable track suit, sprawled in front of the fire, Hannah
Bernstein in the chair opposite. He had just finished his
account of the day's events and Ferguson was pouring
drinks at the cabinet in the corner.

'Anything for you, Chief Inspector?'

'No thank you, sir.'

'Well, the boy here could do with a brandy, I'm sure.'

'It was rather a long walk,' Dillon said and accepted the
glass. 'What do you think?'

'About Morgan? Oh, he knows, that was totally apparent
from our little exchange.'

'So what will his next move be?' Hannah asked.

'I'm not sure, we'll see what tomorrow brings.' Ferguson sat down. 'It's an interesting situation, by the way, the shooting rights and the fishing. Kim tells me he was fishing in Loch Dhu on the day before we arrived when some damn rascals who work for this Murdoch fellow as keepers turned up and suggested he leave, and not too pleasantly.'

'Who are they?'

'I've made enquiries. Tinkers – the last remnants of a broken clan. You know, a touch of all that Scottish romantic nonsense. They've wandered the Highlands since Culloden and all that sort of tosh. Old Hector Munro and his brood. I saw them in Ardnamurchan Village yesterday and there's nothing romantic about them. Bunch of ragged, foul-smelling rogues. There's old Hector, Fergus . . .'

'He'll be the one I had the run-in with.'

'Then there's the other brother, Rory, big rough-looking lout, hair tied in a pony tail. I mean, why do they do that, Dillon? Earrings as well. After all, it's not the seventeenth century.'

Hannah burst out laughing and Dillon said, 'They broke the mould with you, Brigadier. And you say they ran Kim off the place?'

'Yes, I sent him round to the Castle with a stiff letter of complaint to this Murdoch chap, the factor; told him I was considering laying a complaint with the Chief Constable of the county.'

'What happened?'

'Murdoch was round like a shot, full of apologies. Said he'd keep them in line. Gave me some cock and bull story about Arctic tern nesting near Loch Dhu and not wanting to disturb them. Apologised for the Munros. Said he'd kick their backsides and so on.'

Dillon went and helped himself to another brandy. He

came back to the fire. 'We're entitled to be here, to shoot deer in the forest, to fish in the loch?'

'Of course we are,' Ferguson said. 'Mind you, Morgan doesn't like it; I mean, he made that clear on the doorstep, didn't he?'

'Let's draw his teeth, then. I'll put my head in the jaws of the tiger tomorrow. You've got all we need for the fishing?'

'And the shooting.'

'Good, I'll try Loch Dhu in the morning; plenty of trout, I suppose?'

'Masses, dear boy. Quarter pounders – or occasional pounders.'

'Good, I'll take a rod down there after breakfast.'

Hannah said, 'The Munros could prove unpleasant if they catch you, especially after your bout with Fergus. I was with the Brigadier when we saw them in Ardnamurchan village. They really are a fearsome looking clan. I'd say they are the sort who don't take kindly to being beaten.'

'And neither do I.' Dillon finished his drink. 'I'll see you at breakfast,' and he went up to bed.

At the same moment Asta was sitting opposite Morgan by the fire in the great hall at the Castle when Marco came in, a piece of paper in his hand.

'Fax from London, *signore*.'

Morgan read it quickly, then laughed out loud. 'Dear God, listen to this. The Bernstein woman is a Detective Chief Inspector, Special Branch, at Scotland Yard, but it's Dillon who takes the biscuit. Sean Dillon, once an actor, RADA and the National Theatre; superb linguist, speaks many languages. First class pilot, expert diver. Good God, he worked for the Israelis in Beirut.'

'But what was he doing there?'

'Sinking PLO boats apparently. Not choosy, our Mr

Dillon. He's worked for just about everyone you've ever heard of and that includes the KGB in the old days.'

'You mean he's some kind of mercenary?' Asta asked.

'That's one way of putting it, but before that he was for some years with the Provisional IRA, one of their most feared enforcers. There's even a suggestion he was behind the attack on Downing Street during the Gulf War.'

'Then why would he be working for Ferguson?'

'I suppose the Brits were the only people he hadn't worked for, and you know how unscrupulous they are. They'd use anybody to suit their purposes.'

'A thoroughly dangerous man,' Asta said. 'How exciting.'

Morgan handed the fax to Marco. 'Oh, we've handled thoroughly dangerous men before, haven't we, Marco.'

'Many times, *signore*; will there be anything else?'

'Yes, bring me some coffee and tell Murdoch I'll see him now.'

Asta got up. 'I'm for bed. Can we ride tomorrow?'

'Why not?' He took her hand. 'Sleep well.'

She kissed him on the forehead and went away up the great staircase. Morgan reached for a cigar, clipped it and lit it and Murdoch entered, his oilskin coat wet.

'Well?' Morgan asked.

'No luck, I'm afraid; that old bastard Hector Munro was immovable. He said Fergus had gone off on his evening rounds and they hadn't seen him since. He's lying, of course.'

'What did you do?'

'Searched their stinking caravans, which he didn't like, but I insisted.'

'I want Fergus,' Morgan said. 'I want him where I can deal with him personally. He put his filthy hands on my daughter and no man does that and gets away with it. Try again tomorrow.'

'Yes, Mr Morgan; good night, sir.'

Murdoch went out and Marco came in with the coffee. As he poured it, Morgan said in Italian, 'What do you think of him?'

'Murdoch? A piece of dung, *signore*; no honour, only money counts there.'

'That's what I thought; keep an eye on him. You can go to bed now.'

Marco went out and Morgan sat there brooding, drinking his coffee and gazing into the fire.

He was sitting at the desk in the study at eight the following morning, working his way through various business papers, when there was a knock at the door and Murdoch looked in.

'I have Angus here, sir.'

'Bring him in.'

Angus entered, took off his tweed cap and rolled it between his hands. 'Mr Morgan, sir.'

Morgan looked him over. 'You look like a practical man to me, would I be right?'

'I hope so, sir.'

Morgan opened a drawer and took out a bundle of notes which he tossed across. Angus picked it up. 'Five hundred pounds. Anything unusual happens at Ardnamurchan Lodge, you phone Murdoch.'

'I will, sir.' He was sweating slightly.

'Have you been there this morning?'

'To do the wood supply, sir.'

'And what's happening?'

'Mr Dillon was having an early breakfast before going for the fishing on Loch Dhu. He asked my advice.'

Morgan nodded. 'Good. On your way.'

Angus left and Murdoch said, 'If the Munros come across him, he could be in trouble.'

'Exactly what I was thinking.' Morgan smiled and at that moment Asta came in wearing a hacking jacket and jodhpurs.

'There you are,' she told him. 'You said we could go riding.'

'And why not?' He glanced at Murdoch. 'Get the horses ready, you can come with us.' He smiled. 'We could have a look at the Loch.'

The waters of Loch Dhu were darker than even the name suggested, still and calm in the grey morning and yet dappled by falling rain. Dillon wore waders, an old rainhat and an Australian drover's waterproof with caped shoulders, all of which he had found at the lodge.

He lit a cigarette and took his time over putting his rod together. Behind him the heather was waist deep, a line of trees above, and a plover lifted into the morning. A wind stirred the surface of the loch and suddenly a trout came out of the water beyond the sand bar, a good foot in the air, and disappeared again.

Suddenly Dillon forgot everything, remembering only his uncle's sheep farm in County Down and the lessons he'd given his young nephew in the great art. He tied the fly Ferguson had recommended, apparently one of his own manufacture, and went to work.

His first dozen casts were poor and inexpert, but gradually, as some of the old skill returned, he had better luck and hooked two quarter pounders. The rain still fell relentlessly. He let out another couple of yards of line, lifted his tip and cast out beyond the sand bar to where a black fin sliced through the water. His cast was the most accurate he'd ever made, the fly skimming the surface; the rod bent over and his line went taut.

Two pounds if it was an ounce. His reel whined as the hooked trout made for deep water and he moved along the sand bank, playing it carefully. The line went slack and he thought he'd lost it, but the trout was only resting and a moment later the line tightened again. He played it for a good ten minutes before turning to reach for his net. He lifted the floundering fish, removed the hook and turned back to shore.

A harsh voice said, 'Well and good, me bucko, a fine dinner for us.'

The man who had spoken was old, at least seventy. He wore a tweed suit that had seen better days and white hair showed beneath his Glengarry bonnet. His face was weather-beaten and wrinkled and covered with a heavy stubble and he had a shotgun crooked in his right arm.

Behind him two men stood up in the heather. One was large and raw-boned with a perpetual smile, and that would be Rory, Dillon told himself. The other was Fergus, a livid bruise down one side of his face, his mouth swollen.

'That's him, Da, that's the bastard who attacked me,' and he raised his shotgun waist high.

Rory knocked it to one side and it discharged into the ground. 'Try not to play the fool as usual, little brother,' he said in Gaelic.

Dillon, an Irish speaker, had no difficulty in understanding, especially when Hector said, 'He doesn't look much to me,' and swung a punch.

Dillon ducked, avoiding it, but his foot slipped and he fell into the shallows. He scrambled up and the old man raised his shotgun. 'Not now, my brave wee man,' he said in English. 'You'll get your chance. Slow and easy. Walk on.'

As Dillon moved forward, Fergus said, 'Wait till I've done with you,' and swung the butt of his shotgun. Dillon avoided it easily and Fergus went down on one knee.

Rory lifted him by the scruff of his neck. 'Will you listen or must I kick your arse?' he demanded in Gaelic and pushed him ahead.

'God help him but he never will learn, that one,' Dillon told him in Irish. 'Some men stay children all their lives.'

Rory's mouth went slack with astonishment. 'By God, Da, did you hear that; the strangest Gaelic I ever heard.'

'That's because it's Irish, the language of kings,' Dillon said. 'But close enough that we can understand each other,' and he walked on ahead of them.

There was smoke beyond the trees, the sound of children's voices, so they were not taking him to Morgan and he realised he had made something of a miscalculation. They moved down into a hollow containing the camp. The three wagons were old, with canvas tilts and patched many times, far removed from the romantic idea of a caravan. There was an air of poverty to everything from the shabby clothes worn by the women, who squatted by the fire drinking tea, to the bare feet of the children, who played in the grass beside several bony horses.

Fergus gave Dillon a push that sent him staggering forward and the women scattered. The children paused in their play and came to watch. Hector Munro sat himself on an old box vacated by one of the women, placed his shotgun across his knees and took out a pipe. Fergus and Rory stood slightly behind Dillon.

'An attack on one of us is an attack on all, Mr Dillon, or whatever your name is. The great pity you weren't knowing that.' He stuffed tobacco into his pipe. 'Rory.' Rory moved fast, pulling Dillon's arms behind him and the old man said, 'Enjoy yourself, Fergus.'

Fergus moved in fast and punched Dillon in the stomach right and left handed. Dillon made no move except to tense his muscles and Fergus drove a fist into his ribs on the right side. 'Now for that pretty face of yours,' he said. 'Hold his head up, Rory.'

In taking a handful of Dillon's hair, Rory had to release

one of his arms. Dillon flicked a foot forward catching Fergus in the crutch, half-turned, delivering a reverse-elbow strike to the edge of Rory's jaw. The big man released him, staggering back, and Dillon ran for it and stumbled headlong as one of the women stuck out a foot.

He rolled desperately as they all kicked at him, even the children, and then there was the drumming of horses, a voice called, 'Stop that, damn you!' and a shotgun was fired.

The women and children broke and ran and Dillon got up to find Murdoch on horseback, a shotgun braced against his thigh. Behind him Carl Morgan and Asta rode down into the hollow. Dillon was aware of Fergus slipping under one of the wagons.

'Stay there, you silly bastard,' Rory hissed in Gaelic then glanced at Dillon in alarm, realising he had heard.

Carl Morgan urged his mount down into the hollow. The hooves of his horse scattered the fire and he pulled on the right rein so that the animal turned, its hind quarters catching Hector Munro a blow that sent him staggering.

He reined in. 'Tell them who I am,' he ordered.

'This is Mr Carl Morgan, new tenant of Loch Dhu Castle,' Murdoch said, 'and your employer.'

'Is that so?' Hector Munro said.

'So bare your head, you mannerless dog,' Murdoch told him, leaned down from his horse and plucked the old man's bonnet from his head and threw it down.

Rory took a step forward and Dillon said in Irish, 'Easy boy, there's a time and a place for everything.'

Rory turned, frowning, and his father said, 'The man, Dillon, was fishing in the loch, we were only doing our duty.'

'Don't lie to me, Munro,' Murdoch told him. 'Mr Dillon is nephew to Brigadier Ferguson, tenant at Ardna-murchan Lodge, and don't tell me you didn't know that.

You scoundrels know everything that goes on in the district before it bloody well happens.'

'Enough of this,' Morgan said and looked down at Munro. 'You wish to continue to work for the estate?'

'Why yes, sir,' the old man said.

'Then you know how to behave in future.'

'Yes, sir.' Munro picked up his bonnet and put it on.

'And now that son of yours, Fergus. He assaulted my daughter. I want him.'

'And we have not seen him, sir, as I told Mr Murdoch. If he gave offence to the young lady, I'm sorry, but the great one for wandering is Fergus.'

'Away for days sometimes,' Rory said. 'Who could be knowing where he might be?' He glanced at Dillon briefly, but Dillon said nothing.

Morgan said, 'I can wait. We'll go now, Mr Dillon.'

'I'll be fine,' Dillon said. 'I want to get my fishing tackle. I can walk back.' He moved to Asta's stirrup and looked up at her.

'Are you all right?' she asked.

'Just fine,' Dillon said. 'I do this kind of thing most mornings, it gives me an appetite for lunch.'

Morgan said, 'I'll be in touch, Dillon. Come on, Asta,' and he cantered away.

Dillon turned to look down into the hollow at the Munros. Fergus crawled out from under the wagon and Dillon called in Irish, 'So there you are, you little rascal. I'd take care, if I were you.'

He went down to the shore and retrieved his rod and fishing basket. As he turned to go Rory Munro moved out of the trees. 'Now why would you do a thing like that for Fergus, and you and he bad friends?' he asked in Gaelic.

'True, but then I dislike Morgan even more. Mind you, the girl is different. If Fergus touches her again I'll break both his arms.'

Rory laughed. 'Oh, the hard one are you, small man?'

'You could always try me,' Dillon told him.

Rory stared at him, frowning, and then a slow smile appeared. 'And perhaps that time will come,' he said, turned and walked back into the trees.

Dillon drank tea by the fire at Ardnamurchan Lodge while he detailed the events of the morning to Ferguson and Hannah Bernstein.

'So, the plot thickens,' Ferguson said.

'Lucky for you that Morgan turned up when he did,' Hannah said. 'You might have been a hospital case by now.'

'Yes, a useful coincidence,' Ferguson said.

'And you know how much I believe in those,' Dillon told him.

Hannah frowned. 'You think Morgan was behind the whole thing?'

'I'm not sure about that, but I believe he expected it. That's why he turned up.'

'Very possibly.' Ferguson nodded. 'Which raises the question of how he knew you were going to go fishing this morning.'

'I know; life's just one big mystery,' Dillon said. 'What happens now?'

'Lunch, dear boy; I thought we might venture into Ardnamurchan Village and sample the delights of the local pub. They must offer food of some sort.'

'Pub grub, Brigadier; you?' Hannah Bernstein said.

'And you, Chief Inspector, although I hardly expect it will be kosher.'

'I'll find out,' she said. 'I think that chap Angus is working in the garden.' She opened the french windows and went out, returning a few moments later. 'He says the Campbell Arms does do food. Shepherd's Pie, things like that.'

'Real food,' Ferguson said. 'How wonderful. Let's get going then.'

Morgan was standing on the terrace at the top of the steps with Asta when Murdoch joined them. 'I've just had a phone call from Angus. Our friends are going to the Campbell Arms for lunch.'

'Really?' Morgan said.

'It could lead to an interesting situation. The day after tomorrow is the local fair and Highland Games. There are tinkers around, horse traders and so on. The Munros will probably be there.'

'Is that so?' Morgan smiled and turned to Asta. 'We couldn't possibly miss that, could we?' He raised his voice and called, 'Marco!' Russo appeared in the open windows. 'Bring the estate car round, we're going to the village for a drink and you drive. I've a feeling we might need you.'

The Campbell Arms was very old, built of grey granite, but the sign that hung above the door was freshly painted. Dillon parked across the street and he and Hannah and Ferguson got out and crossed, pausing as a young gypsy rode by bareback on a pony, leading three others behind. There was a poster on the wall advertising the Ardnamurchan Fair and Games.

'That looks like fun,' Ferguson said and opened the door and led the way in.

There was an old-fashioned snug bar, the type that in the old days was for women only. This was empty, but a further door gave access to a large saloon, beams in the ceiling. There was a long bar with a marble top, scores of bottles behind, ranged against a great mirror. There was a peat fire on an open hearth, tables, chairs, booths with high-backed wooden settles. It was not exactly shoulder-to-shoulder, but perhaps a crowd of thirty or more, some obviously gypsies to do with the fair, others more local, old men wearing cloth caps and leggings or, in some cases, Highland bonnets and plaids, like Hector Munro, who stood at one end of the bar with Rory and Fergus.

There was a buzz of conversation that stopped abruptly as Ferguson stepped in, the others at his shoulder. The woman behind the bar came round, wiping her hands on a cloth. She wore an old hand-knitted jumper and slacks. 'You are welcome in this place, Brigadier,' she said in a Highland accent and took his hand. 'Ny name is Molly.'

'Good to be here, my dear,' he said. 'I hear your food is excellent.'

'Over here.' She led them to one of the booths by the fire and turned to the room. 'Get on with your drinking while I handle the damned English,' she told them in Gaelic.

Sean Dillon said in Irish, 'A bad mistake you make in my case, woman of the house, but I'll forgive you if you can find me a Bushmills whisky.'

She turned, her mouth open in surprise, then put a hand to his face. 'Irish is it? Good lad yourself and I might surprise you.' They settled down and she added in English, 'Fish Pie is what there is today, if you have a mind to eat. Fresh cod, onions and potatoes.'

'Which sounds incredible to me,' Ferguson told her. 'I'll have a Guinness, lager beer for the lady and whatever you and my friend here have decided.'

'A man after my own heart and a good Scots name to you.'

She went off and, as the conversation flowed again, Dillon lit a cigarette. 'The old man with the granite face and the bonnet at the end of the bar is Hector Munro, the damaged one is Fergus and the bit of rough with the good shoulders that's looking at you so admiringly, Hannah, my love, is Rory.'

She flushed. 'Not my type.'

Dillon turned and nodded to the Munros. 'Oh, I don't know, with a couple of drinks in you at the shank of the night, who knows?'

'You are a bastard, Dillon.'

'I know, it's been said before.'

Hector Munro wiped his mouth with the back of his hand and came over, shouldering men aside. 'Mr Dillon, you did my son a service,' he said in English, 'and for that I thank you. Maybe we got off on the wrong foot.'

'This is my uncle, Brigadier Ferguson,' Dillon said.

'I ken the name Ferguson,' Munro said. 'There are a few not many miles from here Tomentoul way, they were on our left flank at Culloden fighting King George's bloody Germans.'

'You do have a lengthy memory,' Ferguson observed. 'Almost two hundred and fifty years long. Yes, my ancestors did fight at Culloden for Prince Charles.'

'Good man yourself.' Munro pumped his hand and went back to the bar.

'My goodness, we are trapped in memory lane,' Ferguson said as Molly brought the drinks. She put them on the table when the door opened and Morgan and Asta walked in, Murdoch and Marco behind them.

There was another silence, Morgan surveying the room, and then he came forward with Asta. Behind him Marco stayed at the bar and Murdoch approached Molly. Morgan and Asta sat on the settle opposite Ferguson and his party.

'Brigadier, what a pleasure. I didn't have a chance to introduce you to my daughter last night. Asta – Brigadier Ferguson.'

'A pleasure, my dear,' Ferguson told her. 'You know my nephew. This charming lady, by the way, is my secretary, Miss Hannah Bernstein.'

Murdoch came from the bar with glasses and a bottle of white wine. 'Not much choice, sir, it's a chablis.'

'As long as they didn't make it in the back yard it will be fine,' Morgan said. 'What about the food?'

'Fish and potato pie, old boy,' Ferguson said. 'They only have one dish a day.'

'Then fish and potato pie it is,' Morgan told him. 'We're hardly having lunch at the Caprice.'

'Indeed not,' Ferguson said. 'Very different waters.'

'Exactly.' Murdoch poured the wine and Morgan raised his glass. 'What shall we drink to?'

'Confusion to our enemies,' Dillon said. 'A good Irish toast.'

'How very apt.'

Asta drank a little wine and said, 'How nice to meet you, Miss Bernstein. Strange, but in the time we were together, Dillon never mentioned you. Having met you, of course, I understand why.'

'Try and behave yourself, why don't you,' Dillon told her.

Her eyes widened in outrage and Morgan frowned; then Murdoch leaned over and whispered in his ear and Morgan looked round at the bar. At that moment Fergus was sliding towards the door.

Morgan called in Italian, 'Stop him, Marco, that's the one I want.'

Marco put a hand to Fergus's chest and pushed him back and Hector Munro and Rory took a step forward. 'Leave my son be or you answer to me,' the old man said.

Morgan called, 'Munro, I asked for your son earlier and you claimed no knowledge as to his whereabouts. As your employer, I expected better.'

'My son is my business. What touches him touches us all.'

'Please spare me that kind of peasant claptrap. He assaulted my daughter and for that he must pay.'

And Fergus was frightened now, his face white and desperate. He tried to dodge around Marco who caught him with ease, grabbing him by the neck, turning him, sending him to his knees before Morgan.

The bar was totally silent. 'Now then, you animal,' Morgan said.

Rory came in on the run. 'Here's for you,' he cried and swung a punch into the base of Marco's spine. The Sicilian shrugged it off, turned, blocking Rory's next punch, and gave him a right that landed high on the left cheek, sending Rory staggering back against the bar.

Fergus, cowering in fear on the floor, saw his chance, got up to make for the door. Marco, turning, was already moving to block him off when Hannah Bernstein stuck out a foot and tripped him. Marco went sprawling and Fergus was out of the door like a weasel.

'Dreadful, isn't it,' Ferguson said to Morgan. 'I can't take her anywhere.'

As Marco got up, Rory moved in from the bar and Dillon jumped in between them. 'This dog is mine,' he said in Irish to Rory. 'Now drink your beer like a good lad and let be.'

Rory stared at him, rage in his eyes, then took a deep breath. 'As you say, Irishman, but if he lays a hand on me again, he is my meat,' and he turned and went back to the bar.

'Strange,' Ferguson said to Morgan, 'but since meeting you life's taken on an entirely new meaning.'

'Hasn't it?' Morgan said amiably and at that moment Molly arrived with a huge tray containing plates of her fish and potato pie.

'My word, that does smell good.' Ferguson beamed. 'Let's tuck in, I'm sure we're going to need all our strength.'

★

Afterwards, standing in the street outside, Morgan said, 'I wondered about dinner tomorrow night, perhaps. I thought it might be nice to invite Lady Katherine.'

'Excellent thought,' Ferguson said. 'Delighted to accept.'

Asta said, 'Do you ride, Dillon?'

'It's been known.'

'Perhaps you could join us tomorrow morning. We could mount you with no trouble.'

'Ah, well there you have me,' he said. 'My uncle promised to take me deer stalking tomorrow. Have you ever tried it?'

'Deer stalking? That sounds absolutely wonderful.' She turned. 'Carl? I'd love to go.'

'Not my style and I've business to take care of tomorrow.'

Ferguson said amiably, 'We'd be delighted to have you join us, my dear; that is if you have no objection, Morgan?'

'Why should I, an excellent idea.'

'We'll pick you up,' Ferguson said. 'Nine-thirty.' He raised his tweed hat. 'Goodbye for now,' and he turned and led the way back to the Range Rover.

'Right, let's go,' Morgan said, and Asta led the way to the parked station wagon.

Murdoch murmured, 'A word, sir; I've an idea where Fergus might have gone.'

'Is that so?' Morgan said. 'All right, we'll take Miss Asta home and then you can show me.'

At Ardnamurchan Lodge Ferguson shrugged off his coat and went and stood with his back to the fire. 'And what do you make of that?'

'The heavy blocking the door, sir, was his present minder, one Marco Russo,' Hannah Bernstein said. 'I checked with immigration. He came in with Morgan.

Information from the Italian police indicates he's a known Mafia enforcer and member of the Luca family.'

'A thoroughly nasty bit of work, if you ask me,' Ferguson said and turned to Dillon. 'What's all this deer stalking nonsense, then?'

'You've never stalked deer, Brigadier?' Dillon shook his head. 'You've never lived, and you a member of the upper classes.'

'Of course I've stalked deer,' Ferguson told him. 'And kindly keep your fatuous comments to yourself. What I want to know is why are we taking the girl tomorrow? You obviously wanted it, which is why I asked her.'

'I'm not sure,' Dillon said. 'I'd like to get to know her a little better. It might lead somewhere.'

Hannah Bernstein said, 'Dillon, get one thing straight, that is one tough, capable and intelligent young lady. If you think she doesn't know exactly how Morgan makes his money you're fooling yourself. Observe them, use your eyes. They're a very intimate couple. I'd give you odds she knows exactly what they're doing up here.'

Dillon said, 'Which is exactly why I want to cultivate her.'

'I agree,' Ferguson said. 'So we go as planned in the morning. Kim can be a gun bearer, you'll stay here and hold the fort, Chief Inspector.'

'As you say, sir.'

Ferguson turned to Dillon. 'Anything else?'

'Yes, I've decided to pay a visit to the Castle tonight. Check things out, see what's going on. Any objections?'

'Not at all. Come to think of it, it's rather a good idea.' Ferguson smiled. 'Strange, but Morgan's actually quite civilised when you meet him, don't you agree?'

'Not really, sir,' Hannah Bernstein said. 'As far as I'm concerned, he's just another gangster in a good suit.'

NINE

Fᴇʀɢᴜs ѕǫᴜᴀᴛᴛᴇᴅ ᴏɴ ᴀ truckle bed in the old hunting bothy at the west end of Loch Dhu and drank from a bottle of whisky. He was no longer afraid now, the events at the pub behind him, but he was angry, particularly when he thought of Asta.

'You bitch,' he said to himself. 'All your fault.' He drank some more whisky. 'Just wait. If I ever get my hands on you again.'

There was a sudden creak, the door swung open and Murdoch slipped in. 'Here he is, sir,' he said and Morgan moved through the door behind him, a riding crop in his hand, Marco at his side.

'Now then, you piece of dirt,' Morgan said.

Fergus was terrified. He got up, the bottle of whisky in one hand. 'Now look, there's no need for this, it was a mistake, I didn't know who she was.'

'Mistake?' Morgan said. 'Oh, yes, your mistake, you little swine.' He turned. 'Marco.'

Marco was pulling on a pair of leather gloves. Fergus suddenly smashed the whisky bottle, spraying the bed with its contents and held up the jagged glass threateningly. 'I'll do for you, I swear I will.'

As Marco advanced, Fergus swung the bottle. The Sicilian blocked his arm to one side and punched him with sickening force under the ribs. Fergus dropped the bottle and staggered back on the bed.

Morgan said, 'Leave him.'

Marco stood back and Morgan went forward. 'You put your filthy hands on my daughter.'

He slashed Fergus across the face with his riding crop again and again, and Fergus, screaming, tried to protect himself with his raised arms. Morgan rained blow after blow then stood back and Marco moved in again, punching Fergus in the face, sending him to the floor, kicking him with brutal efficiency.

'Enough.' Marco stepped back and Fergus lay moaning on the floor. Morgan turned and found Murdoch in the doorway looking as frightened as Fergus had done. 'Do you have a problem?' Morgan asked.

'No, Mr Morgan.'

'Good. Let's get going, then.'

He led the way outside and they got into the station wagon, Marco behind the wheel, and drove away.

It was some time later, evening falling, when Fergus appeared in the doorway. He looked dreadful, blood on his face. He stood there, swaying a little, and then staggered down the slope to the loch. He waded into the shallows and dropped to his knees, scooping water over his face and head. The pain in his head was terrible, the worst thing he'd ever known. It was really a merciful release when everything went dark and he fell forward into the water.

It was eleven o'clock and raining hard as Hannah Bernstein turned the Range Rover in beside the wall of Loch Dhu Castle. 'My God,' she said, 'it's a miracle when it does stop raining here.'

'That's bonny Scotland for you,' Dillon said. He was all in black – sweater, jeans, running shoes – and now he pulled a black ski-mask over his head, only his eyes and mouth showing.

'You certainly look the part,' she said.

'That's the idea.' He pulled on thin black leather gloves, took a Walther from the glove compartment and fitted the new short Harley silencer to it.

'For God's sake, Dillon, you aren't going to war.'

'That's what you think, my lovely.' He slipped the gun into his waistband and his teeth flashed in the opening of the ski-mask as he smiled. 'Here we go, then; give me an hour,' and he opened the door and was away.

The wall was only twelve feet high and simple enough to negotiate. A crumbling edge or two for footholds and he was over and dropping into damp grass. He moved through trees, came out into an area of open grass and jogged towards the Castle, finally halting in another clump of trees, looking across smooth lawn towards the lighted windows.

The rain fell relentlessly. He stood there, sheltered slightly by a tree, and the great oaken front door opened and Marco Russo appeared, the Doberman at his side. Marco gave the dog a shove with his foot, obviously putting it out for the purposes of nature, then went inside. The dog stood still, sniffing the rain, then lifted a leg. Dillon gave the low, curious whistle he had used at the hunting lodge, the Doberman's ears went up, then it came bounding towards him.

He crouched, stroking its ears, allowing it to lick his hands. 'Good boy,' he said softly. 'Now do as you're told and keep quiet.'

He moved across the lawn and peered in through french windows and saw Asta in the study reading a book by the fire. She made an appealing figure in a pair of black silk lounging pyjamas. He moved away, the dog at his heels, looked in through a long narrow window and saw the empty hall.

He moved round to the far side and heard voices and noticed a french window standing ajar. Curtains were partly drawn and, when he peered cautiously inside, he saw Morgan and Murdoch in a large drawing room. There were several bookcases against the wall and Morgan was replacing books in one of them.

'I've been through every inch in this room, taken down every book, searched every drawer, every cupboard and the same in the study. Not a bloody sign. What about the staff?'

'They've all got their instructions, sir, every one of them is eager to win the thousand pound reward you promised, but nothing as yet.'

'It's got to be here somewhere, tell them to renew their efforts.'

The Doberman whined, slipped in through the window and rushed up to Morgan who rather surprisingly greeted it with some pleasure. 'You big lump, where have you been?' He leaned down to pat the animal. 'My God, he's soaking, he could catch pneumonia. Take him to the kitchen, Murdoch, and towel him off; I'm going to bed.'

Murdoch went out, his hand on the Doberman's collar, and Morgan turned and walked to the window. He stood there, looking at the night for a moment, then crossed to the door and went out, switching off the light.

Dillon slipped in through the window, went to the door and stood listening for a moment, then he opened the door a crack, aware of voices – Asta and Morgan. The study door was open and he heard Morgan say, 'I'm for bed. What about you?'

'I suppose so,' Asta said. 'If I'm out on the moors tomorrow stalking deer I'll need all my energy.'

'And wits,' he said. 'Listen to everything Ferguson and Dillon say; store it up and remember it.'

'Yes, O Master.'

She laughed and, when they came out, Morgan had an arm about her waist. 'You're a great girl, Asta, one of a kind.'

Strange, but watching them go up the great staircase together was something of a surprise to Dillon; no suggestion of the wrong kind of intimacy at all and at the top of the stairs Morgan only kissed her on the forehead. 'Good night, my love,' he said and he went one way and she the other.

'Well, I'll be damned,' Dillon said softly.

He stayed there for a while, thinking. There was little point in going any further. He'd picked up one useful piece of intelligence, that they hadn't got anywhere as regards finding the Bible, that was a good enough night's work and, the truth was, what he'd done had been more for the hell of it than anything else.

On the other hand, again just for the hell of it, he could do with a drink and he'd noticed through the french windows the drinks cabinet in the study. He opened the door and hurried across the great hall to the study door. As he got it open, the Doberman arrived, skidding on the tiles as it tried to brake, sliding past him into the study.

Dillon closed the door and switched on a lamp on one of the tables. 'You great eejit,' he said to the dog and fondled its ears.

He went to the drinks cabinet and found no Irish whiskey so made do with Scotch. He went and stood looking down into the fire, taking his time, and behind him the door opened. As he turned, drawing the Walther, Asta came in. She didn't notice him at first, closed the door and turned.

And she didn't show any sign of fear, stood there looking at him calmly, and then said, 'That couldn't be you could it, Dillon?'

Dillon laughed softly. 'Jesus, girl, you really are on Morgan's side, aren't you?'

He slipped the Walther back in his waistband at the rear and pulled off his ski-mask.

'Why shouldn't I be? He's my father, isn't he?'

'Stepfather.' Dillon helped himself to a cigarette from a silver box on a coffee table and lit it with his ever-present Zippo. 'Mafia stepfather.'

'Father, as far as I'm concerned; the only decent one I've ever known; the first version was a rat, the kind of man who sniffed around everything in a skirt. He made my mother's life hell. It was a blessing when his car ran off the road one day and he was burnt to death in the crash.'

'That must have been rough.'

'A blessing, Dillon, and then after a year or two my mother met Carl, the best man in the world.'

'Really?'

She took a cigarette from the box. 'Look, Dillon, I know all about you, all about the IRA, all that stuff, and I know who decent old Ferguson really is, Carl told me.'

'I bet he tells you everything. I suppose you could give me chapter and verse on the Chungking Covenant.'

'Of course I could, Carl tells me everything.'

'I wonder. I mean there's the Carl Morgan of the social

159

pages, the polo player, Man of the Year, billionaire, and then back there in the shadows is the same old Mafia sources of cash–flow, drugs, prostitution, gambling, extortion.'

She moved to the french windows, opened one and looked out at the rain. 'Don't be tiresome, Dillon, after all, you can talk. What about all those years with the Provisional IRA? How many soldiers did you kill, how many women and kids did you blow up?'

'I hate to disappoint you, but I never blew up a woman or a child in my life. Soldiers, yes, I've killed a few of those, but as far as I'm concerned that was war. Come to think of it, I did blow up a couple of PLO boats in Beirut harbour, but they were due to land terrorists on the Israeli coast with the deliberate intention of blowing up women and kids.'

'All right, point taken. What are you doing here anyway?'

'Just curious, that's all; I wondered if you were getting anywhere, but I overheard Morgan discussing things with Murdoch, and of the Bible there is no sign.'

'It must be here,' she said. 'Tanner said it came back.' She frowned. 'I'm not giving anything away am I? I mean, you and Ferguson wouldn't be here if you didn't know.'

'That's right,' he said. 'Lord Louis Mountbatten; the Laird, Ian Campbell; the Dakota crash in India.'

'You needn't go on. Carl would love to know how you found out, but I don't suppose you'll tell me.'

'Classified information.' He finished his drink and there was a noise in the hall. 'On my way.' He pulled on his ski-mask and, as he slipped out of the french window, said, 'See you in the morning.'

The door opened and Morgan came in. He looked surprised. 'Good God, Asta, you startled me. I thought you'd gone to bed.'

'I decided to come down for my book and, guess what, Dillon was here.'

Morgan's eyes narrowed. 'Really?'

'He looked terribly dramatic. All in black with a ski-mask. Looked like Carlos the Jackal on a bad Saturday night in Beirut. He's just gone.'

'What was he after?'

'Just prowling around to see what was happening. Apparently he overheard you discussing with Murdoch your lack of success at finding the Bible.' Morgan poured a brandy and came over to stand beside her at the windows. 'They know everything, Carl – Mountbatten, Corporal Tanner, the Laird – everything,' she said.

'You got that much out of him?'

'Easy, Carl; he likes me and he wasn't giving anything away. He wouldn't tell me how they found out and you said yourself it was obvious they knew, otherwise why would a man like Ferguson be here.'

He nodded. 'And they don't care that we know. Interesting tactics.' He swallowed some brandy. 'Are they still picking you up in the morning?'

'Yes.'

'Good.' He emptied his glass and closed the window. 'Bed, then, and this time let's mean it.'

'So, the decks really are cleared for action now,' Ferguson said.

'You did say you wanted him to know we were breathing down his neck,' Dillon reminded him.

'Yes, it's a good tactic, don't you agree, Chief Inspector?'

He turned to Hannah Bernstein who was leaning against his desk. 'I suppose so, sir; if we're playing games, that is.'

'So that's what you think we're doing?'

'I'm sorry, sir, it's just that I don't feel we're really

getting to grips with this thing. We know what Morgan is up to and he knows what we are; I'm not sure it makes sense.'

'It will, my dear, when that Bible turns up.'

'Will it? Let's say he suddenly found it at the back of a drawer tonight, Brigadier. They could be into his Lear and flying out of the country in the morning and nothing we could do about it.'

'Well, we'll just have to see, won't we.' Kim came in with tea on a tray. Ferguson shook his head. 'It's bed for me, I'll see you in the morning.'

He went out and Kim poured the tea and retired. Hannah said to Dillon, 'What do you think?'

'You could be right, but I've a hunch it isn't so.' He moved to the window, opened it and looked at the rain bouncing on the flagged terrace. 'I don't think that Bible is tucked away in some casual spot so that a maid might find it while she's dusting.' He turned. 'Remember what Tanner said when the doctor asked him if the Bible had been returned to Loch Dhu?'

'Yes, his answer was: "You could say that".'

'And then he laughed. Now why would he do that?'

Hannah shrugged. 'Some private joke?'

'Exactly. Quite a mystery, and I came across another tonight.'

'What was that?'

Dillon said, 'When I was snooping around earlier at the Castle I saw Morgan and Asta going up to bed.'

'So?'

'It wasn't what I expected, not a hint of a sexual relationship. At the top of the stairs he kissed her forehead and they went their separate ways.'

'Now that *is* interesting,' Hannah Bernstein told him.

'It is if you consider any theory that says his motive for killing the mother was because he had designs on Asta.'

Dillon finished his tea and grinned. 'You can put that fine Special Branch mind to work on that one, my love, but, as for me, I'm for bed,' and he left her there.

The following morning it had stopped raining for the first time in two days. As the Range Rover drove up to Loch Dhu Castle, Kim at the wheel, Asta and Morgan came out and stood waiting. She wore a Glengarry bonnet, leather jacket and a plaid skirt.

'Very ethnic,' Dillon said as he got out.

'Morning,' Ferguson boomed. 'A good day's sport, with any luck. I'm glad this damn rain's stopped.'

'So am I,' Morgan said. 'Did you have a good night, Brigadier?'

'Certainly. Slept like a top. It's the Highland air.'

Morgan turned to Dillon. 'And you?'

'I'm like a cat, I only nap.'

'That must be useful.' Morgan turned back to the Brigadier. 'Dinner tonight? Seven o'clock suit you?'

'Excellent,' Ferguson said. 'Black tie?'

'Of course, and bring that secretary of yours and I'll try and persuade Lady Katherine to join us.'

'Couldn't look forward to it more. We'll see you this evening, then,' and Morgan ushered Asta down the steps into the Range Rover.

As the sun came up and the morning advanced Dillon almost forgot why he had come to this wild and lonely place, as they proceeded on foot, climbing up and away from the glen. He and Asta forged ahead, leaving Ferguson and Kim to follow at their own pace.

Dillon was aware of a kind of lazy contentment. The truth was that he was enjoying the girl's company. He'd never had much time for women, the exigencies of his calling, he used to say, and no time for relationships, but there was something elemental about this one that touched him deep inside. They didn't talk much, simply concentrated on climbing, and finally came up over an edge of rock and stood there, the glen below purple with heather and the sea in the distance calm, islands scattered across it.

'I don't think I've ever seen anything more beautiful,' Asta said.

'I have,' Dillon told her.

The wind folded her skirt about her legs, outlining her thighs, and when she pulled off her Glengarry and shook her head, her near-white hair shimmered in the sun. She fitted the scene perfectly, a golden girl on a golden day.

'Your hair and mine are almost the same colour, Dillon.' She sat down on a rock. 'We could be related.'

'Jesus, girl, don't wish that on me.' He lit two cigarettes, hands cupped against the wind, gave her one then lay on the ground beside her. 'Lots of fair hair in Ireland. A thousand years ago Dublin was a Viking capital.'

'I didn't know that.'

'Did you tell Morgan about my visit last night?'

'Of course I did. In fact you almost came face-to-face. The noise you heard in the hall was Carl.'

'And what did he have to say?'

'My goodness, Dillon, you do expect a lot for your cigarette.' She laughed. 'All right, I told him everything you told me, the Chungking Covenant and so on, but that was because you wanted me to, didn't you?'

'That's right.'

'Carl said he didn't mind. He checked on Ferguson the moment he discovered he was at the Lodge, knew who he was in a matter of hours, and you. He knew you must have been aware of what was going on, otherwise why would you be here. He's no fool, Dillon; he would hardly be where he is today if he was that.'

'You really think a great deal of him, don't you?'

'As I said last night, I know all about you, Dillon, so don't waste time telling me what a bad man Carl is. It would be the pot calling the kettle black, don't you agree?'

'A nice turn of phrase you have.'

'I had an excellent education,' she said. 'A good Church of England boarding school for young ladies. St Michael's and St Hugh's College, Oxford afterwards.'

'Is that so? I bet you didn't get calluses on your knees from praying.'

'You are a bastard,' she said amiably and at that moment Ferguson came over the rise, Kim following with the gun case, a pair of old-fashioned Zeiss binoculars round his neck.

'There you are.' Ferguson slumped down. 'Getting old. Coffee, Kim.'

The Gurkha put down the gun case, opened the haversack that hung at his side and took out a Thermos flask and several paper cups which he filled and passed around.

'This is nice,' Asta said. 'I haven't been on a picnic in years.'

'You can forget that notion, young lady,' Ferguson told her. 'This is a serious expedition, the object of which is to expose you to the finer points of deer stalking. Now drink up and we'll get on.'

And so, tramping through the heather in the sunshine, he kept up a running commentary, stressing first a deer's incredible sense of smell, so that any successful approach could only be made downwind.

'You can shoot, I suppose?' he asked her.

'Of course; Carl trained me; clay pigeon shooting mostly. I've been out with him after grouse during the season many times.'

'Well, that's something.'

They had been on the go for a good hour when Kim suddenly pointed. 'There, *sahib*.'

'Down, everybody,' Ferguson told them and Kim passed him the binoculars.

'Excellent.' Ferguson handed them to Dillon. 'Three hundred yards. Two hinds and a Royal Stag. Quite magnificent antlers.'

Dillon had a look. 'My God, yes,' he said and passed the binoculars to Asta.

When she focused them, the stag and the hinds jumped clearly into view. 'How marvellous,' she breathed and turned to Ferguson. 'We couldn't possibly shoot such wonderful creatures, could we?'

'Just like a bloody woman,' Ferguson said. 'I might have known.'

Dillon said, 'The fun is in the stalking, Asta; it's like a game. They're well able to look after themselves, believe me. We'll be lucky to get within a hundred yards.'

Kim wet a finger and raised it. 'Downwind, *sahib*, OK now.' He looked up at the sky where clouds were forming. 'I think wind change direction soon.'

'Then we move fast,' Ferguson said. 'Pass me the rifle.'

It was an old Jackson and Whitney bolt action. He loaded it carefully and said, 'They're downhill from us, remember.'

'I know,' Dillon said. 'Shoot low. Let's get going.'

Asta found the next hour one of the most exhilarating she'd ever known. They moved through gulleys, crouching low, Kim leading the way.

'He certainly knows his stuff,' she said to Dillon at one point.

'He should do,' Ferguson told her. 'The best tracker on a tiger shoot I ever knew in India in the old days.'

Finally, they took to the heather and crawled in single file until Kim called a halt and paused in a small hollow. He peered over the top cautiously. The deer browsed contentedly no more than seventy-five yards away.

'No closer, *sahib*.' He glanced up. 'Wind changing already.'

'Right.' Ferguson moved the bolt and rammed a round into the breech. 'Your honour, my dear.'

'Really?' Asta was flushed with excitement, took the rifle from him gingerly, then settled herself on her elbows, the stock firmly into her shoulder.

'Don't pull, just squeeze gently,' Dillon told her.

'I know that.'

'And aim low,' Ferguson added.

'All right.' What seemed like rather a long time passed and suddenly she rolled over and thrust the rifle at him. 'I can't do it, Brigadier, that stag is too beautiful to die.'

'Well we all bloody-well die sometime,' Ferguson said and at that moment the stag raised its head.

'Wind change, *sahib*, he has our scent,' Kim said and in an instant the stag and the two hinds were leaping away through the bracken at an incredible speed.

Dillon rolled over, laughing, and Ferguson said 'Damn!' And then he scowled. 'Not funny, Dillon, not funny at all.' He handed the rifle to Kim. 'All right, put it away and break out the sandwiches.'

On the way back some time later they paused for a rest on a crest that gave an excellent view of the glen below the Castle, with Ardnamurchan Lodge on the other side. Dillon noticed something he hadn't appreciated before. There was a landing stage below the Castle, a boat moored beside it.

'Give me the binoculars,' he said to Kim and focused them, closing in on a twenty-five-foot motor launch with a deckhouse. 'I didn't know that was there,' he said, passing the binoculars to Ferguson.

'The boat, you mean?' Asta said. 'It goes with the Castle. It's called the *Katrina*.'

'Have you been out in it yet?' Dillon asked.

'No reason. Carl isn't interested in fishing.'

'Better than ours.' Ferguson swung the binoculars to the rickety pier below Ardnamurchan Lodge on the other side of the loch and the boat tied up there, an old whaler with an outboard motor and a rowing boat beside it. He handed the binoculars to Kim. 'All right, let's move on.'

'Frankly I'm getting bored with this track,' Asta said. 'Can't we just go straight down, Dillon?'

He turned to Ferguson who shrugged. 'Rather you than me, but if that's what you want. Come on, Kim,' and he continued along the track.

Dillon took Asta by the hand. 'Here we go, and watch yourself, we don't want you turning that ankle again,' and they started down the slope.

It was reasonably strenuous going for most of the way, the whole side of the mountain flowing down to the loch below. He led the way, picking his way carefully for something like a thousand feet and then, as things became easier, he took her hand and they scrambled on down together until, suddenly, she lost her balance, laughing out loud, and fell, dragging Dillon with her. They rolled over a couple of times and came to rest in a soft cushion of heather in a hollow. She lay on her back, breathless, and Dillon pushed himself up on one elbow to look at her.

Her laughter faded, she reached up and touched his face and, for a moment, he forgot everything except the colour of her hair, the scent of her perfume. When they kissed, her body was soft and yielding, everything a man could hope for in this world.

He rolled on to his back and she sat up. 'I wondered when you would, Dillon. Very satisfactory.'

He got a couple of cigarettes from his case, lit them and passed one to her. 'Put it down to the altitude. I'm sorry.'

'I'm not.'

'You should be. I've got twenty years on you.'

'That must be some Irish thing,' she said. 'All that rain. Is it supposed to have a dampening effect on love?'

'What's love got to do with it?'

She blew out cigarette smoke and lay back, a hand behind her head. 'Now there's romantic for you.'

He sat up. 'Stop indulging in flights of fantasy; Asta, you aren't in love with me.'

She turned to look at him. 'You said it yourself. What's love got to do with it?'

'Morgan wouldn't think very much of the idea.'

She sat up and shrugged. 'He doesn't control my life.'

'Really? I'd have thought that's exactly what he does do.'

'Damn you, Dillon!' She was angry and stubbed her cigarette out on a rock. 'You've just ruined a lovely day. Can we go now?'

She got up and started down the hill and, after a while, he got up and followed her.

They reached the edge of the loch about thirty minutes later and started to follow the shoreline. They hadn't spoken since the incident in the hollow and now Dillon said, 'Are we speaking again, or what?'

She laughed and took his arm. 'You're a pig, Dillon, but I like you.'

'All part of my irresistible charm,' he said and paused suddenly.

They were close to the west end of the loch, the old hunting bothy where Morgan and Marco had dealt with Fergus on their left. He was still lying down on the shoreline, face in the shallows.

Asta said, 'My God, isn't that a body?'

'That's what it looks like.'

They hurried down the slope and reached the sand bar.

She stood there while Dillon waded in and turned Fergus over. Asta gave a sudden exclamation. 'Fergus.'

'Yes.' Dillon waded back. 'I'd say he was given a thorough beating. Wait here.'

He went up to the hunting bothy. She watched him go in. A moment later he returned. 'From the state of things that's where the fight was. After they'd gone he must have come down to the shore to revive himself and fell in. Something like that.'

'An accident,' she said, and there was a strange calmness on her face. 'That was it.'

'You could describe it that way,' Dillon said. 'I'm sure Carl Morgan would.'

'Leave it, Dillon.' She reached out and grabbed his lapel. 'Do this for me, just leave it, I'll handle it.'

There was a fierceness to her that was something new. He said, 'I'm beginning to wonder if I really know you at all, Asta. All right, I'll leave Morgan to stew in it.'

She nodded. 'Thank you, I'll get back now.' She walked away, paused and turned. 'I'll see you tonight.'

He nodded. 'I wouldn't miss it for anything.'

She hurried away. He looked out again at the body by the sand bar, then climbed up the slope and reached the road. He had walked along it for perhaps five minutes when a horn sounded and he turned and found the Range Rover bearing down on him.

Ferguson opened the door. 'Where's the girl?'

'She's cut across to the Castle on her own.'

Dillon climbed in and Kim drove on. 'I must say, you look thoughtful, dear boy.'

'So would you,' Dillon said, lit a cigarette and brought him up to date.

Morgan was in the study when she went in, sitting at his desk and talking to Marco. He turned and smiled. 'Had a nice day?'

'It was until things went sour.'

He stopped smiling and said to Marco, 'You can go.'

'No, let him stay. You found Fergus, didn't you; you beat him up?'

Morgan reached for a cigar and clipped it. 'He had it coming, Asta. Anyway, how do you know?'

'Dillon and I just found his body. He was lying in the shallows down there in the loch just below that old hunting lodge. He must have fallen in and drowned.'

Morgan glanced at Marco, then put the cigar down. 'What did Dillon do?'

'Nothing. I begged him to leave it to me.'

'And he agreed?'

She nodded. 'He said he'd leave you to stew in it.'

'Yes, that's exactly how he would play it.' Morgan nodded. 'And so would Ferguson. It wouldn't suit the dear old Brigadier to have a police investigation, not at the moment.' He glanced at Marco. 'And it wouldn't get anywhere without a body, would it?'

'No, *signore*.'

Morgan stood up. 'All right, let's take care of it. You stay here, Asta,' and he went out, followed by Marco.

In the trees that fringed the loch below Ardnamurchan Lodge, just above the small jetty, Ferguson and Dillon waited, the Irishman holding the Zeiss binoculars. The light was fading, but visibility was still good enough for him to see the motor launch *Katrina* moving along the shoreline on the other side.

'There they go,' he said and focused the binoculars.

Morgan was in the wheel house and he reversed the launch towards the shore, Marco in the stern. Marco jumped over into the water and Morgan went to help him. A moment later Fergus came over the rail. Morgan went back into the wheel house and turned out towards the middle of the loch. Dillon passed the binoculars to Ferguson.

The Brigadier said, 'It looks to me as if Marco is wrapping a length of chain around the body.' He shook his head. 'How very naughty.'

He passed the binoculars back to Dillon who focused them again in time to see Marco slide the body over the side. It went straight under and a moment later the *Katrina* got under way and turned back towards the Castle.

'So that's it,' Dillon said and turned to Ferguson. 'You're happy to leave it that way?'

'I think so. A crime has undoubtedly been committed, but that's a police matter and frankly I don't want the local constabulary swarming all over Loch Dhu Castle. We've bigger fish to fry here, Dillon.'

'I doubt whether the good Chief Inspector Bernstein would agree,' Dillon said. 'A great one for the letter of the law, that lady.'

'Which is why we don't say a word about this to her.'

Dillon lit another cigarette. 'One thing we can count on, he won't be missed, old Fergus, not for a few days. The Munros will think he's just keeping out of the way.'

'Which will be what Morgan is counting on. I would imagine he's hoping to be out of here quite quickly.' Ferguson stood up. 'Let's get moving, we've got dinner to look forward to. It should prove an interesting evening.'

TEN

THEY ARRIVED AT THE Castle only a few minutes
after seven, Dillon at the wheel of the old estate car
that went with Ardnamurchan Lodge. He and Ferguson
were in dinner jackets and Hannah Bernstein wore a
cream trouser suit in silk crêpe. The door was opened
by Marco, wearing his Alpaca jacket and striped
trousers, and he ushered them in, his face expressionless,
to where Morgan stood by the fire in the hall, Asta in
a green silk dress on the sofa beside Lady Katherine
Rose.

'Ah, there you are,' Morgan said genially. 'Come in. I
think you've met Brigadier Ferguson, Lady Katherine?'

'Indeed yes. He called and took tea with me, he and this charming young gel.'

Hannah looked amused and Ferguson took her hand. 'Lovely to see you again. I don't think you've met my nephew, Sean Dillon.'

'Mr Dillon.'

Dillon took the cool, dry hand, liking her immediately. 'A great pleasure.'

'Irish?' she said. 'I like the Irish; charming rogues, the lot of them, but nice. Do you smoke, young man?'

'My one vice.'

'What a liar you are. Give me one, will you.'

'Lady Katherine, I'm so sorry.' Morgan picked up a silver cigarette box and came forward. 'I'd no idea.'

She took one and accepted a light from Dillon. 'I've been smoking all my life, Mr Morgan, no point in stopping now.'

Marco appeared with a bottle of Crystal in a bucket and six glasses on a tray. He placed it on a side table and said in heavily accented English, 'Shall I open the champagne, sir?'

'Not for me,' Lady Katherine said. 'It doesn't go down well these days. A Vodka Martini, very dry, would be just the ticket. That's what got me through the war; that and cigarettes.'

'I'll get it,' Asta said and went to the drinks cabinet as Marco uncorked the champagne bottle.

'You served in the war, then, Lady Katherine?' Ferguson asked her.

'By God I did. All this nonsense about young gels being allowed to fly in the RAF these days.' She snorted. 'All old hat. I was a pilot from nineteen-forty with the old Air Transport Auxiliary. They used to call us the Attagirls.'

Asta brought the Martini and sat beside her, fascinated. 'But what did you do?'

The old lady sampled the drink. 'Excellent, my dear.

We ferried warplanes between factories and RAF stations to free pilots for combat. I flew everything, we all did. Spitfires and Hurricanes and once a Lancaster bomber. The ground crew at the RAF station I delivered it to couldn't believe it when I took off my flying helmet and they saw my hair.'

'But all-in-all, it must have been extremely dangerous,' Hannah said.

'I crash landed once in a Hurricane, wheels up. Not my fault, engine failure. Another time an old Gloucester Gladiator, they were biplanes, started to fall apart on me in mid-air, so I had to bale out.'

'Good God!' Morgan said. 'That's amazing.'

'Oh, it was hard going,' she said. 'Out of the women in my unit sixteen were killed, but then we had to win the war, didn't we Brigadier?'

'We certainly did, Lady Katherine.'

She held up her empty glass. 'Another one, somebody, and then I'll love you and leave you.'

Asta went to get it and Morgan said, 'Lady Katherine doesn't feel up to dinner, I'm afraid.'

'Only eat enough for a sparrow these days.' She accepted the drink Asta brought and looked up at Morgan. 'Well, have you found the Bible yet?'

He was momentarily thrown. 'The Bible?'

'Oh, come on, Mr Morgan, I know you've had the servants turning the place upside down. Why is it so important?'

He was in command again now. 'A legend, Lady Katherine, of great importance to your family. I just thought it would be nice to find it and give it to you.'

'Indeed.' She turned to Hannah and there was something in her eyes. 'Amazing the interest in the Bible all of a sudden, and I can't help. Haven't seen it in years. I still think it was lost in the air crash that injured my brother so badly.'

Morgan glanced at Ferguson who was smiling and made a determined effort to change the subject. 'Tell me, just how old is the Castle, Lady Katherine?'

Asta got up and moved to the french windows at the end of the hall and opened them and Dillon went to join her, moving out on to the terrace as she did, the murmur of voices behind them.

The beech trees above the loch were cut out of black cardboard against a sky that was streaked with vivid orange above the mountains. She took his arm and they strolled across the lawn, Dillon lighting a cigarette.

'Do you want one?'

'No, I'll share yours,' which she did, handing it back to him after a moment. 'It's peaceful here and old; the roots go deep. Everyone needs roots, don't you agree, Dillon?'

'Maybe it's people not places,' he said. 'Take you, for instance. Perhaps your roots are Morgan.'

'It's a thought, but you, Dillon, what about you? Where are your roots?'

'Maybe nowhere, love, nowhere at all. Oh, there's the odd aunt or uncle and a few cousins here and there in Ulster, but no one who'd dare come near. The price of fame.'

'Infamy more like.'

'I know, I'm the original bad guy. That's why Ferguson recruited me.'

'You know, I like you, Dillon; I feel as if I've known you a long time, but what am I going to do with you?'

'Take your time, girl dear, I'm sure something will occur to you.'

Morgan appeared on the terrace and called, 'Asta, are you there?'

'Here we are, Carl.' They walked back and went up the steps to the terrace. 'What is it?'

'Lady Katherine's ready to leave.'

'What a pity. I wish she would stay, she's wonderful.'

'One of a kind,' Morgan said, 'but there it is. I'll run her down to the lodge.'

'No you won't,' Asta told him. 'I'll see to it. You've got guests, Carl. We mustn't forget our manners.'

'Shall I come with you?' Dillon asked.

'It's only three hundred yards down the drive, for heaven's sake,' she said. 'I'll be back in no time.'

They went inside and Lady Katherine said, 'There you are. Thought we'd lost you.'

She pushed herself up on her stick and Asta put an arm round her. 'No chance, I'm taking you home now.'

'What a lovely girl.' Lady Katherine turned to them all. 'Such a delight. Do come and see me any time. Good night all.'

Morgan had a hand on her elbow and he and Asta took her out of the front door. A moment later the Castle's station wagon engine started up and Morgan returned.

He snapped his fingers at Marco. 'More champagne.'

Marco replenished the glasses and Ferguson looked around the great hall, the weapons on the wall, the trophies, the armour. 'Quite an amazing collection, all this. Fascinating.'

'I agree,' Hannah said. 'If you're into death, that is.'

'Aren't you being a little harsh?' Morgan said.

She sipped some of her champagne. 'If it was a museum exhibition they'd probably call it "In praise of war". I mean, look at those great swords crossed under the shields? Their only purpose was to slice somebody's arm off.'

'You're wrong,' Dillon said amiably. 'The backstroke was intended to remove heads. Those swords are Highland claymores and the shield was called a targ. That's where the word "target" comes from.'

'Actually, the particular one you're looking at up there was carried at the Battle of Culloden by the Campbell of the day,' Morgan said. 'He died fighting for Bonnie Prince Charlie.'

'Well, I don't consider that much of an ambition.'

'Haven't you any sense of history?' Ferguson demanded.

'I can't afford one; I'm Jewish, remember, Brigadier. My people have always had enough on to simply survive in the present.'

There was a silence and Dillon said, 'Well, that's a showstopper if ever I've heard one.'

As he spoke the door opened and Asta came in. 'That's done. I've left her in the hands of the redoubtable Jeannie. Can we eat now? I'm starving.'

'Only waiting for you, my love,' Morgan said, and he gave her his arm and led the way in.

The dining room was quite splendid, the walls lined with oak panelling, the table decorated with the finest crystal and silver, candles in great silver sticks flaring. Marco served the meal aided by two young housemaids in black dresses and white aprons.

'We've kept the meal relatively simple as I wasn't sure what everyone would like,' Morgan said.

His idea of simplicity Beluga caviar and smoked salmon followed by roast pheasant with the usual trimmings, all washed down with vintage Château Palmer.

'Absolutely wonderful,' Ferguson said as he tucked into his pheasant. 'You must have an extraordinary cook here.'

'Oh, she's all right for the simple things, but it's Marco who roasted the pheasant.'

'A man of many talents.' Ferguson glanced up as Marco, face imperturbable, refilled the glasses.

'Yes, you could say that,' Morgan agreed.

Marco disappeared shortly afterwards; Dillon noticed that as the two maids cleared the plates. Asta said, 'And what delight do you have for the climax?'

'Hard act to follow with a simple pudding,' Ferguson observed.

'Nothing simple about this, Brigadier; something Marco specialises in,' Morgan told him.

Marco entered the room at that moment with a large silver chafing dish, the maids behind him. He removed the lid and a most delicious smell was released.

'Cannolo,' Asta said in delight.

'Yes, the most famous sweet in Sicily and so simple,' Morgan said. 'A tube of flour and egg filled with cream.'

Ferguson tried a spoonful and shook his head. 'Nothing simple about this. The man's a genius. Where on earth did he learn to do such cooking?'

'His father had a small restaurant in Palermo. As a boy, he was raised to it.'

'Amongst other things,' Dillon said.

'Yes, my friend,' Morgan told him calmly. 'I suspect you and Marco would have a great deal in common.'

'Now then, Dillon, let's concentrate on the meal,' Ferguson said, 'there's a good chap.'

Which they did, returning to sit round the great fireplace in the hall for the coffee which was Yemeni *mocha*, the finest in the world.

Ferguson accepted a cigar. 'Well, I must tell you this, Morgan, that was the best simple meal I've ever had in my life.'

'We aim to please.'

'A most pleasant evening,' the Brigadier replied.

Dillon felt like laughing out loud at the insanity of it, the pretence of this amazing game they were all playing, the urbanity of the Brigadier's exchanges with a man who only a few hours earlier he had seen dispose of Fergus Munro's body.

'Well, now,' he said, 'if we're going to play patty fingers here I'll use mine on the piano, if you don't mind.'

'Be my guest,' Morgan told him.

Dillon moved to the grand piano and raised the lid. It was very old, a Schiedmayer, but the tone wasn't too bad when he tried a few chords. He lit a cigarette and sat there with it drooping from the corner of his mouth and started to work his way through a few standards.

Hannah came and leaned on the piano, sipping her coffee. 'You consistently surprise me, Dillon.'

'The secret of my fatal charm. Any requests?'

Asta was watching, a slight frown on her face, and Hannah murmured, 'Now that's interesting, I do believe she's jealous. What have you been up to, Dillon?'

'You should be ashamed, you and your bad thoughts,' Dillon told her.

Behind them Morgan said, 'Asta tells me you had an excellent day with the deer.'

'Yes,' Ferguson said. 'Only, when we got close enough to a King Stag to see the damned eyes and I lined her up with my gun she wouldn't pull the trigger. She said she couldn't kill such a magnificent creature.'

Hannah turned. 'Good for you,' she said to Asta.

'Well it *was* magnificent,' Asta said.

'Still a damn silly attitude,' Ferguson told her.

'No, I think the Chief Inspector has a point,' Morgan told him. 'The deer can't fight back. At least in the ring the bull has a chance of sticking his horn in.'

There was silence and Dillon said, 'Sure and you put your foot in it there, old son.'

'Dear me, so I did.' Morgan smiled at Hannah. 'So sorry, Chief Inspector, I wasn't supposed to know, was I?'

'Oh, I wouldn't say that,' Ferguson told him.

'All out in the open so we all know where we are,' Dillon said.

'And on that note we'll say good night.' Ferguson stood up. 'Whatever else, you're an excellent host, Morgan. You must allow me to do the same for you sometime.'

'I'll look forward to it.'

Marco opened the door and they moved out on to the steps. The sky was dotted with clouds and yet undulated with strange shimmering lights.

'What's that?' Hannah demanded.

'The Aurora Borealis,' Dillon told her. 'The Northern Lights.'

'It's the most beautiful thing I've ever seen,' Asta said. 'What a night for a drive. Can we, Carl?'

'Asta, be reasonable. It's late.'

'Oh, you're no fun, you.' She turned to Ferguson. 'Can I come with you, Brigadier? You could have that wonderful Gurkha of yours bring me back.'

'Of course, my dear, if you'd like that.'

'It's settled then.' She ran indoors.

Dillon said to Morgan, 'Don't worry, I'll bring her back myself.'

'Now that I am worried about,' Morgan said and Asta re-appeared wearing a blue mink coat.

'I'm ready when you are.' She kissed Morgan on the cheek. 'I won't be long,' then she got in the rear of the estate car with Hannah.

Dillon got behind the wheel, Ferguson joined him in front and they drove away.

The drive along the side of the loch was pleasantly eerie, the Northern Lights reflected in the dark water so that they seemed to sparkle with a kind of strange silver fire.

'Wonderful,' Asta said; 'I'm so glad I came.'

Dillon changed down to climb the hill up through the trees as they rounded the eastern end of the loch. The old estate car responded well; they went over the crest and started down. It was very steep, with a bend or two below. As their speed increased, Dillon put his foot on the brake pedal. There was no response and the pedal went right down to the floor.

'Damn!' he said.

'What is it?' Ferguson demanded.

'The brakes have failed.'

'Good God, man, how? They worked perfectly well on the way here.'

'Since when we've been parked outside Loch Dhu Castle,' Dillon told him and desperately tried to change down.

They were going very fast indeed now. There was a grinding of gears as he wrestled with the stick and then he did manage to force it into third as they came to the first bend.

'Hang on!' Ferguson called as Dillon worked the wheel and just managed to scrape round.

'For God's sake stop it, Dillon!' Asta cried.

Not that he had any choice, and the estate car hurtled down the straight, another considerable bend waiting for them. Again he worked the wheel hard, trying the old racing driver's technique of driving into the bend, and almost made it, and then they scraped against a granite wall on the left and bounced away. And it was that which saved them for Dillon got control again as they went down another slope into a hollow and started up a gentle incline. Gradually the speed slowed, he changed down to bottom gear and applied the handbrake.

There was silence and Ferguson said, 'Now that could have been very nasty indeed.'

'Let's take a look,' Dillon said.

He found a torch in the dashboard locker and went and raised the estate car's bonnet, Ferguson at his side. A moment later, Hannah and Asta joined them.

Dillon peered into the engine and nodded. 'There you are.'

'What is it?' Hannah asked.

'See that kind of canister there? It holds brake fluid, only it doesn't any longer. The valve's been ripped off at the top, probably with a screwdriver. No fluid, no brakes. It's a hydraulic system.'

'We could have been killed,' Hannah said. 'All of us, but why?'

'I think Asta knows why,' Dillon said.

Asta pulled the collar of her mink round her throat and shivered. 'But why would Carl do that?'

'More important, why would he do it to you, my dear?' Ferguson asked her. 'After all, he made no attempt to stop you coming with us.' And to that she had no reply. He turned to Dillon, 'Will it still work?'

'Oh, yes, it's a straight road to the lodge on the other side of this hill and I'll stay in bottom gear.'

'Good. Let's get moving, then,' and Ferguson ushered the two women back into the estate car.

'I think you could probably do with this,' Ferguson said to Asta who was sitting by the fire in the sitting room at the lodge, still hugging her mink round her.

It was brandy he was holding out and she took the large crystal tumbler in both hands, staring into it, then swallowed it down. She sat there, still holding the glass, and Dillon took it from her gently and turned to Ferguson.

'She's a little in shock,' he said.

She stood up then, took off her mink and tossed it over a chair. 'Shock be damned. I'm angry, Dillon, bloody angry.'

At that moment Hannah came in from the kitchen with Kim who started pouring coffee. The Chief Inspector took a cup to Asta. 'Just sit down, Asta, and take it easy.'

Asta took the cup of coffee and did as she was told. 'The rest of you would make some kind of sense, but why me? I don't understand.'

'I think you will if you pause and think about it, Asta,' Dillon said.

'His connection with Mafia and all that stuff? You mean I know too much? But I always have.'

'Yes, but something more important than that has cropped up, you know that.'

Hannah Bernstein looked puzzled and Ferguson said, 'You signed the Official Secrets Act when you joined me which means anything which takes place during your duties with me is sacrosanct. Am I correct?'

'Of course, sir.'

'Dillon?' he said.

'I found Fergus Munro's body earlier today in the shallows by Loch Dhu. Asta was with me. By my observation he'd been given a severe beating. I'd say he'd collapsed in the water afterwards and drowned.'

'My God!' Hannah said.

Dillon turned to Asta who said, 'I asked Dillon to let it go.'

'Why?' Hannah said.

'Because in a way it was my fault. It was because of me Carl wanted to teach him a lesson.'

'I see.' Hannah turned to Ferguson. 'On the face of it, you've condoned a criminal offence, sir; manslaughter at the very least.'

'Absolutely right, Chief Inspector. If you want the sordid details, Dillon and I observed Morgan and the man Marco recover the body in the motor launch *Katrina*. They then disposed of it wrapped in a length of chain in the middle of the loch.'

She said, 'You've stood by and let him get away with it?'

'You've got it wrong, girl dear,' Dillon said. 'Retribution can come later.'

'Exactly,' Ferguson told her. 'More important things to

consider.' He took her hand, sat on the couch and pulled her down beside him. 'I chose you to assist me in my work because you're one of the most astute brains at Scotland Yard.'

'Now it's flattery, Brigadier?'

'Nonsense. Look at your background. Your grandfather is a highly respected Rabbi, your father a brilliant Professor of Medicine. You have a Cambridge MA in Psychology. You could have been anything. You chose to be a police-woman on the beat in Brixton and have risen because of your own abilities. I need you and I want you, but this isn't normal police work. This is a rather complicated game, our kind of work. We only have the end in view.'

'Because the end justifies the means?'

It was Dillon who leaned down, took her hands and pulled her up. 'God save us, girl, but he's right, sometimes it does. It's called the greater good.'

He actually put an arm round her and she leaned against him. Then she straightened and managed a faint smile. 'They must have loved you at the National Theatre, Dillon, you'd have ended up with a knighthood. Instead you chose the IRA.' She turned to Ferguson. 'No problem, sir, anything I can do?'

He inclined his head towards Asta and Hannah sat beside her and took her hand. 'When you told Morgan you wanted to come with us he didn't say no. Am I right?'

'I suppose so,' Asta said.

'Let's be logical. He was after us, hadn't counted on you being involved, but when the chance came, when you said what you did, he didn't say no.'

Asta sat there staring at her mutely. She moistened her lips. 'Why? He loves me.'

'His account with you was full, Asta. Oh, you knew all about the Mafia background and so on and what you don't realise is that was always a liability. But Fergus.' Hannah

Bernstein shook her head. 'Even if he drowned because of the beating, the charge would be manslaughter; that would get Carl Morgan seven years at the Old Bailey, and Mafia lawyers don't enjoy the same kind of success in court in England as they do in America. Seven years, Asta. Seven years for a billionaire polo player used to the good things of life. There was no way he could take that chance. You knew too much.'

Asta jumped up and paced across the room and turned. 'He's always been so good to me. I can't believe this.'

Ferguson turned to Dillon. 'Would you say it's time?'

'I think so.'

Ferguson said to Hannah, 'The Greek file, Chief Inspector.' Hannah went to the desk and he carried on, 'You take over, Dillon.'

Dillon took Asta's hand and brought her back to the sofa by the fire and sat down with her. 'What we've got to show you now is bad, Asta, as bad as anything could be. It's to do with Hydra and your mother's scuba diving accident.'

She frowned. 'I don't understand.'

'You will, my dear.' Ferguson took the file from Hannah Bernstein and passed it to her. 'Read that.'

Asta put the file to one side and sat there, her hands clenched. 'It doesn't seem possible.'

'You've seen the file,' Ferguson told her. 'The technical details are beyond dispute. Someone interfered with your mother's equipment.'

'An accident?' she said desperately.

'No accident.' Dillon sat down beside her and took her hand. 'I'm an expert diver, Asta. Believe me, what was done to your mother's gear was deliberate. Now you tell me who was responsible. Can you think of anyone who wished your mother harm?' He shook his head. 'Only

Carl, Asta. We think she knew too much and that's the truth of it.'

She closed her eyes and took a deep breath and when she opened them again she was remarkably in control. 'I can't let him get away with that – not that. What can I do?'

'You could help us,' Ferguson said. 'Keep us informed of the situation up there at the Castle. Most important thing of all, you could let us know the moment he finds the Bible.'

She nodded. 'Right. I'll do it.' She took another deep breath. 'Could I have another brandy?'

'Of course, my dear.' Ferguson nodded to Dillon who got up and went to the drinks cabinet. He returned with the brandy and Asta took it from him.

Hannah sat beside her. 'Look, Asta, are you sure you can go through with this? I mean, you've got to go back and smile in his face and act as if nothing's changed.'

Asta said, 'We buried my mother back home in Sweden, flew her body there from Athens and, do you know something? He stood at the side of my mother's grave and he cried.' She emptied the brandy glass with a single swallow. 'I'll see him pay for that if it's the last thing I do.' She placed the brandy glass on the coffee table and got up. 'I think I should go back now.'

'I'll take you,' Dillon said.

She walked towards the door, picking up her mink and pulling it on. She turned. 'All right. So far, the search for the Bible isn't getting very far in spite of the fact that Carl has offered a substantial reward for anyone who finds it.'

'Thank you for that,' Ferguson said.

'As regards future moves, we're supposed to put in an appearance at the Ardnamurchan Fair and Games tomorrow. I don't think there's anything else.'

Dillon said, 'I'll take you now, Asta.'

She turned at the door. 'I've just remembered, Angus the gardener, he's on Carl's payroll now.'

'We'll bear that in mind,' Ferguson said.

She went out and Dillon followed her.

On the way back to the Castle in the Range Rover she sat beside him, clutching the collar of her mink coat round her neck, saying nothing.

'Are you all right?' he asked as they neared the gates.

'Oh, yes.' She nodded. 'Don't worry about me, Dillon. I'll play my part.'

They drove along the drive and he braked to a halt at the steps. Before they could get out the front door opened and Morgan appeared.

'I was beginning to get worried,' he said as Dillon went round and opened the door for Asta.

'Sorry, Carl,' she said as she went up the steps. 'But we nearly had a nasty accident.'

He was immediately all concern. 'What happened?'

'The brakes failed on the estate car,' Dillon said. 'Some sort of rupture in the canister so we lost the hydraulic fluid. It's been around a few years, that car.'

'Dillon was wonderful,' she said. 'Drove like Nigel Mansell going down the hill. I really thought we'd had it.'

'My God!' He gave her a squeeze. 'How can I thank you, Dillon?'

'Self-preservation,' Dillon told him. 'I always struggle to survive, Mr Morgan.'

Asta said, 'I'll go in, Carl. I think I'll go to bed.'

She went inside and Morgan turned as Dillon got in the Range Rover. 'Thanks again. Will you be at the Fair tomorrow?'

'I should imagine so.'

'Good, we'll see you then.' He went in and closed the door.

'And I'll see you, you bastard,' Dillon said as he drove away.

ELEVEN

THE FOLLOWING DAY was a local holiday, Ardnamurchan Village awash with people from the surrounding
district and others who had driven many miles to see the
fair and take part in the games. And there were the tinkers
and the gypsies with their ponies and horses to trade.
Ferguson, Dillon and Hannah arrived just before lunch,
parked the Range Rover at the church and walked down
to the Campbell Arms.

'A little bracer, I think, then all the fun of the fair,'
Ferguson said.

'Ten minutes short of noon, Brigadier,' Hannah reminded him. 'That counts as morning drinking.'

'If the booze was going to get me, Chief Inspector, it would have done so long ago, the Korean War, to be exact, as a twenty-year-old subaltern. I sat in a trench in the snow, twenty degrees below, with the Chinese attacking ten thousand at a time. Only the rum kept me going.'

He pushed open the door and led the way in. The saloon bar was packed, nowhere to sit, but he shouldered his way through cheerfully to the bar where Molly worked feverishly with four local women to aid her.

'Guinness,' Ferguson called. 'Three.' He turned to Hannah. 'Extremely nourishing.'

Molly served them herself. 'Were you hoping to eat, Brigadier?'

'It's an idea,' he said.

'Nothing fancy today, just hot Cornish pasties.'

'A unique thought as we're in Scotland, but why not? We'll have one each.'

'Right. There's someone moving from the settle by the fire right now. You sit yourselves down and I'll bring them.'

She was right, three men getting up at that moment and moving off and Ferguson pushed through the crowd to secure the places. He sat down and rubbed his hands. 'Nothing like a day out in the country.'

'Shouldn't we have more important things to do, sir?' Hannah asked.

'Nonsense, Chief Inspector, everyone needs a break now and then.'

Molly brought the Guinness and the three pasties, which were enormous. 'If that isn't enough for you there's the refreshment tent,' she said, as Ferguson paid her. 'Up at the fair.'

'We'll bear it in mind, my dear.'

Ferguson sampled his drink and then tried the pasty. 'My goodness, this is good.'

Hannah said, 'All right, sir, but what happens now?'

'What would you like to happen?' Dillon asked her.

'I don't know. In fact all I do know is that Morgan took care of Fergus rather permanently and then tried to kill the lot of us last night. I'd say that amounts to open warfare.'

'Yes, but now we've got Asta on our side,' Ferguson told her and at that moment Asta came in followed by Morgan and Marco.

She saw them at once and came straight over. She was wearing the bonnet she had worn when deer stalking and the plaid skirt and there wasn't a man in the room who didn't look her way.

She smiled. 'There you are.'

Dillon stood up to let her sit. 'You're looking particularly fragrant this morning.'

'Well, that's how I feel. Fighting fit, Dillon. It seems to me that's the way I need to be.'

Behind her Morgan spoke to Marco who went to the bar and Morgan crossed to join them. 'How are you? Asta was describing what happened last night. That's terrible.'

'Exciting, to say the least,' Ferguson told him. 'But the boy here kept his head and drove like Stirling Moss in his prime.' He smiled. 'A long time ago, but still the only British racing driver worth his salt, as far as I'm concerned.'

Marco brought two lagers, gave one to Morgan and the other to Asta and retired to the door. Asta said, 'All the fun of the fair. I'm looking forward to it.'

The door opened again and Hector Munro entered with Rory. On seeing them by the fire he paused and put a finger to his forehead. 'Ladies,' he said courteously and started to the bar.

'No sign of that son of yours, I suppose,' Morgan said.

'Ah, well, Fergus is away to see relatives, Mr Morgan,' Hector told him. 'I doubt he'll be back for a while.'

He moved off to the bar and Ferguson finished his drink. 'Right, let's get moving.' He stood up. 'See you later, Morgan,' and he led the way out.

There was a refreshment tent, two or three roundabouts for children and a primitive boxing ring which for the moment was empty. The main event taking place when they arrived was the horse sale and they stood on the edge of the crowd and watched the gypsy boys running up and down, clutching the horses' bridles as they showed their paces. Dillon noticed Hector Munro and Rory at one point, inspecting a couple of ponies.

He strolled over, lighting a cigarette, and said in Irish, 'Dog meat only, those two.'

'Do I need telling?' Hector replied in Gaelic.

Rory grinned. 'Expert, are you?'

'I spent enough time on my uncle's farm in County Down as a boy to know rubbish when I see it.'

Dillon smiled amiably and returned to the others. 'Games just starting,' Ferguson said. 'Come on.'

There were fifty-yard dashes and sack races for the younger children, but the adult sports were more interesting. Large men tossed the caber, an object resembling a telegraph pole. There was hammer throwing and the long jump, even Scottish reels danced to the skirl of the bagpipes.

Morgan and Asta, Marco behind them, appeared on the other side of the crowd. She saw Dillon and waved. He waved back and then turned to watch as the wrestling began. Brawny men in kilts with thighs like tree-trunks grappled with the power and striking force of Sumo wrestlers, the crowd urging them on.

'Rather jolly, all this.' Ferguson produced a hip flask. He unscrewed the top and took a swallow. 'Just like Samson. Didn't he smite the Philistines hip and thigh, Chief Inspector?'

'I believe he did, sir, but, frankly, it isn't my cup of tea.'

'No, I don't suppose it would be.'

And then the crowd moved away towards the boxing ring, carrying them with it. Dillon said, 'Now this looks more like it.'

'What is it?' Hannah demanded.

'Old-style prize fighting, I'd say. Let's see what happens.'

A middle-aged man in boxing boots and shorts slipped under the ropes into the ring. He had the flattened nose of the professional fighter, scar tissue around his eyes. On the back of his old nylon robe was the legend Tiger Grant.

'By God, he's seen a few fights,' Ferguson said.

'A hard one,' Dillon nodded in agreement.

At that moment Asta joined them, Marco forcing a way through for her and Morgan. The Sicilian looked up at Tiger Grant, his expression enigmatic.

Dillon said, 'From the look of his face, Marco here has done a bit himself.'

'Light heavyweight champion of Sicily in his day,' Morgan said. 'Twenty-two fights.'

'How many did he win?'

'All of them. Three decisions on points, twelve knock-outs, seven where the referee stopped the fight.'

'Is that a fact?' Dillon said. 'I must remember to avoid him on a dark night.'

Marco turned to look at him, something in his eyes, but at that moment a small man in tweed suit and cap climbed through the ropes clutching a pair of boxing gloves and turned, waving for silence.

'Now there must be a few sporting gentlemen here so I'll give you a chance of some real money.' He took a wad of bank notes from his inside pocket. 'Fifty pounds, my friends, to any man who can last three rounds with Tiger Grant. Fifty pounds.'

He didn't have to wait long. Dillon saw two burly

young men on the other side of the ring talking to the Munros. One took off his jacket and gave it to Rory and slipped between the ropes.

'I'm on,' he said and the crowd cheered.

The small man helped him into the boxing gloves while Tiger Grant tossed his robe to someone acting as his second in the corner. The small man got out of the ring, took a stopwatch from one pocket and a handbell from the other.

'Each round three minutes; let battle commence.'

The young man moved in on Grant aggressively, the crowd cheering and Asta clutching Dillon's arm. 'This is exciting.'

'Butchery would be a better description,' Hannah Bernstein observed.

And she was right for Grant, easily evading the wild punches, moved in fast and gave his opponent a short and powerful punch in the stomach that put him down, writhing in agony. The crowd roared as the second and the small man helped the unfortunate youth from the ring.

The small man returned. 'Any more takers?' But already the other one who had been standing with the Munros was climbing into the ring. 'I'll have you, that was my brother.'

Grant remained imperturbable and when the bell went and the youth rushed him, stepped from side-to-side, blocking wild punches, eventually putting him down as he had the brother.

The crowd groaned and Hannah said, 'This is terrible.'

'It could be worse,' Dillon said. 'Grant could have made mincemeat of those two and didn't. He's all right.'

He was suddenly aware of Morgan saying something to Marco. He couldn't hear what it was because of the noise of the crowd, but the Sicilian stripped off his jacket and was under the ropes and into the ring, beating Rory Munro by a second.

'Another sportsman,' the small man called, although his smile slipped a little as he tied Marco's boxing gloves on.

'Oh, dear, he's not so sure now,' Ferguson observed.

'Care to have a side bet, Brigadier?' Morgan asked. 'Let's say a hundred pounds.'

'You'll lose your money,' Dillon said to Ferguson.

'I don't need you to tell me that, dear boy. Sorry, Morgan.'

The bell jangled, Marco stood, arms at his side, and for some reason the crowd went silent. Grant crouched, feinted, then moved in fast. Marco swayed with amazing speed to one side, pivoted and punched him in the ribs twice, the sound echoing over the crowd. Grant's head went up in agony and Marco punched him on the jaw, the blow travelling hardly any distance at all. Grant went down like a sack of coal and lay there and there was a gasp of astonishment from the crowd.

The small man was on one knee, trying to revive him, helped by the second, and Marco paced about like a nervous animal. 'My money, where's my money?' he demanded and pulled off his right glove and lifted the small man up. He, in his turn, looked terrified, took the notes from his pocket and passed them over.

Marco moved round each side of the ring, waving the money over his head. 'Anyone else?' he called.

There were boos and catcalls as the small man and the second got Grant out of the ring and then a voice called, 'I'm for you, you bastard,' and Rory Munro climbed into the ring.

Marco kicked the spare gloves over to him and Dillon said, 'A good lad in a pub brawl, but this could be the death of him.'

Rory went in hard and actually took Marco's first punch, slipping one in himself that landed high on the Sicilian's right cheek. Marco feinted then punched him again in the side, but once more Rory rode the punch and hit him again on the right cheek, splitting the skin. Marco stepped back, touched his glove to his cheek and saw the blood. There was rage in his eyes now as he came on, head down, and punched Rory in the ribs, once, twice and then a third time.

'He'll break bones before he's through,' Dillon said.

Ferguson nodded. 'And that young fool won't lie down.'

Rory swayed, obviously in real pain, and Marco punched him in the face several times, holding his head with one gloved hand. The crowd roared their disapproval at such illegality and Marco, contemptuous of them, stepped back and measured Rory for a final punch as he stood there swaying and defenceless.

'Oh, God, no!' Hannah cried.

Dillon slipped through the ropes, stepped between Marco and Rory and held his hand out palm first to the Sicilian. 'He's had enough.'

He turned, took Rory's weight and helped him to his corner, taking off his gloves and easing him down through the ropes to his father and willing hands. 'If I was thirty years younger I'd do for that bastard myself,' Munro said in Gaelic.

'Well, you're not.'

Dillon turned and found Marco standing looking at him, gloved hands on hips. 'You fancy some too, you Irish dog?' he said in Italian.

'That could be arranged,' Dillon replied in the same language.

'Then get your gloves on.'

'Who needs them.' Dillon kicked them out of the ring. 'With gloves I can't hurt you.'

It was deliberate baiting and Marco fell for it. 'Delighted to oblige.'

'No, Dillon, no!' Asta called. 'He'll kill you.'

In motion be like water, that's what Yuan Tao had taught him. Total calm, complete control. This was no longer a boxing match and Marco had made a bad error.

The Sicilian came in fast and swung a punch, Dillon swayed to one side, stamping at the left kneecap, pivoted and struck Marco in the side, screwing the punch as Yuan Tao had shown him. Marco cried out in agony and Dillon struck him again in the same manner and then turned his back, delivering a reverse-elbow strike, smashing Marco's mouth.

The crowd roared as Dillon walked away; Marco, with amazing resilience, went after him like a wild man and, as Dillon turned, punched him under the left cheek. Dillon was flung back by the assault, bounced off the ropes, fell over and Marco kicked him in the ribs.

The crowd were going wild now and Dillon rolled away rapidly and got to his feet. 'Jesus, son, this is getting to be a bore,' he said and, as Marco swung another punch, he grabbed the Sicilian's right wrist, swung it round until the elbow locked and ran him head-first through the ropes and out of the ring to fall on his face in front of Ferguson, Morgan and the two women.

As Marco rolled on to his back, Dillon vaulted the ropes and put a foot on his neck. 'You lie still, now, like a good dog, or I'll break it.'

Morgan said in Italian, 'Leave it, Marco, I order you.' He held out the man's jacket and turned to Dillon. 'You are a remarkable man, my friend.'

'A hero.' Asta clutched his arm.

'No he's not, he's a bloody fool,' Ferguson said. 'Now let's go to the refreshment tent, Dillon, I really think we've earned a drink after that little lot,' and he turned and led the way through the crowd of well-wishers, all eager to pat Dillon on the back.

★

It was reasonably quiet in the marquee, most people preferring to take advantage of the good weather. Ferguson went to the bar which was laid out on a large trestle table. Dillon and Hannah sat at another of the tables and she took out her handkerchief and soaked it in the jug of water on the table. 'Dillon, it's split. I think you're going to need stitches.'

'We'll see. I can't feel a thing at the moment.'

'Well, hold that handkerchief to it for a while.'

'Better to let it dry up.' He lit a cigarette.

'And you're slowly killing yourself with those things.'

'A Fascist, that's what you are. It'll be booze you're banning next, then sex.' He grinned. 'Nothing left.'

'I always thought you had a death wish,' she told him, but she was smiling.

Ferguson came back with drinks on a tray. 'Scotch for us, gin and tonic for you, Chief Inspector.'

'I'd rather have tea, sir, and it wouldn't do Dillon any harm either,' and she got up and went to the refreshment bar.

'I knew it,' Ferguson said. 'When that girl marries she'll be one of those Jewish mothers you read about, the kind who rules her husband with a rod of iron and tells everybody what to do.'

'Jesus, Brigadier, but you must be getting old. I've news for you. There's many a man would happily join the queue to be ruled with a rod of iron by Hannah Bernstein.'

At that moment Asta appeared in the entrance, looked around, saw them and came over. 'There you are.'

She sat down and Dillon said, 'Where's Morgan?'

'Taking Marco down to the local hospital at Arisaig. He thinks you may have broken a rib. I said I'd make my own way back to the Castle.'

'What perfectly splendid news,' Ferguson said.

Hannah joined them with a tray piled with cups and

two teapots. 'I saw you coming,' she told Asta. 'Help yourself.'

Asta laid the cups and saucers out on the table as Hannah poured. 'Wasn't Dillon wonderful?'

'I suppose it depends on your point of view.'

'Oh, come now, Chief Inspector, that wretched man had it coming, deserved every minute of it.'

Hector Munro came in and went to the bar. As they watched he purchased half a bottle of whisky and turned to leave. He saw them sitting there, hesitated and came over.

'Ladies,' he said politely and then to Dillon in Gaelic, 'You'll be expecting my thanks, I'm thinking?'

'Not really,' Dillon said in Irish. 'How is he?'

'The hard head, that one, but that bastard hurt him.' He grinned suddenly. 'Mind you, you're a bit of a bastard yourself, Mr Dillon.'

He walked away and Asta said, 'Was that Gaelic?'

'That's right and I used Irish. They're very similar.'

'Was he thanking you for saving his son?' Hannah asked.

Dillon smiled. 'He never thanked anyone in his life, that one.'

Someone called, 'There you are,' and as they turned, Lady Katherine came through the crowd, leaning on her stick, Jeannie holding her other arm.

'My dear lady.' Ferguson got up. 'I'm amazed to see you, and in all this crowd of people.'

Jeannie helped her into a seat and Lady Katherine said, 'I have to put in an appearance; they expect it, you know.' She turned to Dillon. 'I saw you from a distance over the heads of the crowd. Rather a nasty business and hardly sporting. My goodness, he made a mess of your face.'

'True, ma'am, but he looks worse,' Dillon said.

She smiled and turned to Ferguson. 'I really must go, can't afford to overdo it, but I've been thinking.'

'Thinking, Lady Katherine?'

'Yes, the Bible. I've had a thought. Why don't you drop in on your way home? I'll discuss it with you.' She pushed herself up. 'Come on, Jeannie, let's make a move. Goodbye all.'

She moved away through the crowd, leaning on Jeannie's arm, and Hannah said, 'Now there's a turn-up for the book.'

'It certainly is,' Ferguson said. 'Frankly I can't wait to hear what she's got to say. What do you think, Dillon?'

Dillon lit a cigarette, frowning. 'Whatever it is, it's going to be special. I don't think she's going to say look at the back of the third drawer down in the writing desk in the study, or anything like that.' He nodded slowly. 'No, something we haven't even thought of.'

'And neither has Carl.' Asta turned to Ferguson. 'Can I come too, Brigadier? I'd love to see you steal a march on him.'

Ferguson smiled. 'Of course, my dear, why not? After all, you are on our side now.'

Dillon drove the Range Rover on the way to Loch Dhu Castle. Before leaving the fair he'd visited the first-aid tent and now sticking plaster adorned his right cheek, although the lady on duty from the St John's Ambulance Brigade had advised him to seek proper medical attention.

'Are you all right, my boy?' Ferguson asked as they got out in front of the gate lodge.

'I'm fine, just forget it,' Dillon grinned. 'It's all in the mind.'

Ferguson knocked on the door and Jeannie opened it after a few moments. 'Her ladyship is in the drawing room.'

Ferguson led the way in. Lady Katherine sat in a chair

by the fire, a rug over her knees. 'Ah, there you are. Come in, sit down. Tea and biscuits, Jeannie, and open the french windows. It's far too close in here.'

'Certainly, your ladyship.' Jeannie did as she was told.

Everyone settled down; Dillon leaned on the piano and lit a cigarette. 'This is nice,' he said.

'You can give me one of those cancer sticks, young man, and pass around that photo in the silver frame on the end of the piano.'

'Certainly, ma'am.' He did as he was told, lit the cigarette and went and got the photo. It showed a young woman in an RAF flying jacket and helmet of Second World War vintage standing beside a Spitfire. It was quite obviously Lady Katherine.

'You look like some film star in one of those old war films,' he said and passed it to Ferguson.

The Brigadier smiled. 'Amazing, Lady Katherine, truly amazing,' and he handed it to Hannah and Asta who were sitting together on the couch.

'Yes, those were the days. They gave me the MBE, you know. Telling you about it at dinner last night brought it all back. I started thinking about it all in the early hours today, couldn't sleep, you see. So many amazing incidents, all those brave women who died, and I suddenly recalled a rather strange affair. A wonderful flier called Betty Keith-Jopp was piloting a Barracuda over Scotland when she ran into bad weather. Landed in the Firth of Forth and sank forty feet. She got out and made the surface all right. Was picked up by a fishing boat.'

'Amazing,' Ferguson said, 'but what has that to do with the Bible?'

She said patiently, 'Because thinking of that reminded me of the Lysander that crashed into Loch Dhu while trying to land at Ardnamurchan RAF base. You see, I've remembered now; that was the plane carrying my brother's belongings.'

'It was nineteen-forty-six, March, as I recall. I should tell you that, besides the injury to his brain in that terrible crash in India, my brother sustained some quite severe burns to his right arm and hand, so when he was thought fit enough he was transferred to a place called East Grinstead.'

'Now that I do know about,' Ferguson said. 'It was the unit pioneered by Archibald McIndoe. He specialised in plastic surgery for aircrew who'd suffered severe burns.'

'A wonderful man,' she said. 'His patients weren't always RAF. My brother, for instance.'

'What happened?' Dillon asked her.

'Ian suffered a serious relapse that needed further brain surgery. Jack Tanner was with him, still acting as his batman. Anyway, they gave up on him, expecting him to die at any time.'

'So?' Ferguson said.

'At that time he had a visitor, an RAF officer who'd been a fellow patient for some months, but was now returned to duty, a Wing Commander Smith – Keith Smith. I believe he rose to some very senior rank later. It turned out that he had been given command of the RAF station on the Island of Stornoway in the Outer Hebrides and was due to fly up there in a Lysander, piloting himself.'

'A Lysander?' Asta asked. 'What kind of plane was that?'

'It was a high-wing-braced monoplane, a wheels-down job. Flew them myself many times. Room for a pilot and a couple of passengers. They could take off or land on quite a small field.'

Ferguson managed to restrain his impatience. 'I see, but where does Wing Commander Smith fit in?'

'Well, if he was flying to Stornoway, his course would take him right over here, you see, and Ardnamurchan

RAF base was still operational. As it seemed as if my brother was about to die, he told Jack Tanner that, if he gathered all Ian's belongings together, he'd take them with him, land at Ardnamurchan and drop them off. He would then refuel and fly on to Stornoway.'

'My God,' Hannah Bernstein sighed. 'I see it all now.'

Lady Katherine carried on. 'I was at home at the time on leave. The weather was very bad, a thunderstorm and low cloud. I didn't see it happen, I mean it was all so quick. He lost his engine on the final approach across the loch and ditched. It went down like a stone, but he just managed to get out with his dinghy.'

There was silence and it was Asta who spoke. 'It makes sense now. When Tanner was talking to Tony Jackson at Our Lady of Mercy Hospital he told Jackson that he sent all the Laird's belongings home because he thought he was going to die.'

'And Jackson asked him if the Bible had gone back to Loch Dhu,' Dillon put in.

'And Tanner said, "you could say that" and then, according to Jackson, he started to laugh.' Hannah nodded slowly. 'I always did wonder about that.'

'Well all is certainly revealed now.' Ferguson turned to Lady Katherine. 'No attempt at recovery?'

'They didn't have the equipment. Keith Smith came to see me, of course; lovely man. Strange thing about him. He hadn't been in fighters or bombers. He joked about being a transport pilot, but he had a DSO and two DFCs. I often wondered about that. No, as I say, they left the Lysander down there. Checked out its position and so forth, or so he told me.' She smiled. 'So, there you go. Poor old Ian's Bible is down there at the bottom of the loch in one of his suitcases, if there's anything left, of course. Now let's have some more tea.'

'We've taken up enough of your time, dear lady,' Ferguson told her.

'Nonsense, I insist.' She rang the bell for Jeannie.

Ferguson nodded to Dillon and walked to the french windows and Dillon followed him. As they moved out on to the terrace, Ferguson said, 'We've got to move fast now. I'll call in the Lear and I want you and the Chief Inspector to get down to London and check this out with RAF records.'

Dillon put a hand on his arm, frowning, and Ferguson turned to find Angus close to the wall, ivy on the ground at his feet, pruning shears in his hand.

'Why, Angus, it's you,' Ferguson said. 'Have you been there long?'

'Just doing some pruning, sir. I'm finished now.' He hurriedly bundled the clippings up, dumped them in his barrow and wheeled it away.

Hannah appeared in the open window, Asta at her shoulder. 'Do you think we were overheard?' Hannah asked.

'Of course we were,' Dillon told her. 'That's what the bastard was doing there. He'll go straight to Morgan.'

'Undoubtedly.' Ferguson turned to Asta. 'When you see Morgan you must cover yourself by telling him everything, do you understand? It will strengthen your position.'

'Yes,' she nodded.

'Good.' He looked at his watch. 'Three o'clock. If I contact the office now they'll have the standby Lear take off at once. Priority with air traffic control, so no delays.' He shrugged. 'Should be here by five at the latest. Immediate turn round and back to London.'

'And then?' Dillon said.

'Check RAF records and try to establish details of the Lysander's position and procure the right equipment for a search.' He smiled. 'It looks as if you're going diving again, Dillon.'

'So it would seem,' Dillon said.

Ferguson turned and went inside and they heard him say, 'I was wondering, dear lady, if I might use your telephone?'

TWELVE

IT WAS A GOOD two hours later that Asta saw the Shogun draw up in front of the house and Morgan and Marco get out. One side of the Sicilian's face was covered by a dressing and tape. Angus was lurking near the house and he hurried forward as Morgan and Marco started up the steps. They talked for quite a long time and then Morgan took out his wallet and passed several notes across. He started up the steps again with Marco and Asta eased back into the study and sat by the fire.

The moment the door opened and Morgan entered, she jumped up and ran to him. 'Thank God, you're back. Is Marco all right?'

'They took an x-ray. A couple of cracked ribs, but they're only hairline, and he's had stitches in his face.'

'Dillon needs stitches too,' she said.

'You saw him?'

'All of them, Carl. Lady Katherine invited us back for tea and came up with some sensational news.'

'Really?' he said and reached for a cigar. 'Tell me.'

When she was finished he paced across to the window and back again. 'That's it, it's got to be.'

'So what are you going to do?'

'Wait, my love; let them do all the work, Dillon's a master diver, remember. If they can position that plane, he'll go down and bring up what's inside.'

'And then?'

'We'll take it from there. I'll have the Citation standing by at Ardnamurchan so we can get out of here fast.'

'And you think Dillon and Ferguson will just stand by and let you take it.'

'I'll handle it, Asta.'

There was the sound of a plane taking off on the other side of the loch and they went to the terrace in time to see the Lear in the distance lifting into the early evening sky.

'There they go.' He smiled and put an arm about her shoulders. 'I feel good about this, Asta, it's going to work.'

'Of course the document could have rotted away by now,' she said, 'down there in the water.'

'True,' he said, 'but hidden in that Bible I don't think so.' He smiled. 'Trust me.'

In the Lear, Dillon sat on one side of the aisle facing Hannah who sat on the other. 'Exciting, isn't it?' he said. 'Never a moment's peace.'

'It's worse than Scotland Yard,' she said.

He reached for the bar box and found a miniature of whisky which he poured into a plastic cup and added water. 'All the comforts of home.'

'The water on its own would be better for you, especially at this height in an aeroplane, Dillon.'

'Isn't it terrible,' he said. 'I never could do the right thing.'

She settled back. 'So what happens now?'

'We find out what we can about the crash of that Lysander and so on.'

'RAF records from those days may be hard to uncover.'

'Yes, well it was Air Ministry in those days and now it's Ministry of Defence, where you work yourself. So if you can't trace them who can?' He grinned. 'Power, Hannah Bernstein, that's what it's all about. Better get on the phone and start them moving at the Information Centre.'

'No, that comes second,' she said, and reached for the phone. 'First we get your face fixed.'

'God help me,' Dillon said. 'The mother I never had,' and he folded his arms and closed his eyes.

They had a tail wind so strong that they made Gatwick in an hour and twenty minutes and it was only an hour after that, at approximately seven-thirty, that Dillon found himself lying on his back in a small theatre at the London Clinic while Professor Henry Bellamy sat beside him and stitched the split in the left cheek.

'Doesn't hurt?' he asked.

'Can't feel a thing,' Dillon said.

'Well you damn well ought to.' Bellamy dropped the needles into the pan the nurse held out to him. 'Major surgery at the highest level, I do some of my best work, even wrote a paper on your case. They published it in the *Lancet* . . .'

'Marvellous,' Dillon said. 'I'm immortalised for posterity.'

'Don't be silly.' Bellamy swabbed the line of stitches then put a length of plaster along them. 'I put you together again and then you go off and try to commit suicide.'

Dillon swung his legs to the floor, stood and reached for his jacket. 'I'm fine now. You're a bloody medical genius, so you are.'

'Flattery will get you nowhere, just pay your bill and, if you feel like telling me the secret of your remarkable recovery some time, I'd love to know.'

They went out into the corridor where Hannah Bernstein waited. 'Six stitches, Chief Inspector; that'll spoil his beauty.'

'You think that would bother this one?' Dillon asked.

Hannah pulled down the collar of his jacket which was standing up. 'He drinks whiskey of the Irish variety and smokes far too many cigarettes, Professor; what am I to do with him?'

'She didn't tell you I also play cards,' Dillon said.

Bellamy laughed out loud. 'Go on, get out of here, you rogue, I have work to do,' and he walked away.

The night-duty clerk at the Information Centre at the Ministry of Defence usually had little to do. She was a widow called Tina Gaunt, a motherly looking lady of fifty, whose husband, an army Sergeant, had died in the Gulf War. She was rather sweet on Dillon, had seen his confidential report, and, while horrified at his IRA background, had also been secretly rather thrilled.

'Second World War RAF records and the National Service period after the war are still available in the Hurlingham Cellars, as we call them, but they're out in Sussex. We do have a micro-fiche availability on the computer, of course, but it's usually more of an outline than anything else. I may not be able to help.'

'Sure and I can't believe that of a darling woman like yourself,' Dillon told her.

'Isn't he terrible, Chief Inspector?' Tina Gaunt said.

'The worst man in the world,' Hannah told her. 'Let's start with this service record. Wing Commander Keith Smith.'

'Right, here goes.' Her fingers went to work nimbly on the keys and she watched the screen, then paused, frowning. 'Wing Commander Smith, DSO, DFC and Bar, Legion of Honour. My goodness, a real ace.' She shook her head. 'I don't understand. My father was a Lancaster bomber pilot during the war. It's always been a bit of a hobby of mine – all those Battle of Britain pilots, the great aces – but I've never heard of this one.'

'Isn't that strange,' Hannah said.

Tina Gaunt tried again. She sat back a moment later. 'Even stranger, there's a security block. Just his rank and his decoration, but no service record.'

Hannah glanced at Dillon. 'What do you think?'

'You're the copper, do something about it.'

She sighed. 'All right, I'll telephone the Brigadier,' and she went out.

Tina Gaunt stood with the phone to her ear and nodded. 'All right, Brigadier, I'll do it, but you see my back's covered.' She put the phone down. 'The Brigadier's assured me that he'll have a grade one warrant on my desk signed by the Secretary of State for Defence tomorrow. In the circumstances, I've agreed to cut corners.'

'Fine,' Dillon said. 'Let's get moving, then.'

She started on the keyboard again and once again sat back frowning. 'I'm now cross-referenced to SOE.'

'SOE? What's that?' Hannah demanded.

'Special Operations Executive,' Dillon told her. 'Set up by British Intelligence on Churchill's orders to co-ordinate resistance and the underground movement in Europe.'

'"Set Europe ablaze", that's what he said,' Tina Gaunt told them and tapped the keys again. 'Ah, it's all explained.'

'Tell us,' Dillon said.

'There was a squadron at Tempsford, one-three-eight Special Duties. It was known as the Moonlight Squadron, all highly secret. Even the pilots' wives thought their husbands just flew transports.'

'And what did they do?' Hannah asked.

'Well, they used to fly Halifax bombers painted black to France and drop agents by parachute. They also flew them in by Lysander.'

'You mean, landed and took off again in occupied territory?' Hannah said.

'Oh, yes, real heroes.'

'So now we know how Wing Commander Keith Smith won all those medals,' Dillon said. 'When did he die?'

She checked her screen again. 'There's no date for that here. He was born in nineteen-twenty. Entered the RAF in nineteen-thirty-eight, aged eighteen. Retired as an Air Marshal in nineteen-seventy-two. Knighted.'

'Jesus,' Dillon said. 'Have you an address for him?'

She tried again and sat back. 'No home address and, as I said, the information on the fiche is limited. If you wanted more, you'd have to try the Hurlingham Cellars tomorrow.'

'Damn,' Dillon said. 'More time to waste.' He smiled. 'Never mind, you've done well, my love; God bless you.'

He turned to the door and Hannah said, 'I've had a thought, Tina, do you know about this place they had in East Grinstead during the war for burns patients?'

'But they still do, Chief Inspector; the Queen Victoria Hospital. Some of their wartime patients go back every year for check-ups and further treatment. Why?'

'Smith was a patient there. Burnt hands.'

'Well, I can certainly give you the number.' Tina checked the computer, then wrote a number on her note-pad, tore it off and passed it across.

'Bless you,' Hannah said and followed Dillon out.

In Ferguson's office it was quiet and she sat on the edge of his desk, the phone to her ear, and waited. Finally she got her answer.

'I see. Air Marshal Sir Keith Smith,' an anonymous voice said. 'Yes, the Air Marshal was here for his annual check in June.'

'Good, and you have his home address?' Hannah started to write. 'Many thanks.' She turned to Dillon. 'Hampstead Village, would you believe that?'

'Everything comes full circle.' Dillon glanced at his watch. 'Nearly half-ten. We can't bother the ould lad tonight. We'll catch him in the morning. Let's go and get a snack.'

They sat in the Piano Bar at the Dorchester, drinking champagne, and a waitress brought scrambled eggs and smoked salmon.

'This is your idea of a snack?' Hannah said.

'What's wrong with having the best if you can afford it? That thought used to sustain me when I was being chased through side streets and the sewers of the Bogside in Derry by British paratroopers.'

'Don't start all that again, Dillon, I don't want to know.' She ate some of her smoked salmon. 'How do you think we'll fare with the good Air Marshal?'

'I would imagine rather well. Anyone who could win all those medals and rise to the rank he did has got to be hot stuff. My bet is he's never forgotten a thing.'

'Well, we'll find out in the morning.' The waitress brought coffee and Hannah took out her notebook. 'You'd better give me a list of the diving equipment you're going to need and I'll get them started on it at the office first thing.'

'All right, here goes. The suppliers will know what everything is. A mask; nylon diving suit, medium, with a hood because it'll be cold; gloves, fins, four weight belts with twelve pounds in the pockets, a regulator, buoyancy control device and half a dozen empty air tanks.'

'Empty?' she said.

'Yes, we're flying rather high. You'll also get a portable Jackson Compressor, the electric type. I'll fill the tanks using that and an Orca dive computer.'

'Anything else?'

'Three hundred feet of nylon rope, snap links, a couple of underwater lamps and a big knife. That should take care of it. Oh, and a couple of Sterling sub-machine guns, the silenced variety.' He smiled. 'To repel boarders.'

She put the notebook in her handbag. 'Good, can I go now? We've got a big day tomorrow.'

'Of course.' They moved to the door and he paused to pay the bill. As they went out into the foyer, he said, 'You wouldn't consider stopping at Stable Mews on the way?'

'No, Dillon, what I'd really like to do is surprise my mother.'

Ferguson's driver eased the Daimler into the kerb, the Head Porter opening the door for her. 'I think that's marvellous,' Dillon said, 'it shows such an affectionate nature.'

'Stuff you, Dillon,' she said and the Daimler drew away.

'Taxi, sir?' the porter asked.

'No, thanks, I'll walk,' Dillon said and he lit a cigarette and strode away.

The house was in a quiet backwater not far from Hampstead Heath. It was just nine-thirty the following morning when Dillon and Hannah arrived in Ferguson's Daimler.

The chauffeur parked it in the street and they went in through a small gate in a high wall and walked through a small garden to the front door of a Victorian cottage. It was raining slightly.

'This is nice,' Hannah said as she rang the bell.

After a while it was opened by a middle-aged black woman. 'Yes, what can I do for you?' she asked in a West Indian accent.

'We're from the Ministry of Defence,' Hannah told her. 'I know it's early, but we'd very much like to see Sir Keith, if that's possible.'

'Not too early for him.' She smiled. 'He's been in the garden an hour already.'

'In this rain?' Dillon asked.

'Nothing keeps him out of that garden. Here, I'll show you.' She took them along a flagged path and round the corner to the back garden. 'Sir Keith, you've got visitors.'

She left them there and Hannah and Dillon walked to a small terrace with open french windows to the house. On the other side of the lawn they saw a small man in an anorak and an old Panama hat. He was pruning roses. He turned to look at them, his eyes sharp and blue in a tanned face that was still handsome.

He came forward. 'Good morning, what can I do for you?'

Hannah got her ID out and showed it to him. 'I'm Detective Chief Inspector Hannah Bernstein, assistant to Brigadier Charles Ferguson of the Ministry of Defence.'

'And my name is Dillon, Sean Dillon.' The Irishman held out his hand. 'I work for the same department.'

'I see.' The Air Marshal nodded. 'I'm familiar with Brigadier Ferguson's work. I served on the three services joint security committee for five years after I retired. Am I to assume this is a security matter?'

'It is indeed, Sir Keith,' she said.

'But it goes back a long way,' Dillon told him. 'To when you crashed a Lysander into Loch Dhu in the Scottish Highlands back in nineteen-forty-six.'

The old man said in astonishment, 'That *is* going back a bit. You'd better come inside and I'll get Mary to make some tea and we can talk about it,' and he led the way in through the french windows.

'That was so long ago,' Sir Keith said. His housekeeper brought tea in on a tray. 'That's all right, Mary,' he told her. 'We'll manage.'

'I'll pour, if I may,' Hannah said.

'Of course, my dear. Now what is it you want, exactly?'

'You met a Major Ian Campbell at East Grinstead burns unit,' Dillon said.

'I certainly did.' Sir Keith held up his hands. The skin was light and shiny and the middle finger was missing on the left one. 'That was from a run-in with an ME262, that was the jet fighter the Germans did so well with at the end of things. February, nineteen-forty-five. Blew me out of the sky over Northern France. I was in a Lysander, you see; no contest.'

'Yes, we checked your records at the Ministry of Defence,' Dillon said. 'Found out about your work for SOE. We had to pull strings for that. You're still classified.'

'Am I, by God.' He took the cup of tea Hannah offered and laughed.

'We got on to you through Ian Campbell's sister,' Hannah said. 'Lady Katherine Rose.'

'Good Lord, is she still alive? Was an ATA pilot in the war. Wonderful woman.'

'Yes, she still lives up there on the Loch Dhu estate,' Dillon said. 'It was she who told us about you coming down in the loch in a Lysander.'

'That's right, March of forty-six; I was on my way to a

new command at Stornoway; tried to land in damn bad weather at Ardnamurchan and lost my engine on the approach. I was lucky to get out. The plane sank almost at once.' He spooned sugar into his tea. 'But why are you interested in that?'

'Do you remember calling in at East Grinstead and finding Ian Campbell on the point of death?' Hannah asked.

'That's right, though I heard he recovered later.'

'You told his batman you were flying to Stornoway and offered to take his Laird's belongings and drop in at Ardnamurchan.'

'That's right, two suitcases; that was the reason I was going to land there anyway.' He looked slightly bewildered. 'But what's that got to do with it?'

'There was something of vital importance in one of those suitcases,' she said. 'Something of national importance.'

'Good heavens, what on earth could it be?'

She hesitated. 'Well, actually, Sir Keith, the matter is classified. We're acting on the Prime Minister's instructions.'

'Well, you would be if Ferguson's involved.'

Dillon turned to her. 'Jesus, girl, he was decorated from here to Christmas, knighted by the Queen and ended up an Air Marshal. If he can't keep a secret who can?'

'Yes, you're right,' she said. 'Of course you are.' She turned back to Sir Keith. 'Strictly in confidence.'

'My word on it.'

So she told him about the Chungking Covenant – everything.

Sir Keith searched in the bottom drawer of a bureau, found an old cardboard file and a folded map, which he brought across to the dining table.

'The file is a copy of the original accident report. There had to be a hearing, always is, but I was completely exonerated.' He held up his hands. 'The state of these never stopped me flying.'

'And the map?' Dillon asked.

'See for yourself, Ordnance Survey map of the area. Large-scale, as you can see.' He unfolded it. There was Loch Dhu, the Castle and Ardnamurchan Lodge. 'I was meticulous in noting my exact position after the Lysander went down. See the red line from the little jetty at Ardnamurchan Lodge? That's where I landed.'

Dillon ran a finger along the line. 'That seems clear enough.'

'One hundred and twenty yards south from the jetty. X marks the spot and I know I'm right because the boys from the base dragged for her with a grappling hook on a line and brought up a piece of fuselage.'

'How deep?' Dillon asked.

'About ninety feet. The Air Ministry decided it wasn't worth trying to recover her. It would have meant sending up special equipment, and the war, after all, was over. They were scrapping aircraft, so why bother. Different thing if there had been something of value down there.'

'Which there was, only nobody knew about it,' Hannah said.

'Yes, there's irony for you.' He turned to Dillon. 'You intend some sort of recovery, I presume?'

'Yes, I'm an experienced diver. I'll go down and see what I can find.'

'I shouldn't expect too much, not after all these years. Would you like the map?'

'I certainly would. I'll see you get it back.'

Hannah said, 'We've taken up enough of your time. You've really been more than helpful.'

'I certainly hope I have. I'll see you out.' He took them

to the front door and opened it. 'Forgive an old buffer like me, my dear, but I must say the police have improved since my day.'

On impulse, she kissed him on the cheek. 'It's been an honour to meet you.'

'Good luck, the both of you, with this Morgan fellow. Make sure he goes down, Dillon, and give Ferguson my regards.'

'I will,' Dillon said and they went down the path.

'Oh, and Dillon?' Sir Keith called as they reached the gate.

They turned and Dillon said, 'What is it?'

'If they're still there, you won't find two suitcases down there, there should be three and one of them's mine. Can't expect much after forty-seven years, but it would be fun to have it back.'

'I'll see that you do,' Dillon said and they went out.

They got into the Daimler and Hannah said, 'What an absolutely smashing man.'

'Yes, they don't make them like that any more,' Dillon said. 'Now what?'

'A place called Underseas Supplies located in Lambeth. They've got the order for those things you wanted. The manager said he'd have them ready by noon. He'd like you to check them out before he rushes them to Gatwick.'

'And the two Sterlings I asked for?'

'In the boot. I got them from the armourer at the Ministry before I picked you up this morning.'

'What a girl,' Dillon said. 'Let's get moving, then.'

The warehouse in Lambeth was crammed with diving equipment of every kind. The manager, a man called Speke, handled things himself and he and Dillon went through the list, checking each item off as they did so.

'There seems an awful lot,' Hannah said. 'Do you really need all this? I mean what's this thing?'

She held up a yellow coloured Orca and Dillon said, 'That's my lifeline, girl dear; a diving computer that tells me how deep it is, how long I've been down there, how long I've got to go. It even warns me if I'm coming up too fast.'

'I see.'

'I need it just like I need this.' He picked up the heavy nylon diving suit in orange and green. 'It's going to be very cold down there and very dark. It isn't the Caribbean.'

'About the visibility, Mr Dillon,' Speke said. 'The two lamps you asked for. I've given you the new Royal Navy halogen type. Twice the power.'

'Excellent,' Dillon said. 'That's it then. Get this lot up to Gatwick as soon as you can.'

'It'll take at least two hours, sir, maybe three.'

'Just do your best,' Hannah said.

As they got into the Daimler, Dillon said, 'What kind of time do you think we'll get off?'

'Three o'clock,' she said.

'Good.' He took her hand. 'You and I can take a little time off. What about Mulligan's for oysters and Guinness? After all, tomorrow I'll be diving down to God knows what.'

'Dammit, Dillon, why not?' She laughed. 'We've earned it. Oysters and Guinness at Mulligan's it is.'

THIRTEEN

THE FLIGHT FROM London Gatwick was reasonably smooth until the final stages when the weather deteriorated into low cloud and heavy rain. As they made their approach over the loch, Flight Lieutenant Lacey said over the loud speaker, 'Headquarters have notified the Brigadier of our arrival time. He's on his way.'

They dropped in for the touchdown and, as they rolled along the runway, they saw the Citation standing inside one of the hangars.

'Now what's that doing here?' Hannah said.

'I'd say it was on standby for a quick move out,' Dillon said. 'It makes sense. That's what I'd do.'

As he opened the door for them, Flight Lieutenant Lacey said, 'You've got company, Chief Inspector.'

'That's the personal plane of Mr Carl Morgan, presently of Loch Dhu Castle,' Dillon told him.

'The polo player?'

'Jesus, son,' Dillon laughed, 'and isn't that the grand way to describe him?'

The Range Rover was crossing the decaying tarmac towards them, Kim at the wheel, Ferguson beside him. It stopped and the Brigadier got out. 'Everything go well?'

'Couldn't be better,' Dillon told him. 'I've got a map of the loch with the exact location. By the way, guess who the pilot of that Lysander turned out to be?'

'Surprise me?'

'Air Marshal Sir Keith Smith,' Hannah told him.

Ferguson looked genuinely astonished. 'Of course! I didn't make the connection when Lady Katherine told us his name. I mean, nineteen-forty-six, a Wing Commander.'

Lacey said, 'We'll get all this stuff in the back of the Range Rover, Brigadier, if your man could lend a hand.'

'Of course.' Ferguson nodded to Kim then took a large golfing umbrella from inside the Range Rover and put it up against the rain.

'Morgan's plane seems to have taken up permanent residence,' Hannah said.

'Yes, the bastard's there himself keeping an eye on us; I saw their Shogun parked in the hangar beside the Citation. Probably got their field glasses turned our way right now.'

'Let's give them something to see, then,' Dillon said. 'Pass me those two Sterling sub-machine guns, Flight Lieutenant.'

Lacey handed them over and Ferguson smiled. 'What a happy thought. Hold the umbrella for me, Chief Inspector.' He checked one of the Sterlings expertly and then said,

'Right, let's move out into the open so they can see what we've got.'

Which he and Dillon did, standing in the rain for a few moments and then turning back to the Range Rover.

'That should do it,' Dillon said and put the Sterlings on the back seat.

'You looked like a couple of little boys then, playing gangsters in the school yard,' Hannah said.

'Ah, if it were only so, Chief Inspector, but the time approaches when this whole thing becomes serious business. I've just, in a manner of speaking, given Morgan fair warning, but let's make certain. We'll take a walk.'

He moved directly towards the hangar and the Citation and they moved with him, all three sheltered by the huge golfing umbrella. As they got close, they saw the Shogun – Marco and Morgan leaning against it. Two men in flying overalls were hanging around on the other side of the plane. Hannah slipped her right hand inside her handbag which hung from a shoulder strap low on her thigh.

'No need for that, Chief Inspector,' Ferguson murmured. 'He isn't about to declare war just yet.' He raised his voice. 'Ah, there you are, Morgan. Good day to you.'

'And a good day to you, Brigadier.' Morgan came forward, followed by Marco with his battered face who stood there glaring at Dillon.

'Successful trip, Chief Inspector?' Morgan asked.

'Couldn't have been better,' she told him.

'Who would have thought it?' He turned and looked out across the loch, quiet in the rain. 'Down there on the bottom for all these years. Place of Dark Waters, isn't that what the locals call it in Gaelic? Aptly named, Dillon. I should think you'll have problems down there.'

'Who knows?' Dillon told him.

'I see you've got your plane on standby,' Ferguson said.

'Yes, leaving at the crack of dawn. We've got an eight

o'clock start. Let's face it, Brigadier, you've won and I've certainly had enough of the delights of Loch Dhu Castle and this eternal bloody rain.'

'Really?' Ferguson said. 'Carl Morgan giving up? I find that difficult to believe.'

'Oh, he's just being a good sport, aren't you, Morgan?' Dillon said.

'But of course,' Morgan said calmly.

'Well, give our best to Asta as we probably shan't be seeing her again,' Ferguson told him.

'I will.'

'Good, we'll be off now.'

As they walked back to the plane Hannah said, 'I don't believe a word of it. He isn't going anywhere.'

'Or, if he is, he intends to come back,' Dillon said. 'I'm not sure how, but that's what he'll do.'

'Of course he will,' Ferguson said. 'We're back with the kind of games playing that's characterised this affair from the beginning. We know that he intends to return and he knows that we know.' He shook his head. 'Inconceivable that he'd give up now. It's against his nature. Have you ever seen him boot an opponent out of the saddle in a polo match? Well, that's Carl Morgan. He's always got to win, whatever it costs.'

'I'd say this is a situation Asta could help with, sir,' Hannah said.

'Yes, well we'll see.'

They reached the Lear and Lacey said, 'All in, Brigadier; is there anything else we can do?'

'Not at the moment, Flight Lieutenant, except return to Gatwick. As usual, I require a twenty-four-hour standby.'

'I'll see to it, Brigadier.'

'Good, on your way, then.' He turned. 'Come on, you lot. Let's move out.'

They got into the Range Rover, Kim behind the wheel,

and, as they drove away, the Lear was already starting up behind them.

Morgan went into the study and poured himself a brandy, then moved to the fire. He sipped the brandy slowly, savouring it, and the door opened and Asta came in.

'They arrived back, then, I heard the plane.'

He nodded. 'They unloaded a quantity of diving equipment and Ferguson and Dillon rather ostentatiously displayed a couple of Sterling sub-machine guns, all for my benefit. We had a nice chat.'

'And?'

'I told Ferguson I was retiring from the fray, flying out at eight in the morning.'

'And they believed you?'

He smiled. 'Of course not. Ferguson knows damn well I'll return in some way. Of course, the important thing is that I know that he expects that, so it's all a question of timing.'

'How do you mean?'

He smiled. 'There's a bottle of champagne over there in the bucket, my love. Go and open it and I'll tell you.'

At Ardnamurchan Lodge, the light was on in the garage, the diving equipment arranged neatly on the floor. There was a steady hum from the compressor as Dillon showed Kim how to fill the first air tank.

Hannah came in and stood watching, arms folded. 'Does he know what he's doing?'

'Kim?' Dillon laughed. 'I've just shown him, haven't I, and you only show a Gurkha something once. He said to Kim, 'All six.'

'Yes, *sahib*, I'll take care of it.'

Dillon followed Hannah in through the side door and through the kitchen to the sitting room where they found Ferguson sitting at the desk.

'He glanced up. 'All in order?'

'So far,' Dillon said.

'Good, so the plan is simple. As soon as Morgan leaves in the Lear, we get to work. You hold the fort in the house, Chief Inspector, while Kim and myself go out with Dillon in the whale boat.'

'Dillon, I'm totally ignorant about diving,' she said, 'so forgive my questions that seem stupid. Just how difficult will it be and just how long will it take?'

'Well, to start with, I'll go down very fast, my weight belt helps with that. If Sir Keith's positioning is accurate I could be on to the plane in minutes, but it's going to be dark down there and there's no way of knowing what the bottom's like. There could be ten feet of sludge. Another thing, the depth is important. The deeper you go the more air you use. It's astonishing how much ten or fifteen feet reduces your bottom time. Ideally, I'd like to do this dive within sport-diving limits because, if I can't, I'll have to decompress on the way up and that takes time.'

'Why, exactly?'

'The deeper you go and the longer you're there, the more nitrogen you get in your bloodstream. It's like fizz in a bottle of champagne wanting to burst out. It can give you the bends, cripple you and sometimes kill you.' He smiled. 'Here endeth the lesson.'

'I must say, it all sounds rather heavy to me.'

'I'll be all right.' He went and helped himself to a Bushmills. 'I've had a thought, though, Brigadier.'

'What's that?'

'Have Kim up at the airstrip in the morning with a pair of field glasses. I mean, we'll hear that plane leave, but let's make sure it doesn't just have the pilots on board.'

'Good idea,' Ferguson said. He glanced at his watch. 'Eleven o'clock. I've had an even better idea, Dillon;

another of your little night forays up at the Castle. See if you can have a word with Asta.'

'I'm surprised we haven't heard from her,' Hannah said.

'I'm not, too damn dangerous for the girl to use the phone, unless she's absolutely certain Morgan isn't around,' Ferguson told her. 'No, you take Dillon up there like you did the other night, Chief Inspector, and we'll see what happens.'

It was still raining as Hannah turned in at the side of Loch Dhu Castle and switched off the engine. As on the previous occasion, Dillon wore black. He took out his Walther and tested it, then put it into his waistband at the rear.

'Seems to me we've done this before.'

'I know.' Hannah smiled. 'You'll have to think of a variation.'

He pulled the sinister ski-mask on, leaving only his eyes and lips visible. 'I could always give you a kiss.'

'While you're wearing that thing? Don't be disgusting, Dillon. Go on, on your way.'

The door closed gently and he disappeared into the darkness in a second.

He negotiated the wall in the same way as before and made his way through the grounds to the lawn and paused in the trees, looking across at the lights of the Castle. After a while the french windows to the study opened and Morgan appeared smoking a cigar, followed by Asta wearing a sweater and slacks, an umbrella in her hand.

'What are you going to do?' Morgan demanded.

'Walk the dog. You can come too, Carl.'

'In this rain? You must be crazy. Don't be too long,' he told her and turned back inside.

She put the umbrella up and moved down the steps of the terrace. 'Come on, boy,' she called and the Doberman came out of the study in a flash and hurried across the lawn.

There was a small summer house and Dillon moved to stand to one side of it. The dog stopped dead and whined. Dillon gave that peculiar low whistle and it bounded to his side and licked his hand gently.

'Where are you, boy?' Asta said.

'Over here,' Dillon said softly.

'It's you, Dillon.' She hurried forward and stood there, clutching the umbrella. 'What are you up to this time?'

'Oh, I didn't want to let you go without a word,' he said. 'You are leaving in the morning, that's right, isn't it?' He pulled off his ski-mask.

'Eight o'clock,' she said.

'Yes, that's what Morgan told us at the airfield. So graceful in defeat he was. So bloody graceful that we didn't believe a word of it. He's coming back, isn't he, Asta?'

She nodded. 'He didn't expect you to believe him, that's what he told me. He said you'd expect him to return so the only thing to get right was the timing.'

'All right, tell me.'

'We leave at eight in the Citation. Carl said he would anticipate you making the dive the moment we're on our way.'

'Then what?'

'You know how far Arisaig is?'

'About twenty miles.'

'Exactly. There's another ex-RAF airstrip there like Ardnamurchan. He and Marco took the estate car down there and came back in the Shogun. The Citation will land there after leaving Ardnamurchan. We'll come back by road in the estate car. The pilots will give it an hour then fly back to Ardnamurchan.'

'Where we'll have been caught with our pants down?' Dillon said.

'Exactly.'

'Oh, well, we'll have to see what we can come up with.' He put a hand on her shoulder. 'You're managing, are you?'

'Yes,' she said. 'I'm managing just fine.'

'Good for you.' He pulled on the ski-mask. 'Keep the faith,' and he disappeared into the darkness.

Carl Morgan appeared on the terrace. 'Are you there, Asta?'

'Yes, Carl, I'm coming,' she said and went across the lawn, the umbrella raised, her hand in the dog's collar.

Kim was at the airstrip by seven-thirty. He hadn't taken the car, in case he was seen, and lay on the edge of a small copse with a pair of field glasses and observed the Citation in the hangar. He could see the two pilots walking around doing their checks and, after a while, the Shogun appeared. It stopped just outside the hangar and Morgan and Asta got out. The two pilots came forward, there was a brief conversation and they got the luggage out. As Morgan and Asta went into the hangar, Marco drove the Shogun inside.

Kim waited. After a while the engines fired and the Citation moved out into the open and taxied to the end of the runway, turning into the wind. He watched it race to the end of the runway and lift into the grey sky, then got up and ran back to the Lodge.

Dillon had his diving suit on and was already pushing a wheelbarrow loaded with four air tanks down to the little jetty where Hannah and Ferguson waited in the whaler. It was raining unmercifully and yet, in spite of it, there was a cloud of mist ten or twelve feet high rolling across the water, reducing visibility considerably. Ferguson wore an anorak and a rain hat, Hannah was wearing an old raincoat and trilby she had found in the cloakroom. There was a smaller rowing boat, several inches of water swishing around inside it.

As Hannah got out of the whaler to meet him he said, 'Pull that one out of the way.'

She did as he said and, as he started to pass the air tanks down to Ferguson, there was the sound of the plane taking off. 'There they go,' Ferguson said.

'Right,' Dillon told him. 'I'll make do with the four tanks. With any kind of luck I won't even need all of them. I'll get the rest of my gear.'

He pushed the wheelbarrow back up to the lodge, loaded it with everything else, including the two Sterlings. As he started back down to the jetty, Kim came out of the trees on the run. He caught up with Dillon just before he reached the whaler.

'You saw them go?' Ferguson demanded.

'Yes, *sahib*, they arrived in the Shogun. I saw Morgan and the lady get out and go inside to the plane. The man, Marco, was there too. He drove the Shogun into the hangar. The plane came out and took off very quickly.'

'You mean they got on inside the hangar?' Dillon said.

'Yes, *sahib*.'

Dillon frowned, pausing as he handed the rest of the gear down, and Ferguson said, 'You're worried.'

'For some reason, yes.'

'I can't see why. He himself told us he was going. We expected him to try and work a flanker on us and Asta told us exactly what he planned. And Kim did see them leave.'

'He saw the plane leave,' Dillon said, 'but what the hell, let's get moving.'

Kim jumped down into the whaler and Dillon passed everything down. Ferguson put the two Sterlings on the stern seat. 'One thing is certain, dear boy, anyone who tried to take us on when we've got those things to repel boarders would have to be crazy.'

'Let's hope so.' Dillon handed Hannah up. 'Now you take care.'

She took a Walther from her pocket. 'Don't worry, I've got this.'

'Well, I do worry, that's how I've lasted as long as I have.'

He dropped into the boat, went to the stern and started the outboard motor. Hannah unfastened the line and tossed it into the boat. 'Good luck,' she called as they eased away.

'Like I said, take care; the foolish one you can be on occasions, though lovable with it,' Dillon called and took the whaler round in a broad curve.

Hannah watched them go, then turned and walked back up to the lodge. She went in the front door, took off the raincoat and the old trilby hat. She was cold and her feet were damp. She shivered, and decided to make a cup of coffee and went into the kitchen. She started to fill the kettle at the sink. There was a slight eerie creaking behind her. The larder door swung open and Hector Munro stepped out, a sawn-off shotgun in his hands.

And her Walther was in the raincoat. Ah, God, Dillon, she thought, you're right, I am a fool. She turned and darted to the open kitchen door, straight into Rory Munro. Like his father, he carried a sawn-off and he held her easily in one arm.

His face looked terrible, raw and bruised, but he smiled for all that. 'And where would you be going, darling?'

He pushed her gently back into the room where Hector sat on the edge of the table filling his pipe. 'Now be a good lassie and you'll come to no harm. There's a nice dry cellar for you, we've already checked.'

'No windows to break out of, mind you,' Rory said,

'and an oak door with double bolts that you'd need a fire axe to break through.'

'Aye,' Munro told her. 'You'll do well enough, not even a need to tie your wrists.'

'See how lucky you are?' Rory said.

She stepped away from him and went to the other side of the kitchen to face them. 'You're working for Morgan, aren't you? But why?' She gestured to Rory. 'Remember what happened in the boxing ring. Look at what that animal Marco did to your son's face.'

'But Mr Morgan wasn't responsible for that; a bit of sport, surely. My lad can take his knocks.' The old man put a match to his pipe. 'And then there is the question of the ten thousand pounds we're getting for helping him.'

'What does he intend to do?'

'Ah, well, you'll have to wait and see, won't you?' Hector Munro told her.

She took a deep breath. 'I'm a police officer, did you know that?'

Rory laughed out loud and Munro said, 'What bloody nonsense are you trying now, girl? Everybody knows you're secretary to the Brigadier.'

'I can show you my ID, let me get it. I'm a Detective Chief Inspector at Scotland Yard.'

'Detective Chief Inspector?' Munro shook his head sadly. 'Events have turned her wits, Rory.' He got up, walked to the cellar door and opened it. 'Down with her.'

Rory shoved her through, the door closed, the bolts rammed home. She lost her balance and slipped several steps, banging a knee painfully. And then she remembered the one thing she should have said, the one thing that might have had an effect: *Fergus*.

She went up the steps, found the switch and turned it on and light came on down in the cellar. She hammered on the door with clenched fists.

'Let me out,' she called. 'I've got something to tell you. He killed your son, he killed Fergus.'

But by that time there was no one there to answer her.

Hector Munro and his son walked down towards the jetty in the rain. They could hear the whaler's outboard, but couldn't see the boat itself because of the mist. They went along the jetty and paused beside the rowing boat.

'Dammit, there's nine inches of water in the bottom,' Rory said.

'And a bucket under the seat for you to bale her out with, so get on with it.' Hector took out an old silver watch on a chain and consulted it. 'Not that we're in a hurry. We've got thirty minutes to wait, by my reckoning.'

Rory had laid down the shotgun and got into the rowing boat, cursing as water slopped over his boots. He looked up into the rain. 'By God, it's to be hoped Fergus has a roof of some sort over his head, wherever he is.'

'Never mind, he won't need to keep out of the way much longer, they'll all be away out of it,' Hector Munro told him. 'Now get on with it, boy.'

Rory picked up the bucket and started to bale.

Ferguson took over the tiller while Dillon consulted the map. After a while the Irishman said, 'It's got to be about here.' He turned and could just see the chimneys of the lodge above the mist, the wood behind. 'Yes, that's the line according to Sir Keith's notation on this map. Kill the engine.' They almost stopped, drifting slowly, and he turned to Kim to find the Gurkha already putting the anchor over.

Dillon had cut the great coil of nylon rope into two lengths of one hundred feet with snap links on the ends. He tied a weight belt to each of them and turned to Kim who was securing them round the centre seat.

'Over we go,' Dillon said and the Gurkha slipped them over.

Dillon pulled up the cowl of his diving suit, strapped the knife in its orange sheath to his leg. Then he assembled his equipment, clamping a tank to his inflatable. The Orca computer went out on the line of his air pressure gauge then Kim helped him into the jacket, taking the weight of the tank until Dillon had strapped the Velcro wrappers across his chest. He fastened the weight belt around his waist then pulled on his gloves. He sat down to get his fins on. It was all very awkward because of the size and shape of the boat, but that couldn't be helped. He got one of the lamps and looped it round his left wrist. He spat in his mask, leaned over and swilled it in the water and pulled it on. Then he sat on the thwart, checked that the air was flowing freely through his mouthpiece, waved at Ferguson and went over backwards.

He swam under the keel of the boat until he found the anchor line which, adopting the usual procedure, he followed down, pausing a couple of times to equalise the pressure in his ears by swallowing hard. To his surprise, the water was quite clear – dark, but rather like black glass.

He went feet first, hauling himself down the anchor line, aware of the other two lines they had put down close at hand. He checked his Orca computer. Forty, then suddenly sixty, seventy, seventy-five. It was darker here and he switched on the powerful lamp and there was the bottom.

It wasn't as he had expected, nothing like the silt he had looked for. Instead, large patches of sand in between a kind of seagrass, great fronds waving to and fro in the current at least six feet in length.

He hovered, checking the computer to see how long he had, then moved away from the anchor line, the beam of the halogen light splayed out in front of him, and there it was, a dark shadow at first, tilted up on its nose, tail high.

The Bristol Perseus engine was quite visible due to fuselage corrosion and the triple propeller was still there. The canopy had been pushed back, obviously when Smith had got out fast after hitting the surface of the loch. There was a corrugated metal ladder leading up to the passenger section and, beside it, the outline of RAF roundels.

Dillon went into the pilot's section headfirst. It was all still intact in a kind of skeleton form, the instrument panel, the control column. He turned and pressed into the passenger section. There were two seats, only the tubular construction remaining, leather and cloth long since rotted away.

The suitcases were there, as for some strange reason he had always known they would be. One was metal, the other two leather, and when he touched one of those, it started to crumble. He ran his hand across the metal one and the faint etching of a name appeared. There were three words. The first two were hopelessly faded but when he rubbed with his gloved hand, the lamp held close, the name Campbell was plain.

He backed, pulling the metal case out first, depositing it on the sand beside the Lysander, then he went back for the other two. The first one stayed reasonably intact but the second seemed to come apart in his hand. When it burst open, he caught a brief glimpse of decaying clothes, some corroded toilet articles, what was left of an RAF sidecap and the remnants of a tunic with RAF pilot's wings above medal ribbons. Keith Smith's case obviously. Dillon scrabbled in the detritus and came up with a blackened silver cigarette case. Something to take back to the old boy at least. He stuffed it into one of the pockets in his inflatable, then swam back to where the two downlines from the whaler dangled to the bottom. He fastened the case to one of the line's snap links then returned to the metal case, brought it back with him and fastened it to the end of the other line.

234

He paused, making sure that everything was in order, then started up, one foot a second.

Ferguson and Kim, waiting in the heavy rain, suddenly became aware of the sound of an engine. Quickly Ferguson picked up one of the Sterlings, handed it to Kim and reached for the other himself. He cocked it quickly.

'Don't hesitate,' he said to Kim. 'If it's Morgan and the man, Marco, they'll kill us without the slightest hesitation.'

'Have no fear, *sahib*, I have killed many times, as the *sahib* well knows.'

A voice called high and clear, 'Is that you, Brigadier, it's Asta.'

Ferguson hesitated and said to Kim, 'Stay ready.'

The Loch Dhu Castle boat, the *Katrina*, drifted out of the mist, Asta at the wheel in the deck house. She wore rubber boots, a white sweater and jeans.

'It's only me, Brigadier, can I come alongside?'

'What on earth's going on?' Ferguson said. 'Kim saw you leaving in the Citation.'

'Oh, no,' she said. 'That was Carl and Marco. He told me to go back to the Castle in the Shogun and wait for him. Did you see me go into the hangar, Kim?'

'Oh, yes, *memsahib*.'

'It was Morgan and Marco who boarded the plane. I drove back in the Shogun afterwards.'

Kim turned to Ferguson and said awkwardly, 'I am sorry, Brigadier *sahib*, I left as the plane took off. I did not see the *memsahib* drive away.'

'Never mind that now.' Ferguson put down the Sterling. 'Take the line from the *memsahib* and tie her boat alongside.'

She switched off the engine and came to the rail. 'Is Dillon down there now?'

'Yes, dropped in about fifteen minutes ago.'

'How very convenient.' The door to the saloon opened and Carl Morgan emerged, a Browning Hi-Power in his hand and Marco behind him holding an Israeli Uzi sub-machine gun.

FOURTEEN

At that precise moment Dillon broke through to the surface and floated there, looking up at them all. He raised his mask.

'Asta, what is this?'

'It means we've been had, I'm afraid,' Ferguson said.

Dillon looked straight up at her. 'You're on his side, in spite of what he did to your mother?'

Morgan's face turned dark with anger. 'I'll take pleasure in making you pay for that filthy lie. Asta told me all about it. I loved my wife, Dillon, more than anything in this life. She gave me the daughter I'd never had and you think I could have killed her?'

There was silence, only the sound of the rain hissing into the loch. Dillon said, 'I'd say you're well suited to each other.'

Morgan put an arm round her. 'She did her work well telling you about my plan to fly to Arisaig, omitting the fact that we didn't actually intend to get on the plane. I knew one of you would be waiting, probably that man of yours, Ferguson, so we just stayed in the hangar until he'd gone. I saw him running off into the trees through my field glasses. Then all that was needed was Asta to pilot the boat while Marco and I stayed below and the poor old Brigadier fell for it, Dillon. Strange how I always get my way, isn't it?'

'Yes,' Ferguson said. 'I must say you have excellent connections. Probably with the Devil.'

'But of course.' Morgan raised his voice. 'Are you there, Munro?'

'On our way in,' Munro called and the rowing boat appeared, Rory at the oars.

'What about the woman?'

'Locked her in the cellar.'

They bumped against the hull of the motor cruiser and climbed on board.

Morgan looked down at Dillon. 'So here we are at the final end of things. Did you find the plane?'

Dillon just floated there, staring up at him and Morgan said, 'Don't fuck with me, Dillon; if you do I'll blow the Brigadier's head off, and that would be a pity because I've got plans for him.'

'Really?' Ferguson said.

'Yes, you're going to love this. I'll take you back to Palermo with me and then we'll sell you to one of the more extreme Arab fundamentalist groups in Iran. You should fetch a rather high price. They'd love to get their hands on a British Intelligence officer as senior as you, and you know what those people are like, Ferguson, they'll take the skin off you inch by inch. Before they've finished you'll be singing like a bird.'

'What a vivid imagination you have,' Ferguson said.

Morgan nodded to Marco who fired a burst from the Uzi into the water close to Dillon. 'Now don't mess with me, Dillon, or I swear the next burst takes your boss apart.'

'All right, I get the picture.' Dillon put in his mouth-piece, pulled down his mask and let himself sink.

He didn't bother with the anchor line, simply jack-knifed half-way down and continued headfirst, reaching the bottom to the left of the Lysander above a forest of waving fronds. When he turned on his lamp, the first thing he saw was Fergus Munro on his back, a length of chain wrapped around his body. His face was swollen and bloated, the eyes staring, but he was completely recognisable. Dillon hovered, looking down at him, then pulled out his knife and cut the rope that held the chain. The body bounced from the bottom and he got a grip on Fergus's jacket and towed the corpse back to the downlines.

He left it on the sandy bottom, untied the flimsier case and went and clipped it beside the metal case on the other line. Then he went back to the body, towed it across to the second downline and tied it on, winding the rope round the waist and fastening it with the snap link. Then he pulled on the line that secured the cases and started up.

Kim and Ferguson were still hauling the line in when Dillon surfaced. He floated beside the cases, untied the leather one and passed it up to Kim. It was already falling apart and broke in the Gurkha's hands, spilling a mass of rotting clothes on to the deck.

'That's no bloody good,' Morgan said, leaning over the rail and looking down into the whaler. 'The other one, Dillon, the other.'

Dillon pushed the metal suitcase against the hull and Ferguson and Kim reached over to get it. Dillon murmured, 'If you get a chance to jump, I can give you air under the surface, but only one of you. In a minute I'll be going down again and I want you to haul in the other line, Kim, it's vital.'

'Thanks for the offer,' Ferguson whispered. 'But I've never even liked swimming. What you suggest is a quite appalling prospect. Kim might feel differently.'

'Hurry it up!' Morgan called.

They got the suitcase over and into the bottom of the whaler. The metal was blackened and streaked with green seaweed.

'Get it open,' Morgan ordered.

Ferguson tried the clasps on the locks, but they were rigid. 'Damn thing's corroded, won't budge.'

'Well, try harder.'

Dillon pulled the knife from his leg sheath and handed it up to Kim who forced it behind the two clasps in turn and ripped them off, then he worked the point of the knife under the edge of the lid and prised. Quite suddenly, the lid lifted. There were clothes inside, mildewed but in surprisingly good condition. There was a uniform tunic on top, still recognisable with Major's crowns on the epaulettes.

'Come on, damn you!' Morgan was intensely excited as he leaned over the rail. 'Empty it out!'

Kim turned the case over, spilling its contents into the bottom of the whaler and found it at once, a book-size package wrapped in yellow oilskin.

'Open it, man, open it!' Morgan ordered.

It was Ferguson who unwrapped the oilskin, layer by layer, until he held in his hand the Bible, its silver blackened by the years.

'It would seem to be what we've all been looking for,' he said.

240

'Go on, get it open, see if it's still there.'

Ferguson took the knife from Kim and ran its point along the inside of the front cover. The secret compartment flicked open, the folded document inside, immediately apparent. Ferguson unfolded it, read it, then he looked up, face calm.

'Yes, this would appear to be the fourth copy of the Chungking Covenant.'

'Give it to me,' and Morgan reached down. Ferguson hesitated and Marco raised the Uzi threateningly. 'You can die now,' Morgan said, 'it's your choice.'

'Very well.' Ferguson passed up the document.

'Now get up here yourself,' Morgan told him and turned. 'As for you, Dillon . . .'

But Dillon had gone, dropping under the surface. Marco fired a futile burst into the water and Kim ducked and kept hauling on the line and suddenly Fergus Munro's body surfaced, a totally macabre sight.

'God help me, it's Fergus!' Hector Munro called, leaning over the rail.

Rory joined him, staring down into the water. 'What happened to him, Da?'

'Ask your friend Morgan. He and his henchman here beat him to death,' Ferguson said.

'You bastards!' Hector Munro cried and he and Rory turned, their shotguns coming up too late as Marco raked both of them with a long burst from the Uzi, driving them over the rail into the water.

'Get out of it, Kim!' Ferguson cried and the Gurkha dived headfirst from the whaler into the dark water, pulling himself down with powerful strokes as Marco sprayed the water behind him.

There is a technique known to any experienced diver as buddy breathing by which, if there is no alternate source of air available, it is possible to share your air supply with a companion by passing the regulator back and forth between you. Dillon, at twelve feet, reached up and caught Kim by the foot, pulled him close, took out his mouthpiece and passed it across. The hardy little warrior, a veteran of thirty years of campaigning, understood at once, took in a supply of air then passed it back.

Dillon started to kick with his fins, making for the shore, pulling Kim along beside him and sharing the air supply as they went. After a while he raised his thumb and started up, surfacing into a cocoon of mist, no sign of the boats at all. A moment later, Kim came up beside him, coughing.

Dillon said, 'What happened after I dived?'

'When the body surfaced, the Munros went crazy. Marco shot both of them with the Uzi.'

'And the Brigadier?'

'Cried to me to jump, *sahib*.'

Dillon could hear the motor cruiser moving away at high speed, but not across the loch in the direction of the Castle.

'Where in the hell are they going?' he said.

'There is that old concrete jetty the RAF used just below the airstrip, *sahib*,' Kim told him. 'Perhaps they're making for that.'

'And a quick departure,' Dillon said, and at that moment there was a thunder of engines overhead as Morgan's Citation made its approaches.

Dillon said, 'Right, we can't be far from the jetty so let's get moving,' and he made for the shore.

They landed ten minutes later. Dillon stripped off his equipment and ran towards the house, still wearing his diving suit, Kim jogging at his heels. The Irishman flung open the front door, ran into the study and opened the top drawer in the desk. There was a Browning in there. As he checked it, Kim came in.

'*Sahib*?'

'I'm going up to the airstrip. You get the *memsahib* from the cellar and tell her what's happened.'

He ran outside and cut across the back lawn. No point in taking the Range Rover, he'd be quicker on foot, and the rubber and nylon diving socks he wore protected his feet. He ran into the wood, weaving in and out among the trees, aware that the engines of the Citation hadn't stopped. As he emerged from the wood, he could see it taxiing to the end of the runway and turning into the wind. At the same moment, Morgan and Asta, Marco holding the Uzi against Ferguson's back, came round the corner of the main hangar and started towards the Citation. Dillon stopped running and watched helplessly as they boarded. A moment later the Citation roared along the runway and lifted into the sky.

When Dillon arrived back at Ardnamurchan Lodge and went in the door Hannah rushed to meet him. 'What happened? I heard the plane taking off.'

'Exactly. Morgan had it all worked out. He didn't even go back to the Castle. Not a minute wasted. I arrived in time to see them boarding, he and Asta, Marco and the Brigadier. They took off straight away.'

'I've been on to headquarters. I've asked them to check the flight plan they filed.'

'Good. Get straight on to them again and order Lacey to get up here in the Lear like it was yesterday.'

'I've ordered that too, Dillon,' she said.

'Nothing like Scotland Yard training. I'm going to change.'

★

243

When he returned he was wearing black jeans, a white polo neck sweater and his old black flying jacket. Hannah was in the sitting room at Ferguson's desk, the telephone at her ear. Kim came in with a jug of coffee and two cups.

She put the phone down. 'They were routed to Oslo.'

'That makes sense. He wanted to be out of our air space fast. Then what?'

'Refuelling then onwards to Palermo.'

'Well, that's what he said his intended destination was. He's taking the Covenant to Luca.'

'And the Brigadier?'

'Didn't Kim tell you? He's going to sell him to some Arab fanatics or other in Iran.'

'Can't we stop him in Oslo?'

Dillon looked at his watch. 'The rate that thing goes he'll be just about landing. Can you imagine how long it would take to go through Foreign Office channels to the Norwegian Government? No chance, Hannah, he's long gone.'

'Then that leaves the Italian Government, Palermo.'

Dillon lit a cigarette. 'The best joke I've heard in a long time. This is Don Giovanni Luca we're talking about, the most powerful man in Sicily. He has judges killed to order.'

She was upset now and it showed, her face very pale. 'We can't let them get away with it, Dillon; Morgan and that conniving little bitch.'

'Yes, she was good, wasn't she?' He smiled bleakly. 'She certainly fooled me.'

'Oh, to hell with your damned male ego, it's the Brigadier I'm thinking of.'

'And so am I, girl dear. You get back to headquarters and tell them you want to contact Major Paolo Gagini of the Italian Secret Intelligence Service in Palermo. He should be more than interested. After all he's the one who brought the story of the Covenant to Ferguson in the first place. He's also the expert on Luca, according to the file you showed me. Let's see what he can come up with.'

'Right, good thinking.' She picked up the phone and got to work, and Dillon walked out to the terrace, lit a cigarette and looked out into the rain, wondering about it.

He was aware of Hannah's voice on the phone, but was somewhere else, thinking of Ferguson and what would happen to him in Iran, and that was too awful to contemplate. Strange, but it was only now in a situation like this that he realised he actually had a certain affection for the Brigadier. He also thought about Morgan with a kind of cold killing rage, and as for Asta . . .

Hannah came to the open french windows. 'I've got Gagini on the phone from Palermo. I've filled him in on the situation and he wants to speak to you.'

Dillon went in and picked up the phone. 'Gagini, I've heard good things about you,' he said in Italian. 'What can we do in this thing?'

'I've heard of you too, Dillon. Look, you know what the situation is like here. Mafia everywhere. If I get a court order, which would be difficult, it would take time.'

'What about Immigration and Customs at the airport?'

'Half of them have Mafia connections, just like the police. Any move I make at an official level, Luca will know about within fifteen minutes.'

'There must be something you can do.'

'Leave it with me. I'll phone back in an hour.'

Dillon put the phone down and turned to Hannah. 'He's calling back in an hour. He's going to see what he can do.'

'This is nonsense,' she said. 'All they have to do is meet the damn plane with a police squad.'

'Have you ever been to Sicily?'

'No.'

'I have. It's another world. The minute Gagini makes an

official request for the police to meet that plane, someone will reach for a phone to inform Luca.'

'Even from police headquarters?'

'Especially from police headquarters, the Mafia's fingers reach everywhere. Scotland Yard it's not, Hannah. If Luca thought there was a problem he'd contact Morgan and tell him to go elsewhere, perhaps even tell him to fly direct to Teheran and that's the last thing we want.'

'So what do we do?'

'We wait for Gagini to phone back,' he said, turned and went outside again.

And when Gagini did phone just under an hour later he sounded excited. 'My sources tell me the Citation isn't booked to land at Palermo.'

'They must have a flight plan, even in Sicily,' Dillon said.

'Of course, my friend, just listen. Carl Morgan has an old farmhouse inland from Palermo at a place called Valdini. He doesn't use it much. There's just a caretaker and his wife in residence. It's an old family property.'

'So?' Dillon glanced at Hannah who was listening on the extension.

'The thing is, Morgan had an airstrip laid out there the other year, probably to be used for drug deliveries. It's grass, but open meadow about a mile long, so it's perfectly adequate for the Citation to land.'

'Are you saying that's what he intends to do?'

'That's what the flight plan says.'

'But what about Customs and Immigration?' Hannah broke in.

'All taken care of by Luca, Chief Inspector.'

Dillon said, 'Can we get in?'

'I doubt it. That's real Mafia country. You couldn't pass through a village without being noted, every shepherd boy

246

on a hill with his flock is like a sentry. Troop movements, as with the police, are an impossibility.'

'I see,' Dillon said.

There was a sudden roar as the Lear from Gatwick passed overhead to make its landing.

'What do you want me to do, my friend?'

'Let me think about it. Our plane has just arrived. I'll let you know. The only certain thing is that we'll be coming to Palermo.'

He replaced the phone, as did Hannah. 'It doesn't sound too good, does it?' she said.

'We'll see. Now let's get out of here.'

Lacey came along from the cockpit and crouched down. 'An hour to Gatwick. We'll refuel and get straight off to Palermo.'

'Good,' Dillon said. 'Speed is of the essence on this one, Flight Lieutenant.'

Kim lay back in one of the rear seats, eyes closed. Hannah glanced back at the little Gurkha. 'What about him?'

'We'll drop him at Gatwick. Nothing for him to do where I'm going.'

'And where would that be?'

'Valdini obviously.'

'But Gagini has just told us that would be impossible.'

'Nothing's impossible in this life, Hannah, there's always a way.' He reached for the bar box, found a half bottle of Scotch, poured himself a shot into a plastic cup and sat there brooding.

About twenty minutes before they reached Gatwick Lacey patched a call through which Dillon took. It was Gagini.

'An interesting development. I've got one of my under-cover men working at the local garage near Luca's place.

His driver came in to fill up the tank. Told the owner they were taking a run out to Valdini.'

'That makes sense,' Dillon said. 'Everything coming together.'

'So, my friend, have you had any thoughts on how to handle this?'

'Yes, what about flying in?'

'But they would be alerted the moment you tried to land.'

'I'm thinking of something different, a story Ferguson told me once. He had a fella called Egan working for him and he needed to get down fast in a similar sort of situation. That was in Sicily too, about ten years ago.'

'Of course, I remember the case, he parachuted in.'

'That's right.'

'But he was an expert at that kind of thing. He jumped at eight hundred feet, my friend.'

'Well he would, wouldn't he, but I can do that. I've jumped before. I know my stuff, believe me. Can you lay on a plane, parachute, weapons and so on?'

'That shouldn't be a problem.'

'We'll see you at the airport then,' Dillon said and put the phone down.

'What was all that about?' Hannah demanded, but at that moment the seat-belt signs went on and they started to descend towards Gatwick.

'I'll tell you later,' Dillon told her. 'Now be a good girl and fasten your belt.'

The stopover at Gatwick took only an hour. Hannah took Kim across to the small office the Special Flying Unit used and arranged a taxi.

'I would rather come with you, *memsahib*.'

'No, Kim, you go back to Cavendish Square and make things nice for the Brigadier.'

'He will come back, *memsahib*, you swear it?'

She took a deep breath and, against every conviction, lied to him. 'He'll be back, Kim, I promise you.'

He smiled. 'Blessings on you, *memsahib*,' and he crossed to his taxi.

She found Dillon in the waiting room feeding coins into a sandwich machine. 'Plastic food, but what can you do? Would you like something? Personally I'm starving.'

'I suppose so. Anything there is.'

'Well, you won't want the ham so we'll make it tomato and boiled egg. There's tea and coffee on board. Come on.'

As they walked out to the Lear, the fuel truck was just moving away. Lacey stood waiting, the co-pilot already on board.

'Ready when you are,' the Flight Lieutenant said.

'We'll get moving, then,' Dillon told him and went up the steps behind Hannah.

They settled in their seats and a few minutes later the Lear started to taxi.

Dillon waited until they levelled off at thirty thousand feet, then made tea in the plastic cups. He sat there eating the sandwiches without saying anything.

Finally Hannah said, 'You were going to tell me what you were going to do?'

'There was a fella called Egan worked for Ferguson a few years back, ex-SAS. He had a similar problem about getting somewhere fast and that was in Sicily too.'

'How did he solve it?'

'Parachuted in from eight hundred feet from a small aircraft. At that height, you hit the ground in thirty seconds.'

There was genuine horror on her face. 'You must be mad.'

'Not at all. As far as they're concerned it will be just a plane passing overhead, a bit low perhaps, but they won't be expecting what I have in mind and it will be dark by then.'

'And Major Gagini has agreed to this?'

'Oh, yes, he's arranging a suitable plane, equipment, weapons, everything. All I have to do is jump out of the plane. You can follow on and land in the Lear, say thirty minutes later.'

He drank some of his tea and she sat there staring at him and then a curious expression appeared on her face. 'When you were talking to Gagini I heard you say you'd jumped before. I wondered what you were talking about. It makes sense now.'

'Well, it would, wouldn't it.'

'Except that for some strange reason I think you were lying to him. I don't think you've ever made a parachute jump in your life, Dillon.'

He gave her his best smile and lit a cigarette. 'True, but there's always a first time for everything and you be a good girl now and don't speak a word about this to Gagini. I wouldn't want him changing his mind.'

'It's madness, Dillon. Anything might happen. You could break your bloody neck for one thing.'

'Would you listen to the language and you the decent girl?' He shook his head. 'Can you think of an alternative? You have all the facts.'

She sat there quiet for a moment then sighed. 'When you come right down to it, no.'

'It's simple, my love; forget the Chungking Covenant and just think of Ferguson. Never tell him this, but I actually like the old sod and I won't stand by and see him go to hell if I can prevent it.' He leaned across and put a hand on hers and smiled, that special smile, nothing but warmth there and immense charm. 'Now then, could you do with another cup of tea?'

★

They came in over the sea, Palermo on the port side, evening falling fast and already lights twinkled in the city. There were a few cumulus clouds in a sky that was otherwise clear, and a half moon. They landed at Punta Raisa a few minutes later and Lacey, obeying orders from the tower, taxied to a remote area at the far end of the airport where a number of private planes were parked.

The truck which had shown them the way drove off and Lacey killed the engines. There was a small man in a cloth cap and old flying jacket standing in front of the hangar and, as Dillon and Hannah went down the steps, he came forward.

'Chief Inspector Bernstein? Paolo Gagini.' He held out his hand. 'Mr Dillon, it's a real pleasure. Come this way. We believe Morgan landed at Valdini two hours ago, by the way. His Citation put down here a little while ago. It's over there being refuelled, but it isn't going anywhere tonight. I saw the pilots leave the airport.'

Dillon turned as Lacey and the co-pilot came down the ladder. 'You'd better come too.'

They went into the hangar and Gagini led them to a large glass-walled office. 'Here you are, my friend. Everything I could think of.' There was a parachute, a Celeste silenced machine pistol, a Beretta pistol in a shoulder holster, a Walther and a bulletproof vest in dark blue, and a pair of infra-red night glasses.

'Everything but the kitchen sink,' Lacey said. 'Are you going to war, Mr Dillon?'

'You could say that.'

'There's a camouflaged suit for you over here,' Gagini told him, 'and some army jump boots. I hope to God they're the right size.'

'Fine, I'll go and get changed,' Dillon said. 'If you'll point me to the men's room.' He turned to Hannah. 'You fill in the Flight Lieutenant and his friend while I'm gone,' and he followed Gagini out.

And at that same moment at Valdini Luca's Mercedes saloon turned in through the gates in the wall and went up the gravel drive to park at the bottom of the steps leading up to the front door. As the driver helped Luca out, the front door opened and Morgan appeared and hurried down the steps.

'Don Giovanni.'

They embraced. The old man said, 'So you got it, Carlo, against all the odds? I'm proud of you. I can't wait to see it.'

'Come, let's go in, Uncle,' Morgan said and turned to the driver. 'You stay here. I'll have them bring you something from the kitchen.'

He helped Luca up the steps and into the house. Asta came out of the living room and came and put her arms around Luca at once and he kissed both her cheeks.

'Carl did it, Don Giovanni, isn't he clever?'

'Don't listen to her,' Morgan said. 'She played more than her part this time, believe me.'

'Good, you must tell me about it.'

He led the way into the living room where Ferguson sat by the log fire, Marco standing behind him, Uzi in hand.

'So, this is the redoubtable Brigadier Ferguson,' Luca said, leaning on his stick. 'A great pleasure.'

'For you perhaps, but not for me,' Ferguson told him.

'Yes, that's understandable.' Luca eased himself down into a large chair opposite Ferguson and held out his hand. 'Where is it, Carlo?'

Morgan took the document from his inside pocket, unfolded it and passed it over. 'The Chungking Covenant, Uncle.'

Luca read it slowly, then looked up and laughed. 'Incredible, isn't it?' He looked at Ferguson. 'Think of the mischief I'll be able to make with this, Brigadier.'

'Actually, I'd rather not,' Ferguson told him.

'Come, Brigadier.' Luca folded the Covenant and put it in his inside pocket. 'Don't be a spoilsport. You've lost and we've won. I know you face an uncertain future, but surely we can be civilised about it.' He smiled up at Morgan. 'A nice dinner and a bottle of wine, Carlo. I'm sure we can make the Brigadier a happier man.'

Dillon returned in the camouflage uniform and jump boots, picked up the bulletproof vest and pulled it on. He checked the Walther and slipped it under the waistband at the back under the tunic then tried the Celeste. Gagini had some large blow-up photos on the table which he was showing to the two RAF pilots and Hannah.

'What's this?' Dillon asked.

'Pictures of the farmhouse at Valdini taken from the air. I got them from drug squad files.'

'Would you anticipate any problems landing there?' Dillon asked Lacey.

'Not really. That strip across the meadow is one hell of a length and that half moon will help.'

'Good.' Dillon turned to Gagini. 'What about a plane?'

'Navajo Chieftain waiting outside ready to go.'

'And a good pilot who knows what he's doing?'

'The best.' Gagini spread his arms wide. 'Me, Dillon; didn't I tell you I was in the Air Force before I transferred to Intelligence work?'

'Well, that's convenient. How long to get there?'

'With the Navajo's speed no more than fifteen minutes.'

Dillon nodded. 'Right. I need half an hour on the ground.'

'Understood,' Gagini nodded. 'I'll come straight back here and join the others in the Lear. By the time we're landing at Valdini it should be just about right. I'll go and get the engines fired up.'

Dillon said to Lacey, 'I'll leave you that Beretta in the shoulder holster, just in case.' He picked up the parachute. 'Now show me how to put this on.'

Lacey looked shocked. 'You mean you don't know?'

'Don't let's argue about it, Flight Lieutenant, just show me.'

Lacey helped him buckle the straps, pulling them tight. 'Are you really sure about this?'

'Just show me what to pull,' Dillon said.

'The ring there and don't mess about, not at eight hundred feet. The Navajo has an Airstair door. Just go down it, fall off and pull on that ring straight away.'

'If you say so.' Dillon picked up the Celeste machine pistol and slung it across his chest and hung the night glasses around his neck. He turned to Hannah. 'Well, are you going to kiss me goodbye?'

'Get out of here, Dillon,' she said.

'Yes, ma'am.'

He gave her a mock salute, turned and went out and across the tarmac to the Navajo where Gagini sat in the cockpit, propellers turning. Dillon went up the steps and turned. Hannah had a last glimpse of him pulling up the Airstair door and then the Navajo moved away.

FIFTEEN

T HE NIGHT SKY was clear to the horizon and alive with stars and in the light of the half moon the countryside below was perfectly visible. They were flying at two thousand feet along a deep valley, mountains rising on either side and when Dillon looked out of one of the windows he could see the white line of a road winding along the valley bottom.

It was all very quick, Gagini climbed to two-and-a-half thousand to negotiate a kind of hump at the end of the valley and beyond was a great sloping plateau and he started down.

Five minutes later he levelled off at eight hundred,

turned and called over his shoulder. 'Drop the Airstair door. It's any minute now and I don't want to have to go round again, it could alert them. Go when I tell you and good luck, my friend.'

Dillon moved back to the door, awkwardly because of the parachute. He rotated the handle, the door fell out in to space, the steps unfolded. There was a roar of air and he held on to the fuselage buffeted by the wind and looked down and way over on his left was the farmhouse looking just like the photo.

'Now!' Gagini cried.

Dillon took two steps down holding the hand rail and then allowed himself to fall, headfirst, turning over once in the plane's slipstream, pulling the ring of the ripcord at the same moment. He looked up, saw the plane climbing steeply over on his left, the noise of the engine already fading.

In the dining room of the farmhouse they had just finished the first course of the dinner and Marco, acting as butler again, was clearing it away when they heard the plane.

'What in the hell is that?' Morgan demanded and he got up and moved out on to the terrace, Marco behind him.

The noise of the plane was fading over to the right. Asta came out at that moment. 'Are you worried about something?'

'The plane. It seemed so low that for a wild moment I thought it might intend to land.'

'Dillon?' She shook her head. 'Even he wouldn't be crazy enough to try that.'

'No, of course not.' He smiled and they went back inside. 'Just a passing plane,' he said to Luca and he turned to the Brigadier and shrugged. 'No cavalry riding to the rescue this time.'

'What a pity,' Ferguson said.

'Yes, isn't it? We'll continue with the meal, shall we? I'll be back in a moment.' He nodded to Marco and went out into the hall with him.

'What is it?' Marco demanded.

'I don't know. That plane made no attempt to land, but it was certainly low when it made its pass.'

'Someone sniffing out the lie of the land, perhaps,' Marco suggested.

'Exactly, then if someone was approaching by road, they could let them know how the situation looked by radio.'

Marco shook his head. 'No one could get within twenty miles of here by road without us being informed, believe me.'

'Yes, perhaps I'm being overcautious, but who have we got?'

'There's the caretaker, Guido. I put him on the gate and the two shepherds, the Tognolis, Franco and Vito. They've both killed for the Society, they're good men.'

'Get them out in the garden and you see to things. I just want to be sure.' He laughed and put a hand on Marco's shoulder. 'It's my Sicilian half talking.'

He returned to the dining room and Marco went to the kitchen where he found Rosa, the caretaker's wife, busy at the stove and the Tognoli brothers seated at one end of the table eating stew.

'You can finish that later,' he said; 'right now you get out into the garden just in case. *Signor* Morgan was unhappy about the plane that passed over.'

'At your orders,' Franco Tognoli said, wiping his mouth with the back of a hand and he unslung, from the back of his chair, his *lupara*, the sawn-off shotgun that was the traditional weapon of the Mafia since time immemorial. 'Come on,' he told his brother, 'we've got work to do,' and they went out.

Marco picked up a glass of red wine that stood on the table. 'You'll have to serve the food yourself, Rosa,' he said, emptied the glass at a single swallow then took a Beretta from his shoulder holster and checked it as he went out.

The silence was extraordinary. Dillon felt no particular exhilaration. It was a strange black and white world in the moonlight, rather like one of those dreams in which you dreamt you were flying and time seemed to stand still and then suddenly the ground was rushing up at him and he hit with a thump and rolled over in long meadow grass.

He lay there for a moment to get his breath then punched the quick release clip and stepped out of the parachute harness. The farmhouse was two hundred yards to the left beyond an olive grove on a slight rise. He started to run quite fast until he reached the grove, got down in the shelter of trees on the other side and found himself approximately seventy-five yards from the crumbling white wall of the farmhouse.

He focused the night glasses on the gate which stood open and straightaway saw Guido, the caretaker, at the gate in cloth cap and shooting jacket, a shotgun over his shoulder, and yet he wasn't the problem. The problem was the large old-fashioned bell hanging above the gate, rope dangling. One pull on that and the whole place would be roused.

There was a break on the ground to his right, a gully stretching towards the wall, perhaps two feet deep. He crawled along it cautiously and finally reached the wall. The grass was long and overgrown at that point and he unslung the silenced Celeste machine pistol and moved cautiously along the wall, keeping to the grass, but it petered out when he was still twenty yards away.

Guido was smoking a cigarette, his back to Dillon, looking up at the stars, and Dillon stood up and moved quickly, out in the open now. When he was ten yards away, Guido turned, saw him at once, his mouth opening in dismay. He reached up for the bellrope and Dillon fired a short burst that lifted him off his feet, killing him instantly.

It was amazing how little noise the Celeste had made, but there was no time to lose. Dillon dragged Guido's body into the shelter of the wall and dashed through the gate. He immediately left the drive and moved into the shelter of the lush overgrown semi-tropical garden. Here too the grass badly needed cutting. He moved cautiously through it between the olive trees towards the house. Quite suddenly, it started to rain, one of those sudden showers common to the region at that time of year, and he crouched there, aware of the terrace, the open windows and the sound of voices.

Marco, on his way down the drive, cursed as the rain started to fall, pulled up his collar and continued to the gate. It was apparent at once that Guido wasn't there. Marco pulled out his Beretta, moved outside and saw the body lying at the foot of the wall. He reached for the rope, rang the bell furiously for a few moments then ran inside the gate.

'Someone's here,' he called. 'Watch yourselves,' then he moved into the bushes, crouching.

In the dining room there was immediate upheaval. 'What's happening?' Luca demanded.

'The alarm bell,' Morgan said. 'Something's up.'

'Well, now, who would have thought it?' Ferguson said.

'You shut your mouth.' Morgan went to a bureau, opened a drawer to reveal several handguns. He selected a Browning and handed Asta a Walther. 'Just in case,' he said and at that moment a shotgun blasted outside.

★

It was Vito Tognoli who, panicking, made the mistake of calling to his brother, 'Franco, where are you? What's happening?'

Dillon fired a long burst in the direction of the voice, Vito gave a strangled cry and pitched out of the bushes on his face.

Dillon crouched in the rain, waiting, and after a while heard a rustle in the bushes and Franco's voice low, 'Heh, Vito, I'm here.'

A second later, he moved out of the bushes and paused under an olive tree. Dillon didn't hesitate, driving him back against the tree with another burst from the Celeste. Franco fell, discharging his shotgun and lay very still. Dillon moved forward, looking down at him, and behind, there was the click of a hammer going back.

Marco said, 'I've got you now, you bastard. Put that thing down and turn round.'

Dillon laid the Celeste on the ground and turned calmly. 'Ah, so it's you, Marco, I wondered where you'd be hiding.'

'God knows how you got here, but that doesn't matter now. The only important thing is you're here and I get the pleasure of killing you myself.'

He picked up Franco's shotgun with one hand and holstered the Beretta, then he called out, 'It's Dillon, *Signor* Morgan, I've got him here.'

'Have you now?' Dillon said.

'This is the *lupara*, always used by Mafia for a ritual killing.'

'Yes, I had heard that,' Dillon said. 'The only trouble is, old son, it's only double barrelled and it discharged when Franco went down.'

There was one single second when Marco took in what he had said and realised it was true. He dropped the shotgun, his hand went inside his coat to the holstered Beretta.

Dillon said, 'Goodbye, me old son.' His hand found the silenced Walther in his waistband under the tunic at his back, it swung up and he fired twice, each bullet striking Marco in the heart and driving him back.

Dillon stood there looking down at him, then he replaced the Walther in his waistband, reached down and picked up the Celeste. He took a step forward, looking out through the bushes at the terrace, then fired a long burst, raking the wall beside the window.

'It's Dillon,' he called. 'I'm here, Morgan.'

Morgan in the dining room stood by the table, Luca on one side, Asta on the other, holding the Walther in her hand.

'Dillon?' he called. 'Can you hear me?'

Dillon called back, 'Yes.'

Morgan went round the table and got Ferguson by the collar. 'On your feet,' he said, 'or I'll . . .'

He pushed the Brigadier round the table towards the open windows and the terrace. 'Listen to me, Dillon, I've got your boss here. I'll blow his brains all over the room unless you do as I say. After all, he's what you've come for.'

There was a marked silence, only the rain falling, and then incredibly Dillon appeared, coming up the steps to the terrace, the Celeste in his hands. He reached the terrace and stood there, the rain beating down.

'Now what?' he said.

Morgan, the muzzle of his Browning against Ferguson's temple, pulled him back, step-by-step, until he stood at the end of the table, Luca still sitting on one side of him, Asta on the other, her right hand clutching the Walther against her thigh.

Dillon moved into the entrance, a supremely menacing figure in the camouflaged uniform, his hair plastered to his skull. He spoke in Irish and then smiled.

'That means God bless all here.'

Morgan said, 'Don't make the wrong move.'

'Now why would I?' Dillon moved to one side of the table and nodded to Asta. 'Is that a gun in your hand, girl? I hope you know how to use it.'

'I know,' she said and her eyes were like dark holes, her face very pale.

'Then move to one side.' She hesitated and he said, his voice harsh, 'Do it, Asta.'

She stepped back and Morgan said, 'Don't worry. If he fires that thing he takes all of us and that includes the Brigadier, isn't that so, Dillon?'

'True,' Dillon said. 'I presume the overweight gentleman is your uncle, Giovanni Luca. It would include him too. A great loss to this Honoured Society of yours.'

'There is a time for all things, Dillon,' the old man said. 'I'm not afraid.'

Dillon nodded. 'I respect that, but you're living in the past, *Capo*, you've been Lord of Life and Death too long.'

'Everything comes to an end sometime, Mr Dillon,' Luca said and there was a strange look in his eyes.

Morgan said, 'To hell with this, put the machine pistol on the table, Dillon, or I'll spread Ferguson's brains over the cutlery, I swear it.'

Dillon stood there, holding the Celeste comfortably and Ferguson said, 'I abhor bad language, dear boy, but you have my permission to shoot the fucking lot of them.'

Dillon smiled suddenly, that deeply personal smile of total charm. 'God save you, Brigadier, but I came to take you home and I didn't intend a coffin.'

He moved to the table, placed the Celeste down and pushed it along to the end where it came to a halt in front of Luca.

There was a kind of relief on Morgan's face and he pushed Ferguson away from him. 'So, here we are, Dillon. You're a remarkable man, I'll give you that.'

'Oh, don't flatter me, old son.'

'Marco?' Morgan asked.

'He's gone the way of all flesh plus two fellas in cloth caps I found prowling in the garden.' Dillon smiled. 'Sure and I was forgetting the one at the gate. That makes four, Morgan. I'm nearly as good as that tailor in the fairy tale by the brothers Grimm. He boasted six at one blow but they were flies on the jam and bread.'

'You bastard,' Morgan said. 'I'm going to enjoy killing you.'

Dillon turned to Asta. 'Are you taking all this in? It's fun isn't it? Right up your street!'

She said, 'Talk all you want, Dillon, you're finished.'

'Not yet, Asta; things to be said.' He smiled at Morgan. 'A strange one, the girl here. She looks like she's off page fifty-two in *Vogue* magazine, but there's another side to her. She likes the violence. Gets off on it.'

'Shut your mouth!' Asta said in a low voice.

'And why should I do that, girl, especially if he's going to blow me away? A few words only. The condemned man's entitled to that.'

Morgan said, 'You're talking yourself into the grave.'

'Yes, well that's waiting for all of us, the one sure thing, the only difference is how you get there. Now take your wife, for instance; a strange business, that.'

The Browning seemed suddenly heavy in Morgan's hand. It came down and he held it against his thigh. 'What are you talking about, Dillon?'

'She died scuba diving off Hydra in the Aegean Sea, am I right? An unfortunate accident.'

'That's right.'

'Ferguson got a copy of the report compiled by the

263

Athens police. There were you and your wife, Asta and a divemaster on board.'

'So?'

'She ran out of air and the police report indicates that was no accident. The valve system in her equipment had been interfered with. Difficult to prove anything, especially with a man as powerful as the great Carl Morgan, so they put that report on file.'

'You're lying,' Morgan said.

'No, I've seen the report. Now who would want to kill her? Hardly the divemaster, so we can eliminate him. We thought it was you and told Asta as much, but you said on the boat it was a filthy lie and seemed to mean it.' Dillon shrugged. 'That only seems to leave one person.'

Asta screamed, 'You bastard, Dillon!'

Morgan stilled her with one raised hand. 'That's nonsense, it can't be.'

'All right, so you're going to kill me, so just answer one question. The night of the dinner party the brakes were interfered with on our estate car. Now if that was you it would imply you wanted Asta dead because you let her take a ride back to the lodge with us.'

'But that was a nonsense,' Morgan said, 'I'd never do anything to harm Asta. It was an accident.'

There was a silence and Dillon turned to Asta. When she smiled, it was the most terrible thing he'd ever seen in his life. 'You really are a clever one, aren't you?' she said and her hand came up with the Walther.

'You screwed up the braking system and yet you came with us?' he said.

'Oh, I had every confidence in you, Dillon, it seemed likely we'd survive with you at the wheel, but I knew you'd blame Carl and that would strengthen my position with you.' She turned to Morgan. 'It was all for you, Carl, so I could find out every move they were likely to make.'

'And your mother?' Ferguson said. 'Was that also for Morgan?'

'My mother?' She stared at them, a strangely blank look on her face and she turned to Morgan again. 'That was different. She was in the way, trying to take you away from me and she shouldn't have done that. I saved her, saved her from my father.' She smiled. 'He interfered with our lives once too often.' She smiled again. 'He liked fast women and he liked fast cars so I made sure he ran off the road in one.'

Morgan looked at her, horror on his face. 'Asta, what are you saying?'

'Please, Carl, you must understand. I love you, I always have. No one else has ever loved you as I have, just like you love me.'

The look on her face was that of the truly mad and Morgan seemed to come apart. 'Love you? There was only one woman I loved and you killed her.'

The Browning swung up, but already Dillon's hand was on the butt of the Walther in his waistband at the rear. He shot Morgan twice in the heart. Morgan went down and Luca reached for the Celeste. Dillon turned, his arm extended and shot him between the eyes and the *Capo* went back over the chair.

In the same moment Asta screamed, 'No!' She shot Dillon twice in the back, driving him face-down across the table, then she turned and ran out through the french windows.

Dillon had difficulty in breathing, almost unconscious, was aware of Ferguson calling his name, distress in his voice. His hands found the edge of the table, he levered himself up and lurched to the nearest chair. He sat there, gasping for breath, then reached for the Velcro tabs on the bullet-proof waistcoat, opened them and took it off. When he examined it, the two bullets she had fired were embedded in the material.

'Would you look at that now?' he said to Ferguson. 'Thank God for modern technology.'

'Dillon, I thought I'd lost you. Here, have a drink.' Ferguson poured red wine into one of the glasses on the table. 'I could do with one myself.'

Dillon took it down. 'Jesus, that's better. Are you all right, you old sod?'

'Never better. How in the hell did you get here?'

'Gagini flew me in and I parachuted.'

Ferguson looked shocked. 'I didn't know you could do that.'

'There's always a first time.' Dillon reached for the bottle and poured another glass.

Ferguson toasted him. 'You're a remarkable man.'

'To be honest with you, Brigadier, there's those who might think me a bit of a bloody genius, but that could be a subject for debate. What happened to the Covenant?'

Ferguson went to Luca, dropped to one knee and felt in his inside pocket. He stood up, turned and unfolded the document. 'The Chungking Covenant; that's what it was all about.'

'And this is how it ends,' Dillon said. 'Do you have a match and we'll burn the damn thing?'

'No, I don't think so.' Ferguson folded it carefully, took out his wallet and put it inside. 'I think we'll leave that to the Prime Minister.'

'You old bastard,' Dillon said, 'it's a knighthood you're after, so it is.'

He got up, lit a cigarette and went out to the terrace and Ferguson joined him. 'I wonder where she is? I heard some sort of car leave when I was trying to revive you.'

'Long gone, Brigadier,' Dillon said.

There was a roar of engines overhead, a dark shadow swooping down to the meadow. 'Good God, what's that?' Ferguson said.

'Hannah Bernstein coming to pick up the pieces, plus the good Major Gagini. He's been more than helpful on this. You owe him one.'

'I shan't forget,' Ferguson said.

Hannah Bernstein stood just inside the dining room, Gagini at her side, and surveyed the scene. 'Oh, my God,' she said, 'a butcher's shop.'

'Do you have a problem with this, Chief Inspector?' Ferguson asked. 'Let me tell you what happened here.' Which he did.

She took a deep breath when he was finished and on impulse went and kissed him on the cheek. 'I'm glad to see you in one piece.'

'Thanks to Dillon.'

'Yes.' She looked again at Morgan and Luca. 'He doesn't take prisoners, does he?'

'Four more in the grounds, my dear.'

She shuddered and Dillon came in through the french windows with Gagini. The Italian stood looking down at Luca and shook his head. 'I never thought to see the day. They won't believe he's gone in Palermo.'

'You should put him in an open coffin in a shop window like they used to do with outlaws in the Wild West,' Dillon told him.

'Dillon, for God's sake,' Hannah said.

'You think I was bad, Hannah?' Dillon shrugged. 'An animal this one who grew fat, not only off gambling, but on drugs and prostitution. He was responsible for the corruption of thousands. To hell with him,' and he turned and walked out.

★

At Punta Raisi it was raining as they waited in the office. Lacey looked in the door. 'Ready when you are.'

Gagini came through the hangar with them and walked across the apron. 'Strange how it all worked out, Brigadier. I thought I was doing you a favour when I got in touch with you about the Chungking Covenant and, in the end, you do me the biggest favour of all. You got rid of Luca for me.'

'Ah, but that was Dillon's doing, not mine.'

Dillon said sourly, 'Don't get too worked up, Major, there'll be someone to take his place by tomorrow morning.'

'True,' Gagini said. 'But some sort of victory.' He held out his hand. 'Thank you, my friend. Anything I can ever do, you only have to ask.'

'I'll remember that.'

Dillon shook hands, went up the steps into the Lear and settled in one of the rear seats. Ferguson sat opposite him on the other side and Hannah took the seat behind him. They strapped themselves in and the engines turned over. A few moments later they were moving along the runway and lifting into the air. They climbed steadily until they reached thirty thousand and started to cruise.

Hannah sat there, face grave and Dillon said belligerently, 'What's wrong with you?'

'I'm tired, it's been a long day and I can still smell the cordite and the blood, Dillon; is that so strange? I don't like it.' She exploded suddenly, 'My God, you just killed six people, *six*, Dillon. Doesn't that bother you?'

'What am I hearing?' he said. 'Some sort of fine Jewish Hassidic interpretation on this? The kind of morality that says let your enemy do it unto you, but don't do it unto him?'

'All right, so I don't know what I mean.' There was no doubt that she was genuinely upset.

Dillon said, 'Then maybe you're in the wrong job; I'd think about that, if I were you.'

'And how do you see yourself, as some sort of public executioner?'

'Enough, both of you.' Ferguson opened the bar box, took out a half bottle of Scotch, poured some into a plastic cup and handed it to her. 'Drink that, it's an order.'

She took a deep breath and reached for it. 'Thank you, sir.'

Ferguson poured a generous measure into another cup and passed it to Dillon. 'Try that.' Dillon nodded and drank deep and the Brigadier poured himself one.

'It's the business we're in, Chief Inspector, try to remember that. Of course, if you're unhappy and wish to return to normal duty?'

'No, sir,' she said, 'that won't be necessary.'

Dillon reached for the bottle and poured another and Ferguson said, 'I wonder what happened to that wretched young woman?'

'God knows,' Dillon said.

'Mad as a hatter,' Ferguson said. 'So much is obvious, but that isn't our problem,' and he closed his eyes and lay back in the seat.

It was at about the same time that Asta arrived at the gate of Luca's villa. She kept her hand on the horn and the guard appeared on the other side. He took one look and hurriedly opened the gate and she drove through and up to the house. When she got out of the station wagon, the door opened at the top of the steps and Luca's houseboy, Giorgio, appeared.

'*Signorina*. You are alone? The *Capo* and *Signor* Morgan come later?'

She could have told him the truth, yet for some reason hesitated and at the same time realised why. If Luca was still alive she could still use his power and she wanted that power.

'Yes,' she said. 'The *Capo* and *Signor* Morgan are staying at Valdini on business. You will get in touch with the chief pilot of the Lear. What is his name?'

'Ruffolo, *signorina*.'

'Yes, that's right. Find where he is and tell him to get out here as fast as possible and get in touch with our contact at the airport. There is a Lear from England there. It may have already left, but get all the information you can.'

'Of course, *signorina*.' He bowed, ushering her into the house, closed the door and went to the phone.

She went and poured herself a drink and stood sipping it, staring out across the terrace, and was surprised at how quickly Giorgio returned. 'I've found Ruffolo, he is on his way and you were right, *signorina*. The English Lear has departed. There were two pilots and three passengers.'

She stared at him. 'Three; are you sure?'

'Yes, a woman, a stout ageing man and a small man with very fair hair. Our contact didn't get the names, but saw them boarding.'

'I see. Good work, Giorgio. Call me when Ruffolo gets here.'

Asta stripped and stood under a hot shower. It was like a bad dream, so difficult to believe that Dillon was still alive. Carl, her beloved Carl and Luca, and it was all Dillon's fault. How could she have ever liked him? Dillon and Ferguson, but especially Dillon. They'd ruined everything and for that they had to pay.

She got out of the shower, towelled herself down, then oiled her body, thinking about it. Finally, she pulled on a robe and started to comb her hair. The phone rang. When she lifted it up it was Giorgio.

'*Signorina*. Captain Ruffolo is here.'

'Good, I'll be right down.'

Ruffolo was in an open-necked shirt, blazer and slacks when she went into the sitting room. He came to greet her, kissing her hand.

'Forgive me, *signorina*, I'd gone out for a meal, but Giorgio managed to trace me. How can I serve you?'

'Please, sit down.' She waved him to a chair, went and started to open a bottle of Bollinger champagne Giorgio had left in an ice bucket. 'You'll take a glass, Captain.'

'My pleasure, *signorina*.' His eyes fastened on the ripe curves of her young body and he sat up straight.

Asta poured champagne into two crystal glasses and handed one to him. 'This is a delicate matter, Captain. The *Capo* has given me a special task. I am to go to England tomorrow, but not officially, if you understand me.'

Ruffolo sampled a little of the champagne. 'Excellent, *signorina*. What you mean is you would like to land in England illegally, no trace that you are there, am I right?'

'Exactly, Captain.'

'There is no problem on this. There is a private airfield in Sussex we can use. I've done this before. There is so much traffic in the London approaches that if I go in from the sea at six hundred feet there is no trace. Is it London you wish to go to?'

'Yes,' she said.

'Only thirty miles away by road. No problem.'

'Wonderful,' she said, got up and went back to the champagne bucket. 'The *Capo* will be pleased. Now let me give you another glass of champagne.'

SIXTEEN

It was just before six the following evening when the Daimler was admitted through the security gates at Downing Street. Dillon, Ferguson and Hannah Bernstein sat in the back and, when the chauffeur opened the door for them, it was only Ferguson and Hannah who got out.

Ferguson turned. 'Sorry about this but you'll have to wait for us, Dillon. I don't expect we'll be long.'

'I know.' Dillon smiled. 'I embarrass the man.'

They went to the door where the duty policeman, recognising Ferguson, saluted. It opened at once and they passed inside where an aide took their coats and Ferguson's

Malacca cane. They followed him upstairs and along the corridor. A second later and he was admitting them to the study where they found the Prime Minister sitting behind his desk, working his way through a mass of papers.

He glanced up and sat back. 'Brigadier, Chief Inspector. Do sit down.'

'Thank you, Prime Minister,' Ferguson said and they pulled chairs forward.

The Prime Minister reached for a file and opened it. 'I've read your report. An absolutely first-class job. Dillon seems to have acted with his usual rather ruthless efficiency.'

'Yes, Prime Minister.'

'On the other hand, without him we'd have lost you, Brigadier, and I wouldn't have liked that at all, a disaster for all of us, wouldn't you agree, Chief Inspector?'

'Absolutely, Prime Minister.'

'Where is Dillon now, by the way?'

'Waiting outside in my Daimler, Prime Minister,' Ferguson told him. 'I feel it the sensible thing to do, considering Dillon's rather unusual background.'

'Of course.' The Prime Minister nodded and then smiled. 'Which leaves us with the Chungking Covenant.' He took it from the file. 'Remarkable document. It raises such infinite possibilities, but as I said at the first meeting we had about this affair, we've had enough trouble with Hong Kong. We're getting out and that's it, which is why I told you to find the damn thing and burn it.'

'I rather thought you'd like to do that yourself, Prime Minister.'

The Prime Minister smiled. 'Very thoughtful of you, Brigadier.'

There was a fire burning brightly in the grate of the Victorian fireplace. He got up, went to it and placed the document on top. The edges curled in the heat then it burst into flame. A moment later it was simply grey ash already dissolving.

The Prime Minister turned, came round his desk. 'I'd like to thank you both.' He shook hands with them. 'And thank Dillon for me, Brigadier.'

'I will, Prime Minister.'

'And now you must excuse me, I'm due at the House of Commons. An extra Prime Minister's question time. We must let members have their moment of fun.'

'I understand, Prime Minister,' Ferguson said.

Behind them, by the usual mysterious alchemy, the door opened and the aide reappeared to show them out.

'It went well, then?' Dillon said as the Daimler turned out through the security gates into Whitehall.

'You could say that. He enjoyed the pleasure of putting the Chungking Covenant on the fire himself.'

'Well, that was nice for the man.'

'He did ask the Brigadier to thank you, Dillon,' Hannah said.

'Did he now?' Dillon turned to Ferguson who sat with his hands folded over the silver handle of his Malacca cane. 'You didn't mention that.'

'Didn't want it to go to your head, dear boy.' He opened the partition window. 'Cavendish Square.' He sat back. 'I thought we'd all have a drink at my place.'

'Oh, Jesus, your Honour,' Dillon said. 'It's so kind of you to ask us, the grand man like yourself.'

'Stop playing the stage Irishman, Dillon, it doesn't suit you.'

'Terribly sorry, sir.' Dillon was all public school English now. 'But the fact is I'd take it as a real honour if you and the Chief Inspector would have a drink with me at my place.' He opened the partition window again. 'Change of venue, driver, make it Stable Mews.'

As Dillon closed the window Ferguson sighed and said to Hannah, 'You'll have to excuse him, he used to be an actor, you see.'

The Daimler turned into the cobbled yard of Stable Mews and stopped outside Dillon's cottage. 'Wait for us,' Ferguson told his driver as the Irishman unlocked the front door and Hannah followed him in. Ferguson joined them, closing the door.

'This is really rather nice,' he said.

'Come in the sitting room.' Dillon led the way in, feeling for the switch and, when the light came on, Asta Morgan was sitting in the wing-backed chair by the fireplace. She wore a jump suit in black crushed velvet and a black beret. More importantly she held a Walther in her lap, a silencer screwed to the end of the barrel.

'Well, this is nice, here I was waiting for you, Dillon, and I get all three.' Her eyes glittered, her face was very pale, dark shadows under her eyes.

'Now don't be a silly girl,' Ferguson told her.

'Oh, but I've been a very *clever* girl, Brigadier. I'm not even supposed to be in the country and, when I've finished here, my plane's waiting on a quiet little airstrip in Sussex to fly me out again.'

'What do you want, Asta?' Dillon said.

'Turn round and lean on the table. As I remember, you favour a gun in the waistband at the back. That's how you killed Carl.' There was nothing there. She checked his armpits. 'No gun, Dillon. That's rather careless.'

'We've been to Downing Street you see,' Ferguson said. 'Most sophisticated alarm system in the world there. Try passing through the security gates with any kind of gun and all hell would break loose.'

'Yes, well you can bend over too.' Ferguson complied

and when she was finished she turned to Hannah. 'Empty your handbag on the floor.'

Hannah did as she was told and a compact, gold lipstick, wallet, comb and car keys scattered on the floor. 'See, no gun, the Brigadier was telling the truth.'

'Stand over there,' Asta ordered, 'and you move to the right, Brigadier.' Dillon still had his back to her. 'I thought I'd killed you back there at the farm, Dillon. I'd like to know how I failed.'

'Bulletproof vest,' he said. 'They're all the rage these days.'

'Oh, you're good with the one-liners,' she said, 'but you ruined everything for me, Dillon; took Carl from me and for that you pay.'

'And what would you suggest?' Dillon said, easing his feet apart ever so slightly.

'Two in the stomach, that should make you squirm.'

Hannah Bernstein reached for a small Greek statue that stood on the coffee table next to her and threw it. Asta ducked and fired wildly, catching Hannah in the left shoulder and knocking her back across the sofa. Dillon made his move, but she turned, the barrel of the Walther pushing out towards him.

'Goodbye, Dillon.'

Behind her there was a click as Charles Ferguson turned the silver handle of his Malacca cane to one side, the nine-inch poniard it contained flashed out and he plunged it into her back, penetrating her heart, the point emerging through the front of the jump suit.

She didn't even have time to cry out, the Walther falling from a nerveless hand, and she lurched forward, Dillon's hands catching each arm. Ferguson withdrew the poniard. She glanced down at her chest in a kind of amazement, looked at Dillon once more as if she didn't believe what was happening, and then her knees gave way and she went down, rolling on her back.

Dillon let her go and crossed to Hannah who lay back against the sofa, a hand to her shoulder, blood oozing between her fingers. He got his handkerchief out and put it in her hand. 'Hold this against it hard. You'll be all right, I promise you.'

He turned to find Ferguson on the telephone. 'Yes, Professor Henry Bellamy for Brigadier Charles Ferguson. An emergency.' He stood there waiting, the bloodstained poniard in his hand, the cane on the floor. 'Henry? Charles here. Gunshot wound in the left shoulder, Chief Inspector Bernstein. I'll have Dillon bring her round to the London Clinic now. I'll see you later.'

He put the phone down and turned. 'Right, Dillon, into the Daimler and round to the clinic fast. Bellamy will be there as soon as you are.'

Dillon helped Hannah up and glanced at Asta. 'What about her?'

'Quite dead, but I'll see to it. Now get moving.'

He followed them along the hall, opened the door and saw them into the Daimler, then he went back. He had laid the poniard on the desk and now he picked it up, took his handkerchief from his breast pocket and wiped the blade carefully. He replaced it in the Malacca cane, stood looking down at her then picked up the phone and dialled a number.

A calm, detached voice said, 'Yes?'

'Ferguson. I have a disposal for you. Absolutely top priority. I'm at Stable Mews, round the corner from Cavendish Square.'

'Dillon's place?'

'That's right. I'll wait for you.'

'Twenty minutes, Brigadier.'

Ferguson replaced the receiver, stepped over Asta's body, went to Dillon's drinks cabinet and poured a Scotch.

Dillon was sitting in the corridor outside the operating

theatre an hour later when Ferguson joined him. 'How are things?' the Brigadier said as he sat down.

'We'll know soon. Bellamy said a simple extraction job. He didn't anticipate any problems.' Dillon lit a cigarette. 'You moved fast back there, Brigadier, I really thought I was on the way out.'

'Well, you weren't.'

'What have you done about it?'

'Called in the disposal unit. I waited for them. She'll be processed through a certain crematorium in North London that we find rather useful. Six pounds of grey ash by tomorrow morning and, as far as I'm concerned, they can do what they like with it. We won't tell the Chief Inspector until she's back on her feet.'

'I know,' Dillon said. 'That fine Hassidic conscience of hers.'

The theatre door opened and Bellamy emerged, mask down. They got up. 'How is she?' Ferguson demanded.

'Fine. Nice clean wound. A week in hospital, that's all. She'll be on the mend in no time. Here she comes now.'

A nurse pushed out Hannah Bernstein on a trolley. Her face was drawn and pale under a white skullcap. The nurse paused for them to look down and Hannah's eyelids flickered, then opened.

'Dillon, is that you?'

'As ever was, girl dear.'

'I'm glad you're all right. You are a bastard, but for some strange reason I like you.'

Her eyes closed again. 'Take her away, nurse,' Bellamy said and turned to Ferguson. 'I'll get off now, Charles; see you tomorrow,' and he walked away.

Ferguson put a hand on Dillon's shoulder. 'I think we should go too, dear boy, it's been a hell of a day. I think a drink is in order.'

★

'Now where shall we go?' Ferguson said as the Daimler pulled away.

Dillon slid back the glass partition. 'The Embankment, Lambeth Bridge end, will do fine.'

Ferguson said, 'Any particular reason?'

'The night of the Brazilian Embassy Ball, Asta Morgan and I walked along the Embankment in the rain.'

'I see,' Ferguson said and sat back without another word.

Ten minutes later, the Daimler pulled in by the bridge. It was raining hard and Dillon got out and walked to the parapet beside the river. Ferguson joined him a moment later holding an umbrella.

'As I said, she was as mad as a hatter; not your problem, dear boy.'

'Don't worry, Brigadier, just exorcising the ghost.' Dillon took out a cigarette and lit it. 'Actually, she can rot in hell as far as I'm concerned. Now let's go and get that drink,' and he turned and went back to the car.